BONDS
OF
LOYALTY

D0042433

OTHER BOOKS AND AUDIO BOOKS
BY JENNIFER K. CLARK & STEPHONIE K. WILLIAMS:

Mark of Royalty

OTHER BOOKS AND AUDIO BOOKS
BY JENNIFER K. CLARK

Knight of Redmond

BONDS
OF
L**O**YALTY

a novel

JENNIFER K. CLARK &
STEPHONIE K. WILLIAMS

Covenant Communications, Inc.

Cover image *Medieval Princess Reading Old Book* © DianaHirsch and *Knight Brothers* © DianaHirsch; images courtesy of istockphoto.com

Cover design copyright © 2014 by Covenant Communications, Inc.

Published by Covenant Communications, Inc.
American Fork, Utah

Copyright © 2014 by Jennifer K. Clark and Stephonie K. Williams
All rights reserved. No part of this book may be reproduced in any format or in any medium without the written permission of the publisher, Covenant Communications, Inc., P.O. Box 416, American Fork, UT 84003. The views expressed within this work are the sole responsibility of the author and do not necessarily reflect the position of Covenant Communications, Inc., or any other entity.

This is a work of fiction. The characters, names, incidents, places, and dialogue are either products of the author's imagination, and are not to be construed as real, or are used fictitiously.

Printed in the United States of America
First Printing: August 2014

20 19 18 17 16 15 14   10 9 8 7 6 5 4 3 2 1

ISBN: 978-1-62108-419-8

To Julie and Jared, who have been with us from
the beginning of our personal stories.

ACKNOWLEDGMENTS

OUR DEEPEST THANKS AND APPRECIATION go out to those who reviewed the first drafts of *Bonds of Loyalty*, provided valuable feedback, and helped us fine-tune the story—Don and Linda Kilgrow, Julie Zwahlen, Jared and Jennette Kilgrow, Carolynn Jex, and Tristi Pinkston. Thanks to C. Michelle Jefferies who offered words of encouragement when needed most.

CHAPTER 1

SARAH FELT THE CRUNCH UNDERNEATH the sole of her fancy new shoe and didn't have to wait for the shriek of the disease-ridden creature to know what she'd stepped on. She jerked her foot up, hoping the vermin wouldn't turn around and sink its teeth into her ankle. Thankfully, it scurried off to danker places to nurse its wound.

She paused to steady herself and her nerves. "Are you all right, Your Highness?" the accompanying guard asked.

"Rats. I hate rats." Sarah shivered.

"Aye. They are filthy beasts. Would you like to return and have Prince Alexander accompany you?"

"No. I need to do this on my own. Thank you."

The guard nodded, and they proceeded forward.

The lanterns in the room did little to provide light, and the harsh clicking of her shoes on the cold stone floor only intensified her anxiety. She held her hand to her nose to filter the putrid air, keeping pace with the guard as they moved farther into the dungeons.

"Here we are, Your Highness." The guard raised the lantern, letting the light fall over the room's single occupant.

The man sat on a scattering of straw in the corner, and Sarah's stomach tightened. There were no bars or barriers to separate him from her. A single chain ran from the wall and ended with a metal clasp around one of his ankles.

Sarah took a tentative step forward, making sure she was still well out of the man's reach. She had been dreading this meeting, but it eventually had to take place.

"Sarah," the prisoner cried. A wide grin spread across his face. "Your Highness." The title seemed to be added on as an afterthought. He pulled himself forward and knelt in front of her. "I am your most humble servant."

"Get up, Chad." Sarah didn't use his full name: Chadwick. She had known him too long to stand on formalities.

"If it is Your Highness's wish." He pulled himself up to stand before her. "I am at your disposal."

"Chad . . ." Sarah wasn't entirely certain how she was going to finish that sentence before he interrupted her.

"Sarah, I thank you for bringing clarity to my life. I have been meeting with priests regularly; I've been praying nonstop; I know now where I went wrong."

"Went wrong?" Sarah looked into the face she had once considered handsome. His normally blond hair was darkened with oil and grime. The brown eyes that had once intrigued her were now dull. The smile he gave didn't move past his lips and certainly didn't inspire the feelings she'd previously had for him.

"Yes. I know where I made my mistakes, and I . . ." He paused. "I want to apologize for . . . everything. I was hoping that—"

"Don't, Chad." Sarah held a hand up. "I don't want to hear what you were hoping for."

An immediate change came over his face. "All I have done and worked toward, and you won't even hear me out?" His tone had gone cold, but he tried again. "I meant something to you. You loved me once."

"I don't think I ever really loved you. And I'm certain you never truly loved me either."

The chain rattled angrily as Chad tried to step forward. Resisting the urge to move back, Sarah steadied herself. The guard stepped next to her, but the protective gesture was unnecessary. Chad's bindings restricted his movements, leaving her well out of his reach. His brow twisted with irritation. "I could have had it all. We could have been happy!"

"*We*, Chad? There was no 'we.'"

"There was until Miranda died."

A new pain crept up from Sarah's stomach, a mixture of anger and sadness. "Don't mention my mother's name—"

"She may have raised you, but she wasn't your mother. She took you away from your country and hid you from your real family. She kept your identity a secret—even from you. And then she died and left you on your own with no means of finding out who you were and where you came from. *That* is not motherly."

Sarah felt the sting of his words, but he was wrong. Regardless of what he said, Miranda *was* her mother. Even after her royal lineage was discovered a year ago—after she learned there was another woman she should call mother—Miranda still held that place in her heart. "How can you speak so ill of her, Chad? Was she not kind to you? Did she not have the best hopes for you?"

"And you have thwarted those hopes. Miranda worked so hard to create a prosperous match between us, and if she had lived through her bout of sickness, you would have been my wife."

An acrid taste rose in Sarah's mouth. Chad was the king's nephew and would've been a profitable match, but thankfully their relationship wavered after Miranda's death. "Come now, Chad. Miranda would never have approved of our relationship had she known of your plot to depose Alex as heir to the throne. I could never have faith in someone who so easily betrayed his own family."

The chain scratched against the floor again as Chad shifted his feet. "You're right. I never should have courted you. And as for my cousin . . . Alex will regret it soon enough as well. You weren't raised to be royal. You'll never fit that mold."

Sarah tried not to flinch at the barb, but he must have sensed her insecurity. The dungeon walls echoed with his laughter. The guard stepped forward, but she held up her hand, stopping him.

Chad laughed harder. "That mark on your shoulder may proclaim your lineage, but you'll never be able to live up to the position. Even the finest bloodlines turn out a cull now and again."

The sting hit as if he had physically struck her. She reached her hand over her shoulder, slipping her fingers under the neckline of her gown to feel the raised scar of the Kyrnidan crest—the mark of royalty branded onto her skin after her birth.

The unicorn depicted on her shoulder, proof that she was the first born in her royal family and a symbol of her home country, had slightly distorted as she'd grown. That is how she felt—distorted. The discovery that she was a princess had only muddled her self-identity. The life of a royal had been taken away from her at her birth, and she no more fit that part now than she had before she'd known the truth of her origin. And Chad had voiced her greatest fear—that she wouldn't be able to fulfill the role of a princess. But if there was one thing she was good at, it was hiding her fears. Lifting her chin, she buried his insult. "I am not here to discuss my birthright. I came to inform you that I am betrothed to Prince Alexander. We are to be married, and I will no longer accept messages from you."

"Still engaged?" Chad growled and pulled on the chain. "It's been a year and you have yet to marry him. The King's Council will never ratify the union, no matter how long you campaign for it."

"Alex and I *will* be married." She tried to steady her voice. She and Alex had fallen in love before they knew of her linage. Things were simple then. Of course the council abnegated the prince's marriage to a commoner, and things were not any different now. Despite her being declared a princess, the council still withheld their approval. And they would continue to do so until she proved herself worthy of her newfound position.

Chad's eyes flashed, and hate darkened his once-attractive features.

"We're done, Chad." At least in this matter, Sarah had conviction. "What I do with my life is no longer your concern. Do not send me any more messages. I will not respond. I will never see you again." Sarah turned back to the guard. "I'm done."

Chad's chains rattled angrily, but Sarah didn't look back. "You'll never rule!" he called after her. "You don't have it in you!"

CHAPTER 2

Despite the sweet scent of flowers, Sarah couldn't seem to rid herself of the stench from the dungeons. She couldn't rid her thoughts of Chad's cutting words either. She walked down a path in the queen's garden, absently plucking at the leaves on the hedges until she sat on a bench partially hidden under a shade tree. Would she never be suitable as a royal? Perhaps there was some truth in that. She just didn't fit the part. Even though her lineage was irrefutable, there weren't many who accepted her in that role.

Being raised as a nobleman's daughter had not prepared her to be a princess. There were too many flaws in her personality and behavior. She wasn't accustomed to the life, the clothes, or the protocol of royalty. Instead of gossiping over afternoon tea, she preferred the solitude of the apple orchard. She even felt comfortable working alongside the kitchen maids to bake the bread—something hardly befitting her position, or so she'd been told on numerous occasions.

She plucked a leaf from a nearby branch and was tearing it into tiny pieces when she heard footsteps approaching. Sitting up straighter, she smoothed her dress. Pieces of leaf clung to the needle lace. "Propriety," she mumbled. "Always propriety." She brushed at the fragmented foliage as the person turned the corner and came into view. The man's dark hair and fitted waistcoat were distinguishable even at a distance.

"Sarah."

"Prince Alex." Sarah's face flushed, and she stood to greet her fiancé. He glanced at the pieces of leaf still clinging to her skirt but said nothing. Instead, a hint of a smile pulled at the corners of his lips. Alex was not judgmental like others in the king's court, but his smile disappeared too quickly. Sarah shifted her weight and glanced down with a prick of worry. Maybe she was wearing out her grace period of not following proper decorum.

He leaned in and kissed her. As always, his warm lips pressed against hers brought comfort, but he pulled away sooner than she expected. "I came to see how you're doing. How did the conversation with Chad go? Has there been any change in him?"

It was likely that Alex already knew the answer. He kept a very close watch on his cousin, but she answered anyway. "He's still bitter and angry." Alex took her arm and led her down the pathway while she told him about her discussion with Chad. She was careful to leave out the parts where Chad had challenged her right to her position. She buried her fear and frustration about it before it even surfaced, talking fast and purposefully avoiding eye contact.

There was a time when she didn't have to hide her feelings from Alex. She mourned for those lost moments now. Had their relationship changed that much? She couldn't pretend it hadn't. They had been slowly drifting apart over the last few months. She first noticed it when the council members denied support for their espousal, forcing them to campaign for it. She understood why the king required her and Alex to gain the approval of his counselors. Someone destined to become queen, who would have such a highly influential position in the nation, needed to be scrutinized to see if she was equal to the task. Still, it was a distasteful business. But Alex seemed to take it all in stride. She wished she could do the same.

Alex stopped in the middle of the path and took both of her hands. "As much as I would love to continue wandering the garden paths with you, I understand your sister will be arriving any moment to finalize some last-minute wedding details."

"Yes." Sarah swatted at a bug that had flown too close to her—another gesture she knew didn't follow proper decorum. Oh well. She had thought of that too late. "We must return. I don't want to keep Felicia waiting." Even though Felicia was Miranda's actual daughter by birth, they would always be close. And tomorrow her sister was marrying Joseph Savell, the kind, shy son of the high judge, Andrew Barnett Savell. "They make a good pair, do they not—Felicia and Joseph?"

Alex guided her around a tall hedge and back toward the castle. "Yes, I believe so. Have you told Felicia we'll be departing for Kyrnidan in a month's time?"

Sarah's toe caught on a stone in the cobbled pathway, and Alex put an arm around her waist to steady her. "Are you all right?"

"I'm fine." Her mind was jarred more than anything as she remembered the pending trip. "No, I haven't mentioned anything to Felicia. I guess it slipped my mind." She hadn't forgotten, but it was too daunting to let her thoughts dwell on the upcoming trip. She would be traveling back to her country, meeting a family she'd never seen before. Sarah lifted her chin. "Actually, I'm not fine. I'm not ready to go back to Kyrnidan."

"Your brother is becoming king. Surely you're excited to witness such a grand event."

Sarah tried not to appear too unsettled. Michael was her twin and the only member of her family she'd met. He had come to Calibre as a representative of their father when her true identity had been made known, and in the brief time they spent together, they had formed a bond. She didn't mind that he had assumed the role of the firstborn, that her birthright had gone to him. "With my father aging, I suppose it's a good choice for him to pass on the crown now. And I'm sure Michael will make a good king."

Alex gave her hand a squeeze. "Still, you're apprehensive about going, aren't you?"

Sarah looked into his bright-blue eyes. It was hard to hide her feelings when he knew her so well. Still, she couldn't bring herself to share her most inner thoughts. She was more than apprehensive about going to Kyrnidan—she was terrified. If there was something she could do to put the trip off or cancel it completely, she probably would.

Alex bent his head to look at her, and a thin piece of his dark hair fell in front of his eyes. He didn't bother brushing it back into place. "It's all right. I imagine you have mixed emotions about meeting your birth parents and seeing your home country for the first time."

"That would be putting it mildly." Sarah added a laugh to soften her words. Truthfully—she didn't know what her parents would think of her. They were aware that she hadn't been raised in the customary environment for her position, but would they still have those expectations? And how would the people receive her as their princess? Would they press her to stay, or would they reject her? If she had to go, her only comfort was knowing Alex would be with her. Despite the strain on their relationship, he was still her strength.

"The situation is quite unusual." Alex took her hand in his and brushed his thumb across her fingers. "But all things considered, you've taken everything in with grace and poise."

She didn't feel as confident. "I believe you're too kind. I don't handle much of anything with grace. I still lack when it comes to proper protocol. And I don't think I'll ever get used to these fancy shoes and heavy gowns." Sarah lifted her skirt until the toes of her ornate shoes poked out.

Alex smirked. "Well, I don't know what to tell you about the shoes, but the rest will come with time." He took her arm and directed her down the path again. "You shouldn't be concerned about portraying perfection in Kyrnidan. You're just going to visit not to take an active role in their monarchy. Beyond being a loving daughter, those other facets of character won't matter."

Sarah nodded, but the gesture was a lie. Eventually he would have to stop overlooking her inadequacies. Maintaining proper decorum *did* matter. If she was going to marry Alex, she would need to perfect those dignified qualities. She could shoulder the responsibilities—if she worked harder. Civility, posture, and grammar could all be learned. Being delicate and discreet . . . Well, maybe it would come with time. Hopefully then the council would approve their marriage. The last thing she wanted was to find truth in Chad's hateful words that she'd never be worthy of her position—that she'd *never* be allowed to marry Alex.

CHAPTER 3

SARAH STOOD ON HER TOES to get a better look over the gathering crowd, but there was still no sign of Felicia and the wedding precession. The final details for today's ceremony might all be for naught if they were off to a late start. Sarah moved to a higher step, hoping to get a better view over the throng of people, but her shoe slipped on the flagstone, and she knew she was going to make an impressive spectacle.

She tried to grab onto something but couldn't stop herself from cascading down the stairs of the church until she landed at the bottom in front of the gathering well-wishers. Heat rushed into her cheeks as nearby wedding guests gasped and whispered. Quickly she gathered her skirts—and her wits.

"Your Highness."

Sarah knew that voice, and it positively dripped with condemnation. She closed her eyes for the briefest moment before looking up.

"Lord Clemente." Sarah kept her tone even and forced a polite smile. Lord Moret was there as well. She gave the most imperceptible nod toward both men. Disapproval was evident on their faces, yet neither moved to help her. Apparently, noble acts of kindness were no longer required of men belonging to the King's Council.

"If you'll excuse me." Sarah once again tried to gather herself together when another voice close behind her sent shivers over her skin.

The deep tones were not out of the ordinary for a man, but it had been a year since she'd last heard his Kyrnidian accent. "Your Highness, are you injured? Please, allow me to assist you."

Sarah dared not look up, not wanting to confirm that it was really him. His firm hand gripped her elbow, and he assisted her to her feet. Then she had no choice but to face him. "Apollo." She felt herself tremble.

He was tall and thin like she remembered, but he seemed more worn and his hair had grayed considerably since the last time she'd seen him. She had never expected to see him again, so what duty had brought him here this time? Sarah clenched her teeth together. Unlike other honorable men, Apollo's actions weren't always driven by duty. As her father's once closest advisor, placing the mark of royalty upon her shoulder after her birth had been his duty. However, secreting her out of the castle and giving her to the widow Miranda was not. He claimed his actions were necessary because some prophecy implied the firstborn would be a son. But that seemed a poor excuse for such rash conduct.

Sarah could've lived with that single episode. She would've been fine never knowing who she really was. But Apollo had disrupted that a year ago. Although a Kyrnidian seamstress had first recognized Sarah's royal mark while fitting her for a gown, it was Apollo who had accompanied Prince Alex and her brother back from Kyrnidan and confirmed it. He proclaimed to everyone that she indeed was of royal birth—that she was the princess of Kyrnidan. It seemed as though every time his life touched hers, everything she knew was turned upside down. She eyed him now, uncertain of what turmoil he would bring this time.

Apollo turned to the group of people in front of her. Some of them still had peevish smiles on their faces as they darted glances in Sarah's direction. "Lord Hector Clemente, Lord Emanuel Moret." Apollo gave a stiff bow to the closest men. "I am Apollo Kaplan Moylan."

"I remember—from Kyrnidan," Lord Moret said. "Do you come to seek audience with the King's Council?"

"No. I seek audience with Princess Sarah and Prince Alexander."

"I see." Lord Clemente stifled a yawn with the back of his hand. "It must be a trifling matter—no need for authority."

Apollo's face hardened. "It's a fine day for a wedding, which I understand will soon begin. I suggest you take your places before the bride and groom arrive."

Sarah would have moved out of the way, but Apollo held her firmly by the elbow forcing the group to go around them.

"What are you doing here?" Sarah clasped her hands together to keep them from visibly trembling. She had been told his intentions nineteen years ago had been for the best, but he had abducted her, and she wasn't entirely certain what to think about him. The last time she'd seen him, he had turned her world upside down in a matter of minutes, and coming face-to-face with him now was just as disconcerting. She took a step back, increasing the distance between them.

"I've only just arrived and have been informed that your sister is to be married today. Forgive me for intruding upon this happy day, but I must speak with you and Prince Alexander immediately."

Sarah scanned the church courtyard, looking for Alex. She spotted him setting on the dais, the place of honor, surrounded by several lords and ladies, who were no doubt enjoying the notability. Sarah had been expected to sit on the dais as well, but she'd insisted on standing on the church steps in order to be closer to Felicia.

"Alex is over there." Sarah motioned to where he sat.

"You'll excuse me then." Apollo gave a deep bow.

Sarah didn't particularly want to spend any amount of time with him, so she gave a quick nod to dismiss him. Maybe she should've been a little more polite, but there was no disapproval on Apollo's face. Instead he thanked her and hurried through the crowd.

The wedding party was late, but Sarah had more pressing thoughts. Whatever had brought Apollo back to Calibre certainly couldn't be good. She rocked on her heels and wrung her hands together as she watched him greet Alex. The two men stepped off to the side and stood close together to afford a small amount of privacy. Alex's expression turned from cheerful to solemn. Then he glanced toward Sarah.

Finally they walked toward her, the crowd giving way to make a path for their prince. Alex walked up the stairs of the church, and with the wave of his hand, the crowd dispersed so that only he, Apollo, and Sarah stood there. He took her hand, caressing it with his fingertips, then dropped his voice so that no one would overhear. "Sarah, I'm afraid Apollo has grave news." He nodded to Apollo, who stepped closer and lowered his own voice.

"Your Highness." His voice was thick with his throaty accent. "Your mother, Queen Natalia, is gravely ill. Your brother, His Highness, knows you plan to travel to Kyrnidan next month for his coronation, but considering the condition of the queen, he thought an envoy should be sent to bring you back to Kyrnidan as quickly as possible."

Sarah stared at him. Michael corresponded frequently with her but only offered vague details. One of his letters informed her that their mother had recently struggled through an unanticipated pregnancy. However, to everyone's surprise, she *had* carried the child to term and delivered safely.

The baby boy was healthy, but apparently, the queen had never fully recovered.

Alex pulled her closer to him. "Sarah, you'll need to leave first thing in the morning."

"What? No! It's too soon."

"Sarah, we'll send messages to the castle. Your lady's maids can take care of the packing so you don't have to leave the celebration early."

Panic welled up inside her. "I . . . I just can't go now."

"Yes, you can." Alex pulled her into a hug.

Sarah took comfort within the security of his strong arms. She would be fine as long as he was with her. He would be her support. She calculated the days of travel ahead of her. It would give them time to mend their relationship. Let it go back to the way it used to be—before the pressures of the council were upon them. "All right." She sank further into his arms. "At least this journey will afford us some much needed time together."

Alex said nothing, and Sarah felt the slight change in his mood. She tipped her head up and saw him looking at her. That concerned expression was back. She leaned away. "Alex, what's wrong?"

He shifted uncomfortably. "I am not going with you."

CHAPTER 4

Andrew Barnett Savell, the high judge, had an impressive estate. The large courtyard behind the house afforded the extra space needed to hold the crowd that had turned out to celebrate his son's wedding. The day's fading light was brightened by a sea of lanterns, transforming the outdoor setting into a magical, twinkling backdrop for the party.

As hard as she tried, Sarah couldn't feel the magic of the evening. As Joseph and Felicia's distinguished guests, she and Alex were seated above the crowd at a large table placed on a dais. She tried to smile, but she struggled with the growing anxiety of her mother's sickness and her imminent departure. Apollo, who was seated next to her, only added to her apprehension. With so much on her mind, she didn't want to spend her last evening as a spectacle, attracting the attention that should've been directed toward the newly married couple. She forced an agonized smile as she looked out at the people, who constantly kept their eyes on the dais.

Shifting awkwardly in her straight-backed chair, she gave a sideways glance toward Alex. He was leaning forward, his forearms resting lightly on the table, the very essence of confidence and composure. There was no doubt he was well suited for the place of honor.

Sarah tried to ignore her feelings of inadequacy, but she was all too aware that she had not earned her position there. What was she to be honored for? Her royalty wouldn't exist if someone hadn't accidently discovered it. A seamstress in a dim little shop, measuring a girl for a ball gown, and then—

"I'm a royal accident," Sarah muttered under her breath.

"Excuse me, Your Highness? What was that?" Apollo leaned toward her.

"Nothing." She refused to look at him. Why had they seated him next to her? Perhaps the chain of events he had set in motion had turned out for the best, but she couldn't overlook the fact that he, a chief counselor and friend, had betrayed the family he served by taking their daughter away.

"Anything more to eat, Your Highness?"

Sarah turned to the young servant. "Aaron!" She stared at the boy. She hardly recognized him. He must have sprouted at least four inches since she'd last seen him. And his hair was combed. That made a difference. "How are you, Aaron? I didn't know you worked for Judge Savell."

Aaron looked around as if he were unsure if he should answer. "Ummm. I just started, Your Highness. May I get you anything else to eat?"

"No, thank you. Do you still have Purkoy?"

His eyes darted around again. "Yes. He's tied behind the haystack right now. If you don't mind, Your Highness, I need to get back to my chores."

Aaron darted away, and Sarah turned back in her chair. Apollo was staring at her. "And what is a Purkoy?"

"A wild goat. Aaron caught him over a year ago. The name means inquisitive."

Apollo raised an eyebrow. "Indeed."

Indeed? What did he mean by that? Sarah couldn't decipher his expression. Was he being critical? Perhaps he had a right to be. She had been acting below her status again. But she couldn't help it. She couldn't ignore friends simply because her title had changed.

Sarah stood and took several deep breaths. The air felt clearer when she wasn't sitting amongst stuffy society. "I think I'll take a walk." She was careful with her words, making sure they didn't reveal her desperation to get away.

Alex pulled away from his own conversation and looked at her. "Would you like me to get someone to escort you?"

"No. I think I'll just mingle about."

The expression on Alex's face remained poised, but she sensed his approval. She had intended to slip away somewhere isolated so she could clear the thoughts in her head, but Alex would want her to mingle with the dignitaries. Ugh. She dreaded the work of making good impressions—speaking with the right people and saying the right things. But with Alex's approval on her mind, she resigned herself to the task.

She had just joined a group of women when she saw Apollo stand up and approach her. Her pulse began to race. She wasn't ready to talk to him. Turning abruptly, she began threading her way through the crowd. After a moment, she glanced over her shoulder and frowned. He was following her. She quickened her step and slipped through the thinning crowd and around the corner of the manor.

"This was a mistake," she moaned aloud. The side of the house was completely devoid of people. If he caught her there, she would have no way to avoid him, but there was a door leading into the manor, the servants' entrance, no doubt. Quickly she walked to it and slipped inside.

She found herself in a large kitchen with several bustling cooks. Not wanting to explain why she was there, Sarah quickly ducked through the nearest doorway, which led up a dark, narrow stairway to the second floor. A moment later, she emerged into a great hallway. Thankfully, no one was there. She ventured forward with every intention to exit out the front of the house—hopefully without being seen.

She tiptoed down the corridor and was almost to the end when she heard voices. Frantic, she looked around trying to find a place to hide. It would be a huge scandal if anyone found her wandering around the judge's house. Creeping to the end of the hallway, she peeked around the corner and recoiled. It was the judge with Lord Moret and Lord Clemente.

At a loss for what to do, she turned around and nearly ran into a servant. Sarah grabbed the pile of linens, which nearly toppled out of the woman's arms.

"Leah." Sarah recognized her friend's dainty features even though she was partially hidden behind her neatly folded stack.

"Sarah—" Leah's cheeks flushed, and she dropped into a quick curtsy. "Forgive me. I mean, Your Highness." She steadied her bundle. "Excuse me for bumping into you. I was getting the guest quarters ready, and I can hardly see over this mess." She paused and peered over her pile at Sarah.

"I'm just taking a short walk," Sarah explained before Leah could ask what she was doing in the upper corridor of the judge's home. She lowered her voice to just above a whisper. "I thought I could find some privacy up here."

"I see." Leah shook her head, flipping a silver streaked curl away from her face. "I used to flatter myself with dreams of becoming a courtier when I was younger, but it must be troublesome, I suspect. I would not like every aspect of my life under the observations of others." Leah shifted the bundle in her arms. There was a wistful glint in her eye as she looked at Sarah, like one has when coming across an old friend but knowing a parting of ways is near again. "Your sister, Felicia, has been a good landlady to us, but oh, how I miss visiting with you when you used to come by to collect the rent for your father."

"I miss the visits too." Sarah looked over to the end of the hallway. She could still hear the judge. In fact, the voices seemed much closer now. Being caught in the house would be bad enough, but if the men caught her conversing with the hired help, they would be even less forgiving. Lords Moret and Clemente would use it as more evidence that she continued to act below her station, proving she was not ready to marry the prince.

Facing Apollo would be better than being caught by the judge and councilmen. She turned to run back to the kitchen stairway when Leah nudged her. "I know you want your privacy, but I thought you should know—my little Daniela has taken sick again. She's got the cough and fever like the devil himself is holding her."

Sarah suppressed the urge to flee to the stairs and turned her attention back to Leah. "Daniela can't be sick. Did she not just come through a bout of sweating sickness only months ago?"

"Eight months ago now."

"Still, it's too soon to be sick again. What's being done about it?"

"Nothing to speak of. I haven't had time to tend to her with all this preparation for the wedding. Day after tomorrow I'll be able to go to market to buy medicine."

The judge's voice grew louder, and Sarah stiffened. He was right around the corner. She glanced at the stairway at the opposite end of the hall. If she was going to run, this was her chance. She bit the inside of her cheek and groaned. There was nothing for it. She looked back at Leah, fully aware of what she was risking. "I still gather herbs. I keep them at the old manor. When you get a minute tonight, run over there and tell Joshua I sent you. He'll let you into the storage cupboard. Take the yarrow and make a tea. It will help sweat her fever out. There's horehound and horseradish there too. That will help with the cough. On the top shelf you'll find a box of rose hips; take that as well."

Leah's mouth fell open with something of excitement and gratitude. "Thank you, Sarah—I mean, Your Highness. Thank you so much. I'll run over as soon as I finish up here."

She turned to go just as the judge turned the corner. Sarah waited for the harsh criticism, but Leah stepped out of the way of the judge and collided with Lord Moret. Her pile of linens toppled directly onto Lord Clemente. Sarah's eyes widened. The distraction afforded her one more second, and she didn't waste it. As the judge bent to fuss over his guests, she grabbed the handle to the door directly behind her and, finding it unlocked, ducked inside with a flurry.

Quietly shutting the door, she pressed her ear to it and listened. Leah's muffled apologies continued on for several moments. After some sharp words from the judge, the men's conversation picked up where they had left off. Their heavy footsteps came closer then stopped again. They had stopped in the middle of the hallway just outside the room where she hid. She could hear the councilmen laughing and conversing about the wedding, and then one of them mentioned her name. Sarah pressed her ear harder against the door, mortified. Perhaps they'd seen her after all and knew she was hiding. She froze, unsure what to do. Then the men's conversation continued. She felt her face flush. They must not have known she was there after all. Instead they were recounting a little mishap she'd had during a previous state dinner. Again, the men burst out laughing.

The sound settled on Sarah like a heavy weight. She turned her back to the door and dropped her head, letting her hair hide the embarrassment that was burning in her cheeks. After a moment, she steeled herself and looked up. For the first time, she saw the room she was in. Her breath caught in her throat. "No, no, no!" she whispered. "Can this possibly get any worse?"

There was no doubt about it. She was in Judge Andrew Savell's bedchamber. Sarah closed her eyes in humiliation and shook her head. Another boisterous laugh from the hallway made her spring into action. She had to hide again. What if the judge were to come in? She would never outlive the humiliation. She jerked her head as she looked around. There was no other way out. She cringed as she continued to examine the room. The judge was not a clean man. *I know he's widowed, but does he not have a maid?* Sarah tried not to focus on the undergarments strewn on the edge of the bed.

She quickly bent over, pulled up the coverlet, and looked beneath the bed frame, hoping it would offer a place of concealment. The cavity beneath the rope-strung mattress was completely filled with stray bedding and discarded clothes, and the pungent smell made her gag. Disgusted, she stood again and eyed the window. She fairly flew to it and threw it open with a grateful sigh. It was on a secluded side of the manor, and there were no guests walking the lantern-lit path below the window. She looked around, squinting into the darkness. If only there was a tree nearby like the one she had used to climb out her window as a child.

There were no nearby trees, but there was an arbor not too far away. She tried to gauge how to best reach it and determined that the only way would be to carefully walk along the decorative rock edging that ran the length of the manor.

Another bout of laughter set her determination, and she pulled up her skirts and threw her leg out the window. "I hope I don't regret this." She heaved herself all the way outside.

As she placed her foot on the rock ledge, she instantly yearned for the soft, pliable shoes she was accustomed to; it wasn't going to be easy navigating in the elaborately decorative ones she now wore. She shot one last look into the room behind her then carefully eased herself along the edge. It was too late to go back now. She needed to get down quickly before someone saw her—and preferably without falling to her death.

Her fingers clung to the stone wall as she edged her way over to the arbor. She made a mental note of the construction and determined that if she were to ever have an arbor built, she should at least make it a good deal taller than this one. It was made of a sturdy wooden lattice, and she was certain it would hold her weight, but at its tallest point, it still didn't reach the ledge she was on. If she bent down, she would likely lose her grip, but there was nothing else she could do.

Carefully bending her knees, she moved her hands down the wall, but as soon as she did, her foot slipped and she toppled forward, landing squarely on the top of the arbor. The impact was harder than expected, and she let out an involuntary grunt. Sarah had scarcely gained her balance, and her breath, before she began making her way down. Her hands shook as she grabbed the lattice and placed her feet in the nearest crevice she could find. Wedging her toe into a tight opening, she put her weight on it and felt her shoe slide deeper into the groove. After she shifted her body down, she went to pull her foot free, but it didn't budge. Her shoe was caught in the lattice-work. She tugged at it several times with no success. It was no use. She was stuck.

CHAPTER 5

SARAH CLUNG AWKWARDLY TO THE lattice arbor. *Come on! I used to be good at climbing. What's wrong with me? It's these shoes!* She would gladly leave the stuck shoe behind, but then she imagined hobbling around the rest of the night with only one shoe. She could leave both shoes behind. Would anyone notice her going around in her stocking feet? Her dress was almost long enough—she stopped the thought. She couldn't leave so much as a single shoe behind. What if someone came by and noticed it hanging in the arbor? It would certainly incriminate her. No one else at the celebration had high-heeled shoes embroidered with silk and trimmed with lace that fell in a flounce around the top. She shook her head. What was she thinking? She needed to get moving before she got caught.

"The stars are beautiful, don't you agree?"

Sarah froze when she heard the voice, not daring to find out where it came from. She hoped the man wasn't addressing her. Perhaps he didn't see her and, if she didn't move, he would go away. Several tense moments passed as she held her breath.

"I only make the comment as you must have a better view of the celestial realm from your higher vantage point."

Sarah would have thrown her hands up in frustration had she not needed them to keep herself from falling. *After all that work—to be caught now!* Certainly this would not bode well for her reputation. Her last hope was that the man would leave without realizing who she was. She waited, not responding as she offered up a silent prayer asking God to get her out of the predicament. At last she heard the man's footsteps walk away. With a quick glance confirming the pathway was now vacant, Sarah jerked her foot so hard, the wood cracked. Free from her entrapment, she quickly began her descent again. When she was within reach, she jumped to the stone pavers and began brushing at her dress as she looked around.

"Now that you are safely on the ground, Your Highness, will you continue to ignore me?"

Sarah jumped, turning at the sound but seeing no one. She was astounded at the man's casual regard for her in his tone of voice, but when she saw the lean, hard figure emerge from the shadows across the way, she understood. The man's strong physique and sandy-brown hair were familiar. It was Luther Tandy, Alex's private bodyguard. She had spent hours in the same room as him on countless occasions, and she was used to his blunt manner of speaking. His unchecked honesty was one of the things that endeared him to many in the castle.

"What are you doing here?" she asked.

"The prince hasn't seen you for some time and asked me to check on you."

Sarah hated the confident smile that pulled at the ends of his lips. "Well, in the future, announce yourself." She turned to leave and then stopped. "And Mr. Tandy, I see no reason why you should mention this situation to anyone—ever."

Luther cleared his throat. "I fully agree; however, I do have one question." She turned and regarded him with what she hoped was an innocent expression. "Did you find anything interesting in the judge's room? You were in there for what seemed to be a long time."

She quickly walked back to him. "How long have you been watching me?"

"Long enough to find this very entertaining."

Sarah folded her arms in irritation. "Do you realize what it would mean if you were to be caught spying on royalty?"

"Yes. It means I'll get substantially higher pay from the cantankerous women at court who try to bribe me for information about you." He grinned.

Sarah's mouth fell open. "You wouldn't dare—" She broke off and stared at him. "People try to bribe you for information about me?"

Luther folded his arms across his broad chest and leaned casually against the arbor. "Nice to be in the center of society, is it not?"

Sarah wished she could be as casual about it as he was. She shrugged and wrapped her arms around herself. "Truth be told? I could do without it."

"Pity. Don't tell me you're thinking of bowing out of your newfound royal position. Should we call the trumpeters to announce the loss of society's most divine damsel?"

Despite Luther's amusing antics, Sarah caught the sarcasm in his voice, and heat rushed into her cheeks. "Don't tell me that you're one of those who oppose my marrying Prince Alexander."

"Truth be told?" Luther paused, meeting her eyes with a searching gaze of his own.

"I see no reason for deception; let us be honest," she said.

He pushed himself away from the arbor and took a step closer to her. "Then, yes, I am."

Unable to hold his gaze any longer, Sarah looked away, trying to mask her disappointment.

"I'm sorry." His voice was softer now. "I should restrain my tongue."

"I was the one who asked for your honesty."

"Yes, but what is the opinion of a single guard?"

"It is an opinion that is shared by so many others." Sarah tried not to sound bitter, but she was sure Luther sensed her sour mood.

There was a long silence. Luther leaned back against the arbor again, his arms still crossed. His typical bodyguard physique was hard, with chiseled features, but his face was soft with sympathy. "That's not to say there's no place for you," he said.

"And where exactly is my place?" She put her hands on her hips. "What do *you* think I'm suited for?"

Luther placed a finger over his lips, urging her to be quiet. Only then did Sarah hear approaching footsteps. From where she stood, she couldn't see who was coming down the path, but Luther leaned out, taking a quick look; then he crossed over to her, repeating his signal to stay quiet. He took her hand and guided her to the back side of the arbor. Placing her next to the manor wall, he leaned against the lattice work to further hide her. The steps grew louder, and then Apollo's tall figure passed by.

A minute later Luther nodded for her to come out. "That is who you are trying to avoid, is it not?"

Sarah nodded. He wouldn't have known that unless he'd been watching her from the time she left the banquet table, which was probably long before Alex had asked him to go check on her. She regarded him with a raised brow. How often did he watch her? "But if you don't like me, then why did you help by hiding me?"

"I never said I didn't like you." Sarah felt her cheeks flush before he continued. "And actually, I really don't have any arguments to oppose your position apart from my own selfish reasons." He met her eyes again. "Besides, I'm not helping you hide. I'm simply giving you more time to gather your courage before you go talk with Mr. Moylan."

"You think I'm going to talk to Apollo?"

"Yes, I do—unless you're offering to stay here and talk with me, in which case I won't complain."

She couldn't help but smile at his wit, but at the same time, she felt the need to refrain from enjoying it too much. "Very well. I'll consider speaking to him."

Luther gave a short bow. "Then I shall tell the prince that you are in the company of Mr. Apollo Moylan."

Sarah reluctantly agreed and walked back to the large courtyard. She paused at the edge of the crowd and looked back. Part of her hoped that she'd see an empty pathway, that Luther would be gone, but he wasn't. He stood there and then did something terrible—he smiled. It was a nice smile. She quickly turned away and moved into the crowd.

After greeting several people, Sarah took solace in a friendly face: Carlina Sarter Fales, the seamstress who had first discovered her mark of royalty. Crossing the patio, Sarah wove her way past the dancers and minstrels to her elderly friend.

"Your Highness." The old woman's voice sounded thick with her throaty accent. Even though the Kyrnidians shared the same language, the tone was coarser. Sarah didn't mind the sound and actually enjoyed it at times. She leaned over and let the woman kiss her on the cheek.

"I hear you are to depart for Kyrnidan on the morrow," Carlina said.

Sarah felt a pang of dread as she contemplated her inevitable departure. "Yes, I am."

Carlina's fingers went down to Sarah's waist and touched the long belt of pearls and topaz stones. One end hung halfway down her frame, weighted by a silver unicorn. "You still wear it, my dear?"

"Of course. I'll never forget the night you brought me that exquisite gown—a gown fit for a queen." Sarah touched the belt. "This was the pinnacle feature. I always wear it, and it will go with me to Kyrnidan."

Carlina picked up the unicorn and ran her fingers over it—the symbol of their home country. "Oh, I wish I could go with you, my child."

"I wish you could come too." Sarah would so enjoy taking Carlina with her, but there was no use hoping for the impossible. Carlina was expecting a grandchild soon and would not so much as step foot outside the village until her daughter-in-law delivered. "I am certain to take other trips in the future, and I shall make sure that you are among the party."

Carlina looked up at her. "No, child. You should stay in Kyrnidan. I think you do not comprehend the significance of the mark you bear on your shoulder. You are the firstborn, my dear, and are meant to fulfill the prophecy. They'll need you to stay there in Kyrnidan."

Sarah's jaw tightened at the reference to the prophecy. It was the reason Apollo had taken her from her home to begin with. "The prophecy refers to the firstborn *son*," Sarah reminded her.

"Oh, pishposh. The high priest's prophecy refers to the firstborn, and as the firstborn, you are destined to unite the people of Kyrnidan." Carlina waved a hand in the air. "He only assumed the firstborn would be a boy."

"The high priest should not have written an assumption into his prophecy. Either way, you cannot dismiss that the prophecy is incorrect. I am decidedly not a boy. How can the people of Kyrnidan still believe in something that has been disproven?"

"Tisk, tisk." Carlina shook a finger at Sarah. "The high priest had a gift, I tell you, and that gift has proven itself many times. The evidence is on the plates."

"Oh yes, the plates." Sarah tried not to roll her eyes. She had been told about the plates—thinly pounded sheets of metal which were supposedly engraved with the exact words of each prophecy given by the high priest. "Regardless, there is at least one plate that is wrong." Carlina opened her mouth to respond, but Sarah cut her off. "My journey to Kyrnidan is not to fulfill a prophecy. I'm simply going to visit my family and to see my ailing mother. After that I will be returning here." She met the woman's gaze. "I know you love Kyrnidan, but please understand that my loyalty is to Calibre. I was raised here, and this is my country."

Carlina nodded; the gesture said, "I understand you," but there was a distinct sadness behind her eyes.

"Ah, there is Apollo." Sarah motioned in the direction of the tall man making his way through the crowd. "Will you stay with me while I talk with him?"

"Of course. I've heard that you won't have any close friends to accompany you on your journey, but at least you will have Apollo. He is such a good man."

Sarah didn't respond but silently braced herself for the uncomfortable encounter.

Apollo bowed deeply when he reached them. "I'm sorry to intrude on your celebration." His accent was heavier than Carlina's. "I was just wondering, Your Highness, if I can do anything to assist you in preparing for our journey tomorrow?"

Sarah tried not to sigh. He could not help her get ready nor could he make this any easier for her. "No, thank you," she said, trying to keep the conversation short and to the point. The less she had to speak to him, the better. He regarded her with a thoughtful expression, and she shifted under his gaze.

Awkwardness settled over them. At last, Carlina and Apollo began to exchange pleasantries, and Sarah looked around, searching for someone to relieve her from her uncomfortable situation. At last she found Alex. His tall frame made him easy to spot. He stood near a corner, the light from a nearby lantern glistening off his raven-dark hair. He was deep in conversation with a stout, barrel-chested man and several guards. Luther was among them.

Luther, at least, was aware of her torture. He met her eyes, and she tried to communicate her plea. She thought she saw a slight smile cross his face. Then, thankfully, he interrupted Alex and the men. Alex turned and looked at her then spoke to Luther again.

Sarah breathed a sigh of relief when Luther started striding toward her. Suddenly Carlina nudged her, and she became painfully aware that Apollo had been talking to her. "I'm sorry," she said. "These events have me rather distracted."

Apollo gave a courteous bow of his head. "Quite understandable. I was just saying that I will aid you in any way that I can in your preparations for tomorrow. I am at your complete disposal."

"Thank you for the offer." It was the proper thing to say, although the entire trip was going to be awkward enough with him as her escort, and she wasn't going to precipitate it by including him in her preparations.

"Excuse me," Luther said as he stepped between Apollo and Sarah. "I have been asked to accompany you back to the castle, Your Highness."

Sarah looked at him with surprise. She wanted intervention—not to be completely extracted from the celebration. Luther took her arm and began directing her to where Alex stood. "I'm not ready to leave," she said.

Luther looked down at her. "It's for your safety, Your Highness." His voice was low, and his brow wrinkled with concern. "We have just been informed by the bailiff that Chadwick Hill has escaped."

Sarah brought herself up short and stared at Luther. His face was tense, as if he were reluctant to share any more details. But it all seemed impossible. "Is there such a flaw in the king's dungeons to allow Chad to escape?"

Luther pressed his lips together and looked around uneasily. "Unfortunately, that seems to be the case. And from what we can determine, he may be coming after you."

CHAPTER 6

THE LAST OF SARAH'S TRUNKS had long been outside and carefully packed into the carriage. The entire entourage would, at that moment, be gathering in the courtyard readying for their departure. Sarah stood alone in her room and looked out the window. The pink on the horizon indicated that it wouldn't be long before the sun made its appearance. She pulled her traveling cloak tighter. It will be foggy this morning, she thought, gratified that the weather matched her mood. *Have I forgotten anything?* She felt as though she had forgotten a hundred different things, but she couldn't remember a single one. She leaned her cheek against the coolness of the window. Yesterday had been rife with commotion and activity. There had been no time for her to sort through the tempest of emotions she'd been feeling.

"Mother," she whispered to the dark, foggy morning. The word brought images of Miranda reading a book, riding a horse, gathering and preserving herbs, then finally images of a pale, thin, fragile woman, her vivacious spirit gone. Now another woman, one that she couldn't put a face or feeling to, lay sick and possibly dying—her birth mother. Sarah wanted to get to know her, even come to love her. But at the same time, she felt that this stranger would never fill the role of mother.

At least Sarah hadn't been forced to leave on her journey before Felicia's wedding. It was refreshing to see her sister so beautiful and happy. She almost let her thoughts drift to the day when she would be exchanging vows with Alex, but she quickly reined them in. It wouldn't do any good to think so far ahead when the possibilities were so uncertain.

A knock at the door brought her back to the present. "Come!" The door opened, and Alex strode across the room to join her at the window. "I was just thinking about you."

"I am glad to hear that I still occupy your thoughts." He gave her a wink then moved behind her and wrapped his arms around her waist. "Mother told me to give you her sentiments and to wish you a safe journey." He rested his cheek against her hair. "And I am shamelessly using that as my excuse to come and share a few private minutes with you before your departure. Now tell me—are you ready?"

Sarah rocked her weight onto one hip. "How can I be ready for this?" All of the turbulent feelings returned. "I don't know if I can do this." She twisted around in his arms to face him and laid her head on his shoulder.

"You need to. I'll feel better knowing you'll be out of Calibre and out of Chad's reach."

Sarah tensed. "Have you learned anything more?"

"We know that one of the guards in the castle helped him escape. Apparently, we hadn't weeded out all of Chad's supporters. The guard is in custody, but there has been no word on Chad's whereabouts. We suspect he's hiding somewhere in the village."

Sarah gave him a sidelong glance. Would she ever be out of Chad's reach? What if he followed her to Kyrnidan?

"I wish I had some great words of wisdom that would bring you comfort," Alex said. "The only thing I can tell you is that I believe all will be well."

She detected the uncertainty in his voice. It was slight, but it was there nonetheless. "Tell me that you are coming with me," she pleaded.

"All right." He looked into her face. "I'll come with you. Just tell me how long you're willing to wait to get married?"

She groaned.

"I know. I really wish I could go, but the King's Council has finally agreed to put our marriage to the vote at their next meeting. If the majority agrees—and I think they will—then we can be married in a few months. I need to be here to hedge any possible naysayers."

"I know." Sarah was unable to keep the gloomy tone from her voice.

"Everything will be all right. You'll be fine." He bent his head and kissed her. She leaned into it. She wanted it to be fine. She wanted *them* to be fine—like they were before. The council meeting would play a great part in what their future would look like, and it was best that Alex stay. She wanted to postpone her trip herself, but she would deeply regret it if she did. Just as Alex needed to stay for the meeting, she needed to go see her mother. Alex tightened his arms around her and kissed her with more intent. She responded by pouring her heart into the embrace. It would be a long time before they would see each other again.

Finally Alex stepped back, holding her at a short distance. He was breathless and slightly flushed. "We should go out so you can meet the rest of your entourage." Sarah pressed the back of her hand to her lips, trying to compose herself and to keep her tears from falling.

A moment later, Sarah pulled her traveling cloak tight to shield herself from the cool, damp morning. As far as an entourage went, this one was relatively small. As it was, she would be accompanied by Apollo, a designated travel companion, a couple of maid servants, and several guards. The smaller carriage would carry her trunks and the maids, while the large carriage would comfortably seat her, a companion, and Apollo when he wasn't riding horseback, which she hoped wouldn't be often.

She and Alex held hands as they approached the group. Everyone's attention turned to them, and the guards put a clenched fist over their hearts in a salute.

"Your Majesties." A prudish looking gentleman stepped forward. His Kyrnidian uniform, with its embroidered sash and ribbons, bespoke of his elevated status, but the man's physical appearance seemed at conflict with his apparel. His build was not that of the typical tall Kyrnidian, but he was a rather short man with pale hair and a weak chin that seemed to slide into his throat.

He snapped himself to attention with gratuitous pride and bowed deeply. "I am Sir Gilbert Henry," he stated in his guttural accent. "I am a member of your father's council, and he has entrusted this journey into my capable hands." He took Sarah's hand and pressed his flaccid lips to it. "It is my great honor to escort you to your home country, Your Highness."

Sarah pulled her hand back and rubbed away the moisture just as Apollo approached them.

"A good morning to you," Apollo said with a bow.

Sarah thought it best to keep her thoughts on that count silent; it was *not* a good morning.

"I see you have met our honorable Sir Henry." There seemed to be a touch of sarcasm in Apollo's voice, but Sarah couldn't be sure.

Sir Henry sidled up next to her. "We should have met sooner; however, Apollo denied me the pleasure, insisting your schedule wouldn't allow it."

Sarah regarded Apollo for the briefest moment, thankful he had respected her time pending her sister's wedding. But she wouldn't say as much. Despite the fact that he had completely played the hand of fate in her life, she repeatedly told herself he was no one of consequence. His decision to take her from her family had caused him to lose his title and authority. Although he had been exonerated from his crime after she was discovered and her whereabouts made known to her family, he had never fully regained his position.

"Let me introduce you to our party," Sir Henry said, as he took her arm and led her forward. Apollo followed closely behind.

Sarah saw that Alice and Rose were there along with a few other maid-servants from the castle. Sir Henry let her greet the women then motioned toward the guards. The military escort was larger than she had expected.

"Both Calibrean and Kyrnidian guards?"

"Let's just say that both countries have a vested interest in your safety," Apollo said.

Sarah didn't mind the extra protection, especially now that Chad was out there.

Sir Henry began turning an angry shade of red as Apollo proceeded to introduce the Kyrnidian officers. Although Sir Henry was supposed to be in charge, Apollo seemed to assume the role himself. His confident, dignified manner made it seem as though he had never lost his authority.

Each soldier was called out by name and stepped forward with a bow. There were no whispers, but the men shared glances between themselves. Sarah squared her shoulders under their scrutiny. She didn't want to be an oddity to them, but after so many years, they must have regarded her as a myth or a legend. *This is going to be a very long journey.*

Sarah averted her eyes from the group as her attention was drawn to a woman near the back of the carriage. In the gloom of the early morning fog, she could see the woman was fumbling with something. Whatever it was, she hastily shoved it into her satchel then looked around nervously before coming out from behind the carriage. She appeared to be several years older than Sarah. Her dress and travel cloak were a muted brown, and although not fashionable, they accentuated her nicely and gave her a steady, collected appearance.

The woman approached as Apollo gestured for her to join them. "The king allowed me to select your travel companion, so may I have the pleasure of introducing to you, Margaret Antonellis. She is . . ." Apollo paused for a moment. Sarah couldn't quite discern his expression. Was he pleased, or was he saddened? It was always so difficult to tell. "She is Miranda's niece," he said.

Sarah gave a start. He certainly put a great deal of thought into choosing her companion. She turned to Margaret. "It is a great pleasure to meet you!"

"I am most pleased to meet you, Your Highness." Margaret accompanied her words with a curtsy.

"Please, call me Sarah. You are as much family to me as Miranda was." She glanced at Apollo. His eyes brightened, but he didn't smile. The rest of the introductions were made, and then Sir Henry asked to speak privately with Alex. They walked a short distance, and to Sir Henry's obvious dismay, Apollo joined them.

Sarah turned to Margaret when she saw Luther bringing her horse up from the stables. "Margaret, I'm anxious for us to get acquainted, but if you'll excuse me for a minute, I need to speak with someone." Margaret gave a polite nod, and Sarah walked over to Luther.

"Absolutely beautiful," he said, holding the horse still so Sarah could pet the snow-white mare.

"She is, isn't she?" Sarah ran her hand down its silky neck and gave the horse a gentle pat.

Luther stepped closer, leaned toward her, and lowered his voice. "The horse is indeed beautiful, but I was referring to you."

Sarah's blush was quick and intense. She knew Alex hadn't heard the comment, but she cast a glance to where he stood. What would he do if he heard another man commenting on her looks? She should have reprimanded Luther, but she couldn't—not when he was paying her a compliment. Did that make her vain? Her brow furrowed. Still feeling the heat in her cheeks, she moved so that the horse was between her and Luther then attempted to change the conversation.

"I didn't ask for Pearl to be brought from the stables," she said.

Luther tugged at the bridle, and the horse backed up, leaving Sarah out in the open. "It'll be a long trip." He looked pointedly at her. "And since I cannot ride in the carriage with you, I thought you might take an occasional ride with me."

"In the carriage? Ride with you? I . . . I had not . . ." Sarah stumbled over her words.

"From your reaction you either didn't know I was assigned to be your personal bodyguard, or you find the thought of riding with me repugnant."

He stepped closer to her. "I choose to think you didn't know I was going with you." Sarah wasn't sure if she should be flattered or frightened, and seeing her confusion, Luther laughed out loud. It was a good-natured, hearty laugh, and it put her at ease. He meant nothing untoward, she was certain—or at least she hoped.

"Considering the length of this sojourn, I do appreciate your thoughtfulness in bringing Pearl." She continued to stroke the horse as he tied the lead to the back of the carriage. "I understand that the roads are well traveled."

"They are." His brusque manner was not unattractive.

"How often will we need to stop, do you think?"

"Not often. The royal horses are good stock. They're bred and trained for endurance. Breeding isn't everything though." His smile was gone. "Training is often more important. A well-bred horse that has been improperly trained will cause her owner nothing but grief." His gaze was sharp and his expression intent.

Was he referring to something more than the horses—that her lineage wouldn't compensate for her lack of training? Last night he'd admitted he didn't approve of her marrying Prince Alexander. Before she could respond to his musings, his expression changed, and he smiled.

"I anticipate a pleasant and uneventful journey, Your Highness." Was that a glint of mischief or amusement in his eyes? She wasn't entirely certain what to think of Luther Tandy, her new personal bodyguard.

"Sarah," Alex called to her. "Everything is in order."

This was the part that she had been dreading all night. She walked toward Alex, and he took her by the hand and led her to the carriage. As Apollo was assisting Margaret in, Sarah turned to Alex to say her good-byes. He pulled her into an embrace and pressed a kiss to her lips. She felt his love, but his hold on her was entirely too short, and when they pulled apart, she felt as if he were slipping away.

"I love you," Alex whispered. He took her face in his hands. "All will be well. And when you return, we'll plan our wedding."

"I love you too." Sarah thought she was doing a remarkable job of keeping her emotions hidden. As she turned toward the carriage, she caught a glimpse of Luther sitting on top of a large chestnut gelding. He was staring at her, his expression a tangled mixture of yearning and disappointment.

CHAPTER 7

Sarah shifted uncomfortably in her seat, annoyed that the bumpy movement of the carriage had wakened her. The seemingly countless days of travel were taking their toll. Sir Henry was sound asleep across from her, and Margaret—Sarah tried not to smile—Margaret was definitely awake. She had her little palm-sized bottle out and had just taken a long draw from it.

This is what Margaret had been doing behind the carriage the first day they had met—secretly taking a drink from the bottle, but it had taken Sarah three days to figure it out. Since then there had been a dozen times where Sarah had nearly confronted her about it. She thought about sitting up now and catching Margaret in the act, but she didn't want to hurt her companion's feelings. It was obvious the woman didn't want anyone to know about the habit. She was always secretive, glancing nervously around before she pulled it out. Then with lightning speed, she would take one or two swallows before stashing it away. For someone as proper as Margaret, being caught would be humiliating, so Sarah waited until the small bottle was corked and hidden away before she feigned waking up.

"Did you get any rest?" Margaret asked as she straightened into her proper pose now that she knew someone was watching her. "You didn't sleep long."

"Apparently not as much as Sir Henry." Sarah nodded toward the sleeping gentleman.

Margaret lowered her voice. "Yes, none of us ever get as much sleep as Sir Henry. Sometimes I wonder if he's related to a cat."

Sarah laughed. "Yes, but a cat would be better company."

Margaret choked back a giggle as she took out a mint leaf and began chewing it. Sarah had identified this as another one of her companion's habits—one that manifested itself after sneaking drinks from the little bottle. Despite the habits, Sarah had bonded with the woman. Margaret was a wonderful listener, patient, and enjoyable to be around, yet strict with the guards and firm with the maids when the situation called for it. In more ways than one, she reminded Sarah of Miranda.

"I haven't thanked you for coming along on this tedious journey," Sarah said, looking at her new friend. "It has been a blessing to have you with me." Margaret dismissed the comment with a wave of her hand. "But we haven't talked about Miranda yet," Sarah continued.

Margaret turned toward her, and her eyes softened with compassion. "I've wanted to, but I wasn't sure you were ready."

"You were Miranda's niece and have every right to know everything about her." Sarah took a deep breath. This conversation would likely refresh the painful loss she felt for her mother. "Did you know her when she lived in Kyrnidan?"

"Oh yes. I was a young girl—nine, I believe—when she left. We lived in different villages, but we visited her twice a year. I remember how beautiful she was."

Sarah tried to smile but faltered. "I'm sorry. I feel it was my fault she left."

"Don't ever think that!" Margaret's accent caused the words to sound harsher than they were intended. "You were only a baby. Nothing was your fault."

A long moment of silence passed between them, and Margaret's gaze seemed to slide out of focus as if she were looking through Sarah. "I remember the day we received the letter from Miranda. My parents were all in a tizzy over it. It said she was moving to Farellden, but when Father went there, she was nowhere to be found. To think, she was making her way across the countryside with you in her arms. The princess of Kyrnidan." Margaret focused on Sarah again. "Miranda was always up for an adventure, and she had always longed for a child. You gave her both. I'm sure she was happy."

"I believe it was hard for her, but she was a wonderful mother, and we shared many happy moments together." Sarah was surprised how easily they slipped into conversation after that. Margaret was eager to share her memories of Miranda, and Sarah found that she was too. Before long, they were both laughing as they recounted their favorite stories.

An hour later, the conversation lulled, and Sarah pulled the curtain aside to look out the window at the guards who were riding alongside them. She watched them often, especially the Kyrnidian guards, who were particularly entertaining. They were a little rough around the edges compared to the Calibrean men. She expected as much. Kyrnidan was a nation that prided itself on its warriors, and the Kyrnidian guards exemplified those ideals. They brawled each night and sparred whenever they could. Since most of their time consisted of traveling, they had invented a means of practicing their combat tactics even while riding.

Sometimes the men would pair off, galloping side by side, trying to unseat each other—a kind of wrestling, jousting routine. Other times they would take turns wearing a large red feather in their hats. The brave man with the feather would then put one hand on his hip, jutting his elbow out to the side to create an opening between his arm and his body. Taking turns, the soldiers would ride from behind at full gallop and swords drawn. Sweeping close to the red-feathered man, they would pass the blade of their sword cleanly through the small opening his arm created. The rider would then have to let go of his sword and catch it on the other side of the man's arm. Sarah found herself holding her breath every time she watched.

All the men were now riding quietly in uniform lines, so apparently, she had missed their sport for the day. She wasn't disappointed. All the entertainment in the world couldn't replace the conversation she had just had with Margaret.

Sarah let her eyes wander across the craggy landscape. The rocky outcrops had emerged during the previous day of travel when the caravan had officially crossed the border into Kyrnidan. The jagged countryside was fascinating, but after several minutes, she found her gaze shifting to where Luther rode with the other men. Watching him had been another pastime she'd taken up. It helped her endure the many monotonous hours. A few days into their journey, she had accepted his offer and had ridden alongside him on Pearl. That was the day she noticed the fine details of the bodyguard's contagious smile—how it lit up his face and brought out the golden flecks in his brown eyes. She hadn't ridden with him since and had spent more time trying to remember the details of Alex's face.

"You know," Margaret said as she leaned over toward Sarah, "Apollo tells me that Luther Tandy reminds him of your father."

"Really?" Sarah dropped the curtain, slightly embarrassed that Margaret had noticed her looking at Luther. Her curiosity piqued, but it being improper to ask about details, Sarah took the safe approach. "And how long has Apollo known my father?"

"Since they were young. But the specific day Apollo mentioned to me was the day your father was made king. Your grandfather, the overlord, had just passed away. Your father had already proven himself a great leader in battle and would have easily been the next warlord voted in, but the old ways were changing. Your father was already married, and no doubt your mother inspired part of that change as well—her being nobility from a monarchal country. It's funny how we're always trying to adopt the ways of other nations."

Sarah wasn't interested in a lesson about how the old government had changed to the monarchy. "So what happened on the day Father was made king that made Apollo think of Mr. Tandy?"

"Apollo said he remembered seeing your father parade through the streets right after he had been offered the title of king. There had been many overlords before him—warriors who have proven themselves in battle—but Apollo said your father was different, which also contributed to the people wanting a monarchy. There was something truly gallant about your father. He had a compelling nature that distinguished him from other men, and people were drawn to him and were devout to his leadership."

"And Apollo sees that in Mr. Tandy as well?"

Margaret shrugged. "I don't know. Apollo said that Luther sets atop his horse in the same manner."

Sarah pulled the curtain again and looked out. She had no doubt about that. Luther had proven popular among the Kyrnidian guards. Eager, highly skilled, and physically disciplined, he had many warrior-like qualities, something the Kyrnidians highly valued. And he did sit atop his horse well.

The sun was just about to set when the carriage pulled up to a roadside inn. Sarah was familiar with the routine. She waited while Sir Henry paid the innkeeper, and within minutes her maids would have her room ready.

Once inside, Margaret pushed the door open and let Sarah enter the small, bleak chamber. She tried not to cringe as she looked around. She couldn't help but notice that as they drew closer to the heart of Kyrnidan, the quality of the accommodations diminished. She resolved to ask her brother about the well-being of the country's economy. The room was sparsely furnished with only a bed and a narrow, rickety table, and the air was thick with the distinct smell of dirt and sweat. She eyed the bed. It was small, rather lumpy, and sagged dramatically in the middle. The maids had put out fresh linens, but the sleeping accommodations still left something to be desired.

"Don't worry," Margaret said, walking over and pushing on the bed. "I'll have Alice and Rose tighten the ropes, but I don't know what's to be done about this old, prickly straw." She pounded a fist into one of the lumps. "Your accommodations will be much better at the castle, I assure you." She straightened and gave Sarah a sympathetic look. "It still might not be what you're used to, but I'm sure you'll find it pleasant enough."

"How much longer until we arrive?"

"Another day and a half is all. And I can't wait to get you settled in."

"One more inn," Sarah said with a sigh. "I can handle that."

"Yes, we can." Margaret punched another lump.

Sarah watched her with adoration. Margaret's optimism reminded her so much of Miranda.

"Regretfully, hard bread and cheese is all the innkeeper is offering us for tonight's meal." Another lump was pummeled. "But I'll have some fetched up immediately if you're hungry."

"Perhaps a little later." Sarah wasn't really hungry. Sir Henry always had morsels of food to munch on in the carriage and had given her an apple and a couple of strips of dried meat shortly before they'd arrived at the inn. "Right now I think I'll go for a walk."

Margaret put her hands on her hips. "Now do you really intend to go for *a walk*, or do you aim to sneak off to the stables to dote over that horse of yours?"

Sarah replied with a smirk and tried to hide it by walking over to the window and looking out. From the corner of her eye, she caught a glimpse of a rider, and her heart jumped. Even at a distance, the man looked like Chad. She pressed a hand against the thick pane, trying to get a closer look. He was too far away to make out the details of his features, but the outline, the way he set his mount—all of it reminded her of Chad. Had he followed her to Kyrnidan? The rider turned aside, taking another road, and disappeared from sight. She shook her head. She was just tired, and it was nearly dark outside. Perhaps she was just seeing things.

"You don't need me to come with you then?" Margaret asked.

"I'm sorry. What were you saying?" Sarah pulled herself away from the window and focused on Margaret.

"If you're just going to the stables, you won't need me to accompany you."

"Of course not." The Kyrnidians were much more lax in their formalities. For them a short walk didn't warrant an escort. Sarah planned to spend time in the stables with her horse, but she also needed to stretch her legs. After sitting in the carriage for hours, a short stroll was exactly what her stiff body needed. Still, with someone out there resembling Chad . . . She rubbed one arm and glanced back at the window.

Margaret had gone back to punching the clumps of straw in the bed, and Sarah teetered on the idea of asking for her company. It was silly. She shouldn't be scared to go out. Anyway, she wouldn't go far, and if someone were following her, they wouldn't dare come near the inn while a large band of soldiers was lodged there. Sarah resolved to continue with her walk but to keep it short. Besides, Margaret needed some time alone too. The poor woman was always forcing herself to be rigid and poised whenever anyone was around, and it was surprising she hadn't had a fainting spell yet.

"If Apollo comes by making his nightly rounds, I'll tell him you're resting comfortably in this nice lumpy bed." Margaret punched another lump then waved a hand to shoo her out the door.

Strangling a sigh, Sarah walked out and muttered a thank you. "I'll only be a minute." As she pulled the door behind her, she saw Margaret abandon her fight with the mattress and reach for the little bottle in her satchel.

Sarah paused outside the inn's door, tempted to go right back inside. "Coward," she mumbled to herself. She didn't want to go skulking around afraid of her own shadow simply because she had seen someone out the window. There was no use scaring herself over it. It wasn't far to the side street where the rider had gone, so she walked a little way and looked in that direction. The rider was gone. She was just being paranoid, but regardless, she had walked far enough. She quickly turned back toward the inn and headed in the direction of the stables.

The smell of horses and dusty hay settled over her as she slipped in through the large wooden door. The familiar aroma was comforting, and she breathed it in to calm herself. She was safe. With the sun now set and everyone inside for the night, the stable was almost pitch-black. A horse shifted uneasily in its stall. Could it sense her? Not waiting for her eyes to adjust to the darkness, she put a hand on the rough-planked wall and felt her way forward.

By the time she got to the first stall, she was able to make out dark shapes. She stepped around a bucket, a shovel, and a pitchfork when she noticed a bag of grain. *Pearl would like a handful of grain.* She bent down to open the bag when all at once she felt decidedly uneasy. Something was wrong, and an unexplained sense of panic welled up inside her. Not daring to move, she listened.

Boots. Someone was near the back of the stable—hiding in the dark. The feeling that stirred in the pit of her stomach grew into cold fear.

The boots moved again, a quiet, heavy thud as they stepped toward her. She stood, suddenly regretting all the times she had gone off without an escort.

"It's a little late for you to be out here, is it not?"

Sarah almost cried out with relief at the sound of Luther's voice. "Mr. Tandy." She put a hand on her chest to calm herself. "You scared me; I thought you were—" She stopped just short of mentioning Chad's name. She didn't want to appear hysterical over her own imagination.

"You thought I was who? Someone dangerous?" he said dramatically.

"No." His features became clearer as he stepped closer to her.

"I could be dangerous." He sounded a little defensive about it, but Sarah couldn't make out his expression in the darkness to really tell. "What are you doing out here?" he asked.

"I came to see how Pearl is doing. And what about you?"

"The same. But I was checking on *all* of the horses when my lamp ran out of oil." He moved closer to her. "You shouldn't be out here alone."

"I'm not alone. You're here."

He chuckled. "Yes, and I guess if you should be with anyone, it should be me."

Sarah peered at him; his sandy-brown hair looked almost black in the darkness. She dropped her gaze, suddenly feeling a little uncomfortable.

"I mean for your protection," he added. "After all, your safety is my charge."

She only nodded.

"I'm sorry I don't have a light for you." He bent down, opened the bag, and pulled out a handful of grain. "Here." He found her hand in the darkness and poured the grain into her open palm. Taking her other hand, he led her toward Pearl's stall.

She tried to ignore the fact that his fingers were wrapped around hers. She thought about pulling away, but his touch was warm and strong. She liked the reassurance. He probably meant nothing more than to guide her through the darkness. Still, she couldn't help but wish it was Alex holding her hand and giving her comfort. When they reached Pearl, he let go of her hand to open the stall door. The pang of disappointment she felt at the loss of his touch surprised her. She shouldn't be feeling anything at all. She loved Alex. Then why did it feel so good to have Luther's hand envelope her own? Moments ago she had been frightened, and it was understandable that the closeness of her personal guard would console her. She struggled to remember how Alex's touch felt. She missed him so very much, but she couldn't shake the feeling of warmth and concern Luther had shared with her.

"Are you going to give her the grain?"

Sarah stepped in, putting her palm up to Pearl's muzzle.

"Did you know your horse is from Kyrnidan?" he asked.

"Yes. Alex got her for me when he came here last year."

"I accompanied him on that journey."

She couldn't think of a reply. She hadn't known that Luther had come to Kyrnidan with Alex . Luther had found out that she was royalty before she even knew, and yet he still didn't want her to be queen. It was disheartening. If her royal validity wasn't enough for a guard, what hopes did she have to prove it to an entire nation?

She reached up and stroked her horse's forehead. Pearl was a typical example of the high-quality Kyrnidian breed—not like the muscular horses of Calibre, but tall and lean, built for lasting strength and endurance. Sometimes she thought people were like that—built for different purposes. Alex and his majestic black Friesian, she and Pearl. They each had different qualities, and sometimes the pairing didn't always make a good match. Alex had earned his elevated status and filled his role well, but despite her lineage, she just didn't feel regal.

"It's getting late." Luther must have sensed her sullen mood because he reached out, took her by the hand again, and gently squeezed her fingers. "You must be tired. Let's get you back inside. He held her hand until they reached the door of the inn. She didn't complain, and that bothered her. Inside he maintained a hand on the small of her back as he escorted her to her room.

Margaret had a puzzled look on her face as Sarah walked in. "That took longer than I expected. You said you'd only be gone a minute. I was half a hair away from worrying about you. I should have gone with you."

"No need. Luther was with me."

"Good. As your personal guard, Luther is as good as any escort—wouldn't you agree?"

Sarah pursed her lips together. She didn't want anyone encouraging her and Luther being together, but she couldn't admit that out loud—how would she explain it? *I know he's supposed to be protecting me, but he can't be around me?* That would only demand further explanation, and she wasn't about to tell anyone she had conflicting feelings when he touched her hand—that she enjoyed it.

She threw herself down onto the bed and buried a groan in the mattress.

"You're weary of all the traveling, aren't you, my dear?"

Sarah sat up and met Margaret's gaze. This was her companion. If she could share her feelings with anyone, it would be Margaret. And as Miranda's niece, there was already a connection between them. A trust. A friendship.

"Margaret, can I tell you something?"

"Of course."

She paused, second-guessing the wisdom of sharing something she didn't understand herself. Just as she decided to remain silent, heavy footsteps thundered down the hallway. Someone was in a hurry, and they carried the weight of urgency and frustration. They passed by Sarah's room and continued down to the end of the hall. When the tromping stopped, it was followed by a heavy pounding on a door.

"Who has the room at the end of the hall?" Sarah asked.

Margaret's eyes widened. "Sir Henry's is the only other room down there."

Sarah jumped up and ran to the door, placing her ear against it to see if she could hear what was going on.

"Oh no, you don't." Margaret put her hands on her hips and strode across the room. "There will be no eavesdropping—without me." She placed her own head next to Sarah's.

"Gilbert, open this door right now!" Apollo's voice was unmistakable, and from the sound of it, he was furious. Another heavy pounding and then a soft creak sounded as the door was opened. Apollo's voice was quieter this time, and Sarah had to strain to hear what was said. "Gilbert! Tell me it's not true. Tell me you didn't send for Tobias to accompany us to the castle."

"No." Sir Henry's voice was weak in comparison to Apollo's. "I didn't invite him. It's by his own initiative that he's coming. He sent word and is already on his way."

Sarah thought she heard Apollo swear. "You idiot! How can you be so naïve? You should have put a stop to it!"

"Mind yourself," Sir Henry warned. "Tobias is far your superior and won't take kindly to your insubordination. If you want to keep your meager residence in the castle, I suggest you not speak ill of a man so loyal and favored by Prince Michael."

"You blasted whelp!" Apollo's voice rose again. "Everyone has their moments of stupidity, but you seem to outdo yourself."

Sarah turned to Margaret as Apollo's heavy footsteps retreated back the way they'd come and then disappeared down the hallway. "Tobias. That name sounds familiar."

"It should. He's your uncle."

"But why would Apollo disapprove of him coming?"

Margaret slid an arm around Sarah's shoulders. "I suspect, my dear, it's because he's the one that swore to kill your mother's firstborn babe if it were a girl."

CHAPTER 8

"I REALLY DON'T THINK YOU have reason to fear the man," Margaret told Sarah as they walked out to the carriage the next morning. "I don't know what he was like before, but I've been a lady's maid in the castle for several years, and I can tell you that your uncle is devoutly loyal to the king and to your family." Sarah gave her a skeptical look, so Margaret went on. "Your brother met with a bout of pox in his younger years. That was before I came to the castle, but the maids tell me that Tobias didn't leave the prince's side until he was recovered. Now, is that not the sign of a caring man?"

Sarah didn't respond. She just pressed her lips together and stared at Margaret. She wasn't convinced. Margaret took her hand and patted it gently. "I see the worry in your eyes, but there's no need for it. I'm sure we won't even cross paths with him until late this afternoon, and you'll be safe in the carriage next to me. We shan't stop until dark, and at that late hour, he can hardly expect you to converse with him."

Sarah managed a nod this time, although the thought of meeting Tobias still made her sick to her stomach. As admirable as he may be now, it didn't excuse the fact that he had once threatened her very life. She turned toward the carriage just as a large dog came bounding out from the stables. Sarah looked twice, almost mistaking the animal for a small horse. The steel-gray dog was massive yet bounded around like a puppy. Sarah snapped her fingers to see if he would come to her. He loped over to her and sat obediently at her feet while she ran her hand over his rough hair and scratched his ears.

"I think I made a new friend," Sarah said.

Margaret stood rigidly, all color drained from her face.

"It's all right," Sarah assured her. "I know his size is daunting, but he's perfectly friendly." She ruffled the grey hair again. "I believe he's a wolfhound. Many nobles in Calibre own them." She glanced at Margaret, who appeared as if she were about to faint. Sarah almost laughed. Was the dog really that intimidating? "Have you never seen a wolfhound before?"

Margaret swallowed hard. "I only know one man who owns that kind of dog . . ."

"I see you have met Ranger."

Sarah looked up to see a large man striding toward her. He was dressed in the tailored uniform of a Kyrnidian military officer and was possibly the tallest man she had ever seen—a good half a head taller than Apollo, she surmised. He was an older gentleman, yet handsome, with wavy hair that shown like copper in the morning light. The only thing she didn't like about him was the imposing mustache that hid his expression.

Margaret was suddenly nudging her then leaned over and whispered urgently, "The one man I know who owns that kind of dog—"

"Your Highness," Sir Henry interrupted as he appeared beside her. "I would like to introduce you to your uncle, Tobias Delacor."

Sarah clamped her mouth shut to keep from gasping.

"I was trying to tell you," Margaret whispered.

Tobias gave a deep sweeping bow then gently took her hand and politely kissed the air above it. "Let me be the first to welcome you home, Your Highness."

"I thank you," Sarah said, trying not to stumble over her words.

"I know it will take some time for us to get acquainted." He spoke as he opened his coat and withdrew a small wrapped package. "Please accept my gift as a token of celebration. After all, your return to our family is something to celebrate."

Sarah took the offered gift and began pulling the cloth wrapping from it. Tobias had not dispelled all her fears, but he didn't seem to be the treacherous man of her imagination. She would keep her guard up, but at the same time, she would allow the acquaintance. The cloth wrapping held a wooden box, polished to a high luster, with the Kyrnidian crest inlayed in the lid. She ran her fingers across the design. It was identical to the symbol that marked the back of her shoulder. She opened the lid and peered inside.

"Oh my." She stared at the necklace nestled inside. The strand featured alternating stones of red and blue, each skillfully and elaborately set. The whole necklace was accentuated by a large oval center stone—a brilliant, reflective blue gem that was decorated at each end with a pearl.

Tobias pointed at it. "The red stones are rubies, and the blue, sapphires—the colors depicted on the Kyrnidian crest. The two pearls," he pointed at each one, "represent you and your brother, Michael."

Sarah cocked her head to look at him. Was *he* that thoughtful, or was it the artisan who had thought of the arrangement? Tobias gently took the necklace and held it so Margaret could clasp it around Sarah's neck.

"It is beautiful. Thank you." Sarah reached up and touched the stone that now rested at the base of her throat.

Tobias held his arm out to her. "I am told the wheels on the servants' carriage are being greased and our party will not be able to leave for another twenty minutes. Would you allow me that time to visit with you?" Sarah hesitated, but there was no obvious reason to refuse.

"Your Highness." Sarah turned to see Apollo standing in the doorway of the inn. His lips were tight with irritation. A crimson color touched his skin, creeping up his neck and into his cheeks as he stared at Tobias. "We'll be leaving soon. Would you and Margaret like to wait in the carriage?"

"Apollo," Tobias chided as he rocked forward on the balls of his feet. The movement made him appear even taller than he was. "Would you deprive me of my first meeting with my niece?"

"I can't help but wonder what your first meeting would have been like had it happened nineteen years ago."

Tobias looked pained. "I admit I was young and headstrong back then. In truth, I had only expressed my concerns at the time. It was others," his eyes locked onto Apollo, "who misconstrued those concerns as actual threats. The truth is I would do anything to protect my family. However, if it will ease your mind, you may send for Mr. Tandy. He is her personal guard, is he not? I am certain he will have no problem with our conversing."

The color slowly drained from Apollo's face, and his eyes deepened with anguish. What must he be thinking? Had he really committed such an unforgivable act of treason over a hollow threat? Was that the reason she could see regret in his eyes every time she looked at him? To make matters worse, she had learned that he had loved Miranda, and that thought only served to make their acquaintance even more awkward. When Tobias put his arm out to her again, she took it, and they walked past Apollo and into the inn.

* * *

"I don't know what to do about the man," Sarah whispered to Margaret. She didn't want to wake Sir Henry, although the rocking of the carriage was probably more than enough to keep him asleep. She had waited the entire afternoon and into the evening for a chance to talk to Margaret privately, and that only happened when Sir Henry slept.

"I understand, dear. It must be very uncomfortable for you to be around him, but Apollo *is* a good man."

"He may have good intentions, but he betrayed my family, and he sent Miranda away. You don't do that to someone you love. I know he believed he was doing the right thing, but even *he* laments those choices."

Margaret patted her hand. "Your father must still trust him; otherwise, he wouldn't be on this journey. If the king sees fit to allow Apollo to accompany you home, then you mustn't be too harsh on the man. We don't know all the details about why he took you away and gave you to Miranda. It's hard to understand someone's actions without knowing the reasons behind them."

Sarah shifted in her seat. Lately she had difficulty understanding her own heart. Tobias, the man she had lost sleep over, had turned out to be nothing but kind. And then there was Luther, whom she knew disapproved of her position, yet there was an undeniable connection between them. She pulled the curtain aside and looked out the window even though it was too dark to see anything clearly. Out of the corner of her eye, she saw Margaret relax her posture and gaze longingly at her satchel. When Sarah dropped the curtain, Margaret quickly returned to her erect position. "It's so late. I was sure we would have reached the inn by now."

A worried look clouded Margaret's face. "I didn't want to say anything, but you're right—we should have stopped some time ago."

"Perhaps they haven't found suitable accommodations yet."

Margaret shook her head. "There are several places in the area where we could've stayed."

"Do you think we should wake Sir Henry and ask him?"

Sarah had tried not to sound too nervous, but Margaret instantly moved across the carriage and shook Sir Henry a little too vigorously. He woke with a start and stared at the small lantern hanging in the corner, its shutter pulled halfway shut, bathing the interior of the carriage in a faint light.

"What time is it?" he asked, rubbing his eyes. "We should have stopped by now."

Sarah tipped her head toward Margaret. "That's why we woke you."

"I don't know anything about it, I'm sure. I wonder if there was a possible threat at the scheduled inn."

Sarah and Margaret exchanged worried looks as Sir Henry pounded on the wall and yelled to the driver to stop. Before the wheels had come to a complete halt, he opened the door and called to Luther.

When Luther appeared in the doorway, a feeling of reassurance washed over Sarah. His eyes instantly sought her out, and he smiled.

"There's no problem," he explained after they had stated their concern. "We're not going to stop for the night. We've decided to continue on to the castle. We should arrive in a few hours."

Sarah furrowed her brow. She had imagined arriving at the castle tomorrow afternoon with a royal fanfare. Although this wouldn't be so bad; she'd be just as happy to have a quiet arrival and avoid the hundreds of curious onlookers waiting to see their lost princess.

Luther offered no more explanation. He looked over his shoulder at the other riders before turning back. "I'm afraid Apollo is weary. There isn't room for him in the servant's carriage. If it isn't too much of a burden, would you allow him to ride with you?"

Sir Henry gave a disgusted humph, and Margaret scowled at the small man. "Of course he is welcome in here," she said then looked at Sarah for confirmation.

Sarah gave an almost imperceptible dip of her head. A minute later, Apollo climbed into the carriage and sat next to Sir Henry. The long days of travel had indeed taken a toll on the older gentleman, and he appeared both physically and emotionally exhausted. His face had a ragged expression accentuated by his tousled, graying hair and dusty clothes. Sarah met his gaze, which seemed to compound his weariness. The pain in his eyes deepened. She could feel the weight hanging in the air around him, and she tried to imagine what he was going through. Her arrival at the castle tonight would have significant meaning to him. After nineteen years, the results of his actions were finally coming full circle.

CHAPTER 9

FEIGNING SLEEP, SARAH WATCHED APOLLO through half-hooded eyes as he pulled the curtain back and looked out at the dark landscape. It wouldn't be much longer, and his part in all of this would finally be at an end. The dark shadows beneath his eyes made him look old and worn, and she wondered if things had not gone quite as he'd hoped, especially with the latest addition to their party—Tobias. It was clear the last nineteen years had done nothing to improve the relationship between the two men, and Apollo still viewed him as a threat, despite how kind Tobias had been to her.

Sarah closed her eyes as Apollo looked toward her. She knew he wished to talk to her, but it was too difficult. She hadn't fully come to terms with her newfound knowledge of the past, and some of her emotions were still raw. She wasn't ready to listen to his reasoning behind taking her. He had done what he had felt was right, and she didn't regret being raised by Miranda, but his actions had hurt other people—the very ones he was supposed to love and care for. He may have been seeking to make reparations, but she couldn't pardon him completely—not yet. And she couldn't dive into that conversation now—not right before she was to meet her family. She needed to keep a tight control of her emotions, and that meant any conversation with Apollo would have to wait.

A moment later, she opened her eyes. Apollo had turned his gaze back to the dark window. It wouldn't be much longer now. The entire caravan had slowed as they passed through the village so as not to draw too much attention. The change of pace had awakened Margaret, but Sir Henry slept on.

"He will, no doubt, be exceptionally well rested," Margaret whispered. The corners of Sarah's lips rose before her thoughts turned to their imminent arrival. She picked at her nails and tried to ignore the nervous tingle in her fingers. The carriage slowed, and she tied the curtains out of the way so she could get a better look as they approached the castle gates. As they pulled into the courtyard, she peered out at the towering castle walls. They were dark and imposing, almost unwelcoming.

"It would seem they're not expecting us." Sarah pulled the curtain back farther to better observe the vacant courtyard. "I feel like we're sneaking in."

Margaret patted her hand. "My dear, that's exactly what we're doing."

"Why?"

Apollo was the one to answer. "Tensions are running high. As I'm sure you've been told, there is some opposition to the monarchy. Tobias thought it best if you arrived without the fanfare."

Sarah sat back as the carriage came to a stop. She took a deep breath trying to steady her nerves. Margaret put an arm around her shoulders, "Welcome home, Princess."

Apollo reached across and took her hand forcing her to look into his eyes. "Welcome to Kyrnidan, Your Highness. It has been my great honor to escort you on your return."

What was that expression in Apollo's eyes? Sarah couldn't determine if it was relief, sadness, or something else. She might have said something, but at that moment her throat was tight with the anxiety and anticipation of what awaited her.

"I suppose we should wake the sleeping cat over there." Margaret pointed at Sir Henry but made it clear she wouldn't be the one assigned to the task.

"Sir Henry." Apollo gave the little man a rough shake. "We've arrived."

Sir Henry sat up a bit bleary-eyed and tried to gain his composure. "Oh . . . oh! Thank you. And may I say welcome home, Your Highness. I hope—" His grand speech was abruptly interrupted as the door was pulled open. Tobias reached in to assist Sarah out of the carriage.

"May I be the first to welcome you home, niece." Sarah suppressed a smile and thanked him as she stepped down from the carriage. She was grateful to finally be able to stretch her legs. "If you'll excuse me." Tobias gave a curt bow then turned and bounded up the stairs to the castle doors.

Sarah waited as the other passengers disembarked. Sir Henry tried to push past Margaret, obviously seeing it as his obligation to escort Sarah into the castle. But Margaret wasn't about to let that happen. She elbowed him, forcing him to stay behind her.

Apollo was the one who stepped next to her. "May I have the privilege of being your escort?" He extended his arm.

Sarah looked back to see Margaret completely blocking Sir Henry. She paused for a moment then took the proffered arm. "Thank you," she managed to whisper. She looked up the long flight of stairs and wondered what that night, some nineteen years ago, had been like, and what Apollo must have been thinking when he took her down those very steps.

Climbing the stairs went by too quickly. Before Sarah knew it, the large, heavily plated doors were opened for her. She hesitated. It was too soon. She wasn't ready. Apollo put a hand on the small of her back and guided her over the threshold. It was cool inside the castle, and Sarah pulled her traveling cloak tightly around her. The stark walls and floors had a harsher appearance than those of the castle in Calibre. Perhaps it was the dim lighting that made everything appear so menacing. The few lit sconces cast foreboding shadows off the displays of armaments. A few banners hung high above them, but there wasn't enough light to make out what was on them.

Tobias walked out of the shadows. His military attire appeared more daunting against the harsh stone surroundings. "I am to take you directly to the king." Margaret and Sir Henry joined them, and Tobias led the entourage down a wide hall and up a flight of stairs.

The air was heavy with silence. Margaret slipped an arm through Sarah's and gave her a reassuring pat on the shoulder. It didn't lend much comfort. Sarah's heart pounded, and she clutched her cloak in order to keep from wringing her hands. As she climbed the stairs, it became more difficult to pull each leaden foot up the treads. Tobias and Sir Henry continued on their way without noticing her slowing pace. However, Apollo and Margaret matched her stride.

Tobias and Sir Henry were waiting for them as they topped the stairs. Their expressions were unreadable, but Sarah's own anxiety was palpable. Apollo stepped closer, and Margaret put her warm hand over Sarah's icy fingers. *He's my father*, she told herself as she thought about the impending meeting with the king. *He wants to see me . . . doesn't he?* She wished more than anything that Alex was with her, or even Luther. She could use some strength right now, as it seemed hers might fail at any moment.

"Sarah." She looked up to see a familiar figure coming toward them down the dimly lit hallway.

"Michael!" A fraction of her apprehension dissolved at seeing her twin brother. His very appearance warmed her. He was very debonair in his stylish puffed sleeves and large feathered hat, and he wore a broad grin to match.

"How was your journey?" he asked as they embraced. It was only then that she noticed the tall, aging gentleman behind him.

"Long," she replied.

The older gentleman approached and stood closely behind Michael. The resemblance was remarkable. There was no doubt—this was her father. His copper hair was laced with the silver of time and encircled by a simple, embellished gold crown. The soft etchings in his face bespoke of a hard life well lived.

"Tobias," the old king acknowledged, greeting his younger brother. He then turned to Apollo and said in a low voice, "I see you have returned to us what you took nineteen years ago." He paused and then added, "Are you certain you want to be here?"

"I will fulfill my responsibility, Your Majesty."

"Indeed. Admittedly, you have faced that responsibility with equanimity." Even though the words seemed to be a compliment, the tone of her father's voice said otherwise.

"Sarah," Michael addressed her. "It is my pleasure to introduce you to our father."

She curtsied but didn't know what else to say or do. The king's eyes scrutinized her carefully, and she tried to stand tall under the weight of his visual examination. Did he see any resemblance to convince him that she was indeed his daughter? For several years he didn't even know of her existence—hadn't known that his wife had given birth to twins.

"So you are Sarah Elizabeth Rankin Delacor." Her father motioned to her with one hand. "At least the woman who raised you was thoughtful in your naming."

"Yes, Your Majesty . . ." Sarah's voice faltered. "Miranda was thoughtful in many ways."

He held her gaze for a moment longer then shifted his eyes to her red-blonde hair. Her long wavy locks didn't boast the coppery tones of his hair, but it was nearly the same shade as Michael's. Still, he examined her, as if he were unconvinced.

"I want to see it." The king clasped his hands behind his back and leaned forward. Sarah was taken aback by the request.

"Father, it's late. Can't we do this tomorrow?" Michael asked in a low voice.

"I want to see it now!"

Sarah turned to Margaret, still stunned and unsure of how she should react.

"He means your mark, dear."

"I thought as much." Sarah's voice faltered as she fumbled with the clasp on her traveling cloak. She hadn't known what to expect, but it certainly wasn't the coolness with which she had been received. Her own words which she had been trying to compose escaped her.

Apollo reached up and helped remove her cloak and then held it for her. She turned around and caught a glimpse of Tobias as he moved in closer too. *Of course he'll want to see it as well*, she thought. Margaret pulled the shoulder of Sarah's dress down far enough so the scar of the rampant unicorn within the Kyrnidian crest could be seen.

Sarah heard her father grunt in satisfaction as the edge of her dress was pulled back into place. She turned to face them again. The king simply nodded. Tobias was quiet, with an indefinable expression pasted on his face.

"I suppose you're wanting to get her settled in," the king said to Margaret.

"Yes, Sire."

"Fine. Go. Tobias and Michael, come with me." He turned and strode down the hallway. Tobias followed without saying a word of parting.

"You must excuse father's behavior," Michael said quietly. "He's been nervous about your arrival."

"I didn't notice." Sarah didn't try to hide her sarcasm. "Are you sure he wants me here?"

Michael hesitated. "I had to convince him to let you come. There will be some political ramifications from you being here, but we'll handle that. It's just . . . awkward for him—emotionally, I mean. Give it some time."

Sarah nodded.

"I shall see you in the morning." Michael embraced her again then turned to follow the king.

His own daughter, and he barely even addressed me. She hadn't expected hugs or a flood of tears, but at the very least, she had expected some cordiality.

"Let's go, dear." Margaret took her arm and encouraged her to walk. "We'll have some fruit and cheese brought up to your room. You'll feel better after you eat, and then you can get some decent sleep, in a real bed."

All at once, Sarah felt the culmination of the stressful trip weigh on her. She was tired, and a good, long sleep was all she really wanted.

CHAPTER 10

SARAH RUBBED HER THUMB GENTLY across Nathaniel's tiny fist and pressed a kiss to his pudgy cheek. Her little brother was completely angelic and serene in sleep. It was a total transformation from fifteen minutes ago when the castle walls echoed with his cries. At nearly seven months old, he was a spirited child who Sarah was sure could rival any herald or bugler in the country. She couldn't believe how peaceful he was in her arms now.

"He's an angel." She ran her fingers through his wispy, red hair.

"Yes," Sybil replied. The wet nurse had not stopped smiling since she'd proudly introduced Sarah to her baby brother that morning.

Sarah hadn't stopped smiling either, even during Nathaniel's short bout of vocal complaints. She would simply love to hold him all day, but there was someone else she needed to meet. She pressed another kiss to the sleeping boy's cheek then handed him over to Sybil. "I think it's time I go in."

"I was wondering when you'd be ready," Margaret said as she stood and crossed the room then slid an encouraging arm around Sarah. "Come on. I'll take you to her room."

Sarah followed Margaret down a series of corridors before they approached a group of people who huddled together in quiet groups—both servants and nobility. Their whispers died as she drew near. Margaret didn't offer an explanation, but Sarah guessed they had arrived at the queen's chamber.

She didn't get a good look at her mother's room as she walked in. The physician stood in front of her, blocking her way, and three maids stood behind him, gaping at her. Margaret gave her a little nudge. "Go on. It'll be fine. I'll wait for you out in the hall."

When Margaret was gone, the physician addressed Sarah. "I'm sorry, but Her Majesty is delirious much of the time. She won't respond to you."

He stepped out of her way and ushered her next to the bed. Queen Natalia's frail body was hidden under thick covers, and it brought back frightening memories of Miranda. "May I sit with her for a while?" Sarah placed her hand on the back of a chair that was obviously positioned for visitors.

"Of course, Your Highness." He looked a little uncertain and then finally gave an awkward bow and moved over to a table, where he began organizing the tinctures sitting there. Sarah watched him, uncomfortable at sharing this moment with her mother while other people were in the room. The man, like everyone else in the castle, kept looking at her with curiosity. He seemed to sense the awkwardness of the situation and cleared his throat. "I don't think you need me here."

She shook her head gratefully.

"Well, I shall be back in an hour then. If you need anything, send one of the maids for me." Sarah wished he would order the maids out of the room as well, but he left by himself.

After he left, Sarah sat down next to her mother and took her hand. She realized that her own sun-kissed hair was a combination of her father's red and her mother's blonde, which had now faded to mostly gray.

"Hello, Mother," she whispered. The reunion was easier than she'd hoped for. Partly because of her mother's lack of awareness. And that caused a sad prick in Sarah's heart. There should have been some sacredness to their first meeting, yet it was somehow lacking. After several long minutes, Sarah glanced across the room at the three maids who were standing in the corner whispering. They were gossiping about her. Sarah couldn't hear everything, but she did hear her name, and she was growing tired of them staring at her as if she were something on display. "Do you mind?" she finally asked. "May I have some time alone with my mother?"

The maids nodded, and Sarah turned her attention back to the queen. Moments later she heard the door close, and she quickly glanced over her shoulder to make sure they were gone. She stroked her mother's hand, not quite knowing what to do or say. This woman was a stranger to her, yet she could feel a bond between them.

Several more minutes passed with only the sound of her mother's labored breathing. Then Sarah heard a slight noise behind her as if someone else were in the room. She turned to look but didn't see anything that would have made the noise. Perhaps it was just the sounds that came with old castles. The room wasn't very elaborate, but it was an improvement from what she had seen so far. No doubt this chamber had been the first to be renovated, probably at her mother's request, yet it still lacked the comfort she had grown accustomed to in the palace at Calibre.

She stood up and walked over to the large tapestry hanging on the stone wall. It depicted a rampant unicorn similar to the one on the Kyrnidian crest. When she looked down to compare it to the weighted unicorn hanging on the end of her belt, she gasped. Shoes were sticking out from under the tapestry.

Slowly she reached out, grabbed the edge of the thick woven cloth, and threw it aside. The woman hiding there jumped, her cheeks flushing red with embarrassment.

"What are you doing?" Sarah demanded. "Who are you?"

The woman, who appeared to be quite a bit older than Sarah, stepped out with her hand on her heart, trying to regain her composure. Sarah hoped the maid wasn't about to faint, but then again, fainting might be a suitable consequence for scaring her like that.

"My name is . . . is Grace, Your Highness."

Sarah glared at her. "What in heaven's name were you doing?" Grace pinched her mouth shut unwilling to answer. Perhaps, like in Calibre, there were women in Kyrnidan's court who were willing to pay the servants to spy on her. "Who put you up to this?"

Grace began to sputter. "No one." She shook her head. "I'm so sorry. I'll leave now." She gave a quick curtsy and ran for the door.

"Wait!" Sarah followed the woman into the hallway, past a bewildered Margaret, and down the corridor until she disappeared around a corner. "These shoes!" Sarah looked down at her elaborate footwear. "I couldn't catch a turtle in these things." She stopped at the corner and looked around. The woman was gone.

"My word, what was that all about?" Margaret asked when she joined Sarah.

"I think that maid was spying on me."

"Are you sure she wasn't just curious? You've seen how everyone's been watching you."

"I don't know. Perhaps." Sarah turned to walk back to her mother's room when other voices drew her attention. Apollo and Tobias were coming down the corridor with Ranger jogging behind them, his tongue hanging out. The dog seemed quite content despite the arguing going on between the two men he was following.

"Ah, Your Highness," Apollo said when he looked up and saw her. "I was wondering if I could have a minute to talk to you."

Tobias reached her first, however, with his long stride. "Perhaps that can wait. I was planning on showing my niece the castle grounds. You didn't get to see anything last night due to our late arrival; and since the king and Prince Michael have been attending to affairs of state this morning, I feel you have been left quite alone."

"Not quite," Margaret chirped in.

"I beg your pardon." He offered a slight bow of his head. Sarah thought she saw him wink. "Shall we?" He stuck his arm out to her. Sarah hesitated. She hadn't spent much time with her mother, but that moment had already been ruined.

She looked at Margaret, who shrugged. "You can always come back and spend more time with the queen this afternoon."

"All right." A walk around the castle wasn't a bad idea, and with luck she might find the maid that had run away. Sarah took her uncle's arm, and he directed her past Apollo. The subdued look and disappointment on Apollo's face did not go unnoticed.

CHAPTER 11

SARAH TOOK IN HER SURROUNDINGS. The castle was an antiquated concentric design with walls inside of walls for maximum protection. The old-style square keep towered above them, dotted with overly small windows. This fortress was built for defense. It wasn't surprising, coming from a country that prized militarism and had been ruled by warlords not too long ago—her grandfather being one of them. Sarah let her eyes wash across the battle-worn walls. It seemed strange that the old ways were still so much alive here.

"A chapel?" Sarah asked when her eyes fell upon the spire-crowned building across the courtyard. It stuck out from its primal surroundings. Elaborate columns and arched stained glass windows bespoke of modern and skilled architecture, something she had seen little of in Kyrnidan.

"Yes." Tobias seemed reluctant to discuss the building, but at last he consented. "Of course, the idea was inspired by the queen, but Prince Michael oversaw all the construction. It is one of his most gratifying achievements—in his own eyes."

Sarah looked at him. "Don't you think it's beautiful?"

He took her arm again and began walking her toward the building. "Of course it is, but does beauty really matter?"

"It inspires and lifts one's soul."

Tobias traced his mustache with his thumb and forefinger. The gesture was probably intended to make him appear thoughtful, but instead it made him look sad. "You really are your brother's twin."

Sarah tried not to smile. She and Michael had been raised apart, but she often wondered if they inherently shared similarities.

Tobias opened the door to the chapel, and they walked in with Ranger following closely at their heels. The dog apparently followed Tobias wherever he went, so it shouldn't have surprised Sarah when her uncle allowed him inside the Lord's house.

She looked around. The room was large and open with elaborate scripture scenes painted on the walls. A finely crafted altar stood at the head of the room with a large, ornate stained glass window behind it, featuring a detailed depiction of the Savior. Sarah could hardly pull her eyes away from the arresting image, but when she did, she noticed the silver plates that hung on either side. "Are those . . ." Sarah walked forward.

"The prophecy plates," Tobias said.

"I've heard about them." Sarah took a closer look, noticing a distinguished pattern in the metal sheets—silver lines waved across the surface, reminiscent of flowing water. Adding to the exquisite design were the thin, contrasting strands of gold woven throughout the silver waves. The words were etched into the surface and inked black for distinction.

There were just over a dozen plates, and Sarah examined all of them. It only took a few minutes to read the prophecies as they only consisted of two or three sentences each. One specifically mentioned a change in the government. Another stated the abolishment of the warlords, and another mentioned the split among the people.

After Sarah had read the last one, she turned to Tobias. "These are beautiful, but I thought there would be more."

"That's a common misconception. The high priest gave many prophecies, but only the ones that were specifically denotable to our country were made into plates, and those consist of what you see here." Tobias clasped his hands behind his back and walked over to stand beside her. "Your father always valued the high priest's advice and allowed him to sit in on council meetings where these prophecies were revealed. The late councilman Simon Cuthbert was the scribe at those meetings. He took it upon himself to make a lasting record of the prophecies referring to the kingdom. His craftsmanship is unparalleled, as you can see."

Sarah nodded and looked over the plates again. "I don't see the one that mentions the firstborn uniting the kingdom. That's specific to the country. Why is it not here?"

Tobias cleared his throat and began to rock on the balls of his feet. "It is the only one missing from the collection. You see, Simon always took his documentation to the high priest after the meetings to confirm the exact wording. Only when they were confirmed would he make the plate. However he passed away shortly after that prophecy was given. It was never found at his estate, so we assume he hadn't had time to engrave it before his passing."

Silence fell over them, and Sarah looked over at her uncle. He was gazing reverently at the metal plates on the wall. "It wasn't long after Simon's death that the high priest himself passed away. He was very old, and it was expected; nevertheless, he has been greatly missed."

Sarah turned back and stared at the open space on the wall where the last plate would have hung. It seemed odd no one else had taken it upon themselves to make one so the collection could be complete. Sir Cuthbert's craftsmanship would be hard to match, but that shouldn't have stopped them from displaying the last prophecy.

Perhaps they didn't want it there for all to see. It was obvious the high priest had made a mistake, and engraving his words would only remind everyone of his obvious blunder. Even without a plate, she wondered at the people's belief in it. The other predictions the high priest had made had come true, but anyone with access to the King's Council could guess where the future of the country was going and make similar prophecies. Why did the people not see through this fraud?

Surely someone besides her could admit the prophecy was wrong. If she could find someone of prominent status who had heard the exact words, she could question them about it. And if they would concede that their faith had been misplaced, then others would follow suit. Eventually the prophecy would drift into obscurity. Sarah took a deep breath, a thread of hope building inside her. Perhaps she could do something useful after all while in Kyrnidan.

"Were there other councilmen, besides Sir Cuthbert, who heard that particular revelation?" she asked.

Her uncle must not have guessed her motive for the question and answered frankly. "There were several other councilmen present when it was given."

"Does anyone remember the exact words the high priest said?"

"Oh yes. It is well known. In fact, I myself have a tapestry hanging in my private chamber with the exact words embroidered on it." He let his eyes drop to meet hers. "It shall be the son, the firstborn in the new monarchy, who shall quiet the fears and unite the nation again."

Sarah glanced away. She didn't understand how everyone could base all their hopes in something so decisively wrong. *The son, the firstborn in the new monarchy*. She was the firstborn in the new monarchy. Granted, she and Michael were born only minutes apart, but if the high priest was truly inspired by God, he would've known which of them would be first. He would have declared twins would be born and the second one—the son—would receive the birthright and unite the kingdom.

"Come," Tobias said, taking her arm. "There's much more to see." He led her outside and directed her toward the smithy and kennels. They hadn't gone far when a sudden racket of clashing swords made Sarah stop short. Worry creased her brow. It sounded as if a battle was being waged right around the corner. Ranger barked and jumped around, wagging his tail with excitement. She looked at her uncle for an explanation.

Tobias grinned. "Ah, yes. You'll want to see this."

Sarah had to jog to keep up with his long stride, but as they rounded the corner, Tobias slowed. His face lit up with approval. "This is the finest of Kyrnidan." He waved a hand, motioning to the large group of men vigorously sparring in the compound before them.

If Sarah hadn't known better, she would have thought they were really battling, as if for their very lives. Far advanced, the Kyrnidian army was an asset that drew the attention of every surrounding nation, and within minutes she determined that they lived up to the lofty tales. She watched in awe as the men moved with precision and skill. "They are an impressive group," she said after a moment.

"They should be." Tobias gave a proud nod toward the men. "We don't rely on reluctant knights to fight our battles as other countries do." She knew Calibre was included in *other countries*. "Each man is paid and rigorously trained. If one wishes to gain prestige and be gifted lands, he must excel on the battlefield. Every household in the country hopes to raise great warriors. As a result, our army has an abundant and constant supply of young fighting men, yet only the best are kept."

"I can see it's an accomplished art to your people—to our people."

"Your brother, when we can get him to join in, is among the most skilled."

"Michael?" Sarah tried not to sound too astonished. "I didn't know."

"You wouldn't, would you? He spends far too much time indulging his other curiosities—music, architecture, diplomacy—but when you put a sword in that boy's hands . . ." Tobias paused. "That's when his true talents emerge."

Sarah had a hard time picturing Michael as a warrior. Her eyes narrowed. "I didn't think fighting was his specialty."

"Of course! Think of who he is and the stock he comes from. His grandfather was one of the greatest warlords ever known, and his own father—"

Sarah had expected Tobias to continue on, talking about her father and the great things he had done in battle. Margaret had told her some stories glorifying her father and Tobias in the campaigns of their youth. And wasn't this the perfect time for her uncle to boast of their great accomplishments—their fierce loyalty, risking their very lives for the cause, their celebrated victories?

When Tobias cut his sentence short, she looked at him, expecting misty eyes as he reminisced about the past, but instead his face was hard and the muscles in his jaw were flexing and tight with irritation. Whatever was tormenting him was firmly shut inside behind his clamped teeth.

"There aren't as many men here as I expected," she said, trying to draw his attention away from his inner plight.

Another moment of silence passed before he spoke. "This is only a small part of our forces. The army is too large to be completely housed here; we have garrisons established throughout the country."

Sarah turned her attention back to the men and spotted Luther in the mix of it all. A sense of comfort washed over her when she saw him. He was someone familiar in this strange land. She watched him for several minutes, pleased that he could hold his own among the Kyrnidians.

"Ah, yes. Mr. Tandy does enjoy the sparring." Tobias motioned to where Luther was fighting. "I have to say he is rather good."

"He is," Sarah agreed. Thankfully, Tobias's mood seemed to be lifting again. But she was still concerned. He had just mentioned her father when his spirits had suddenly darkened. She hated to think that something pernicious had happened while he and her father campaigned together. She would ask about it later. Right now his mind seemed pleasantly occupied as he watched Luther. She hated to admit it, but she was pleasantly occupied too.

"I have spent quite a bit of time with your personal guard these last two days." Tobias tipped his chin toward Luther. "He quite impresses me. We met last year when he came to Kyrnidan with Prince Alexander, but I had no idea he was such a fighter."

Sarah bit the inside of her cheek to keep from commenting. When it came to Luther, she had a hard time controlling her mouth. Let alone her thoughts. Was it being disloyal to Alex to think about Luther? She diverted her attention away and stared at the ground. Was she really at risk of being disloyal? She loved Alex, and it sickened her to think her devotion might not be as deep as it once had been.

She admitted she had pulled away from Alex because of her own anxieties. The more people questioned her worthiness to be with him, the more she withdrew from him. Maybe everyone was right—she wasn't ideal for the position. But royalty was too stuffy. They could use someone who wasn't pressed into that rigid mold. Sarah turned and looked at the sparring soldiers again, and the lump in her throat solidified. The councilmen wouldn't accept her any more than these soldiers would accept an untrained boy in their ranks. There were standards and expectations to meet, and no one would lower them for her sake.

She let her gaze settle on Luther again.

The silence between her and Tobias had drifted on too long, and he cleared his throat. "I guess I better get you back inside." They continued to watch the men spar for a few moments; then he took her arm and led her back to the castle. "I hope you don't mind me cutting the tour short, but I should be going through these drills with the soldiers. Perhaps we can meet later and I'll show you—" The heated sound of an argument cut him off as they entered the great hall.

The king's voice boomed against the walls, and Michael shouted back.

"What would you have me do? Send her back to Calibre?" As Michael's voice rose in pitch, a tight knot formed in Sarah's chest.

"That would hardly help. Their plan has already been set in motion!"

"My point exactly! We will just have to make sure she doesn't—"

Sarah walked farther into the room, finally catching their attention, and the argument ended abruptly, leaving the echo of their shouts hanging in the air.

CHAPTER 12

"I REALLY DIDN'T INTEND FOR you to hear that."

The king and Tobias had exited together, leaving Sarah and Michael alone in the great hall. She crossed her arms, not caring that her irritation was showing through. "*You* are the one who asked me to come to Kyrnidan. Is my presence here really causing that much trouble?"

Her heart wrenched when her brother didn't respond. He just looked at her, struggling to keep his face expressionless. There was no use in sparing her from the truth. She knew what it was like to be out of place and causing problems in the royal court.

"If I'm complicating situations here, then I must go back to Calibre. Better to cause discontent in one country rather than two." She turned to walk away, but Michael caught her by the arm and turned her around. She refused to look at him. She didn't want him to see the tears forming in her eyes.

"You must let me explain." He paused, as if he didn't know where to start. With each passing moment, Sarah had to restrain herself from walking away because if she did, she would never come back.

Michael drew a breath and released it before speaking. "There are complications surrounding the monarchy."

Sarah threw her hands out. "I know that. And I know there are a lot of people who oppose me coming here. Will you please just tell me what is going on?"

Michael drummed his fingers on his leg. "There is a large, powerful family in the province—the Moylans. They oppose everything about our family and the monarchy, and their influence is wide reaching."

The family name of Moylan didn't go unnoticed by Sarah. Apollo was a Moylan. Most likely he was related to this group. However, Apollo was still ardently loyal to the Delacor family, so it was probably one of those third or fourth cousins once removed type situations. Sarah wanted to hear what Michael had to say, so she saved her questions about it for later. "Go on," she said, bracing herself.

"We just received word that they're planning a large function at their estate, a rally of sorts. They're using your arrival to their advantage and are bringing people in from all over the country. They have many supporters already, and this will allow them to gain many more."

"But what exactly are they trying to achieve? How does my arrival help them?"

Michael took off his large feathered hat and slapped it against his leg several times. "When I returned from Calibre last year, I declared we had at last found you—that you really were the lost princess. I had a statement signed by everyone who had been in attendance at the council in Calibre, witnessing that they saw the mark of the Kyrnidian crest on your shoulder. I had the statement published and posted all over the kingdom."

Unable to stand still any longer, Sarah began pacing in short spans as she shook her head. Michael had every right to announce it, but she found it incredibly frustrating. Was there no end to the political flaunting?

"Everyone in Kyrnidan knows you have the mark." Michael lowered his voice and continued, "Which means they know I was given the same one after the fact—that I'm not truly firstborn." Their eyes met, and his brow furrowed with worry. "My supporters are dividing as we speak. Many wonder if you are here to claim the throne."

Sarah recoiled and her throat seemed to close off. "Of course I would never—"

"Many openly oppose your involvement; however, others expect, even *want* you to be heiress."

Sarah opened her mouth, but no words came out.

"Many aspects of this monarchy are new and untested, and many feel things are . . . still open for debate." Michael began slapping his large hat against his leg again. The gesture was not becoming and made him appear nervous rather than the composed prince she knew him to be. "I'm sure you're aware that there are many countries where women are allowed to inherit," he said. "You are the firstborn, and many people believe that you *are* the natural heiress."

Sarah closed her eyes in disbelief. It was that abominable prophecy again. *The firstborn.* Now that they knew she was the firstborn, were they expecting her to rule and unite the people? It was preposterous! Didn't they see that the prophecy was wrong? "Michael, let me make this abundantly clear." She emphasized each word. "I have no intention to do any such thing! I only came to see my family. You know my support is behind you. I would never get involved with your affairs of state."

"I know." Michael's voice was tight. "Regardless, the Moylans are using the divide to further weaken support for the monarchy. It's possible that, in a matter of weeks, they'll have the majority."

"What will happen then?"

Michael's shoulders sagged and with them her heart dropped. "Sarah, they loathe our family. I believe it is their intention to mount a revolt and overthrow the government. Then they will reestablish the old ways and vote in another warlord."

"But you have the army on your side. No one can defeat the army of Kyrnidan."

"The army belongs to the people. I won't have them fight their own families."

Sarah looked at a small window and the craggy Kyrnidian landscape in the distance. "In a matter of weeks . . ." The words fell softly from her mouth and seemed to hang in the air. In a matter of weeks, there could be a revolt, and all because of her. She knew what the result would be. Her family would die in the battle or be captured and killed later.

She reached over her shoulder and felt the raised bump of the mark that had been burned into her flesh at birth. "All this because of my mark," she whispered. She tried to remain calm, but inwardly she wanted to claw at the scar—to tear at it until not a single shred of it remained. She was tired of being presented, paraded, and forced into uncomfortable situations. She wanted to return to her simple life where weighty decisions that affected the lives of so many people were not laid upon her shoulders. She didn't have the training for this, and she didn't know how to manage this kind of exposure, adoration, and disdain.

"What are you going to do?" she asked.

Michael folded his arms with a determined look. "We're going to follow protocol. We're holding a banquet—for you—this evening."

Sarah's mouth fell open.

"Good or bad"—he pointed at her—"you must be presented to society."

CHAPTER 13

SARAH WAS AMAZED. MICHAEL'S EFFORTS in achieving the cultural sophistication he knew Kyrnidan was capable of was clearly depicted in the atmosphere of the great hall. Elegant table settings, beautiful flower arrangements, and exquisite foods were all set against a backdrop of enchanting melodies and the finest-dressed of society.

"Stop fidgeting," Margaret whispered in her ear.

"Torture—that is what this is," Sarah replied with a glare. "How can my own family expect me to endure something so agonizing? It's cruel."

"Be that as it may, you should endure your torture with better posture and a smile on your face."

Sarah slumped farther down in her chair.

"Really!" Margaret whispered sharply. "You spent hours with your mother this afternoon—God bless her and bring her through this sickness—but Her Majesty is still unaware of her surroundings, and you need to give *others* audience as well."

"Yes, but—"

Margaret held up a finger cutting her off. "No excuses. You are the first woman I have heard complain about attending a banquet."

Sarah rolled her eyes. "I would enjoy it more if some of them would actually speak to me." She gestured toward the crowd. Margaret looked at her, and Sarah thought she detected some sympathy there.

"I am sorry, my dear. We Kyrnidians are not a very inviting people. It's in our nature to remain distant until we know if we face a friend or a foe."

Sarah wasn't happy with the explanation. The Kyrnidians were a beautiful people, tall and fair-haired; however, they were exactly as Margaret had described. Clustered in groups, they whispered about her in their thick accents and pointed at her. None had invited her to join them or even ventured to talk to her after she had greeted each and every one of them. There were a few people that seemed as though they wanted to approach her but didn't dare. And then there were those who were openly scowling at her. It wasn't easy to endure such ostracism, but more frustrating was that her father and Michael tolerated such unwelcoming behavior from their guests.

She looked around the large banquet room to see where her father had gone. He still seemed withdrawn, but at least he had made it a point to sit next to her during the meal. She spotted him now near the edge of the room speaking with Tobias. At first it appeared to be a pleasant conversation, but Sarah began to pick out the subtle discomfort both men tried to hide. It was something she had witnessed each time they were together. At best they seemed to tolerate each other, so it appeared something had tainted their association. Of course, Tobias had threatened to kill her when she was born, and that was more than enough to force a wedge between the brothers, but Sarah sensed there was more to it than that. It was apparent her uncle had given up any notions of harming her, so the discord between the two men must have stemmed from something more.

Tobias gave a curt nod to her father then drifted off to where Michael was mingling in the crowd. Her brother was trying to ascertain the general opinion about their new-found princess and had vowed to quell any animosity. It appeared he was having a hard time of it and was deep in an animated conversation. He waved his hands to accentuate his words and frequently glanced in her direction.

Trying not to sigh, Sarah let her eyes drift back to where her father was making his way through the crowd. He yawned and waved away several men who were vying for his attention, giving the distinct impression that he was done with the festivities and politics.

He walked behind the table to where Sarah was sitting. There was no smile. No approval that she had done her part at being presented to the public. He only offered a simple explanation as to why he was retiring early. "If you'll excuse me, my dear. I'm an old man, and I'm afraid I don't keep late nights like I used to. I think I'll go look in on the queen." Well, that was something. He at least referred to her as *my dear*. If nothing else, it was a form of endearment—she hoped.

The king left, and Sarah looked back at the crowd just in time to catch a disapproving glare from an older woman in a jade-green dress. Sarah leaned over to Margaret. "I've done my part in greeting the people, so why must I remain propped up here on display? I feel like a fresco being analyzed by art critics."

"Well, I certainly don't fancy you in a Da Vinci," Margaret said. "The maidens in *those* masterpieces have poise and never complain about banquets."

Sarah pulled a face in response.

"Although," Margaret added, "I *would* like to see you plastered to the ceiling with an egg tempera wash over you. Now sit still and smile. At least try to play the part of their princess."

"Is that what I am supposed to do the entire time I'm in Kyrnidan? Will there be no end to the political posturing?"

"Not for one who is royal."

Sarah rose to her feet, letting out an exasperated breath. "This is absurd! My being here is only further dividing the people. My very presence is making the situation worse. Besides, I came to see my mother, not to be a pawn in their royal game of chess."

Margaret gently took her arm and pulled her back down. "Do you realize you don't have a choice in the matter?"

"There's always a choice. I will not be a political object to these people." Sarah glanced at the nearest doorway, trying to formulate an escape. Perhaps she would go and find Luther. She mulled the idea over and was just about to give an excuse to Margaret when she saw a familiar face peek out from the doorway. It was the maid, Grace. Had she been watching the entire time?

Several minutes passed, and the maid continued to watch from the corner. Sarah concentrated on the crowd again, trying not to be completely unnerved by the spying woman. Suddenly she didn't want to go sneaking out by herself to find Luther.

She watched the people mingle and couldn't help but seek out the woman who had so viciously scowled at her earlier. A moment later, she found the older woman in the jade-green dress standing with a small group of people. They seemed to have segregated themselves from the rest of the crowd. "Margaret," Sarah said, nodding toward the particular group clustered together. "Do you know any of those people? Several of them have looked at me in the most hostile manner."

"That is the Moylan family and some of their closest supporters."

"I didn't realize they had been invited."

"Oh yes. His Royal Highness must try to show them his merits. Who better to prove his worthiness to than those who oppose him?"

More political posturing, Sarah thought.

"However," Margaret went on, lowering her voice. "Mr. Robert Moylan, the head of the house, won't set foot in the castle or any place where a member of the Delacor family is. So, of course, he's not here. But his wife is." Margaret pointed out the older woman—the one in the jade-green dress. "That's Catalina Moylan."

Sarah leaned forward in her chair and studied the woman. Her face was marked with the hard lines of age, and she was weighted down with a plethora of jewelry. A distinct air of contempt surrounded everyone in the Moylan group, but Sarah continued to keep an eye on Catalina as she made her rounds. After watching her for several minutes, it was obvious the woman was not simply being sociable. Catalina moved from group to group with a calculating purpose. When she spoke to someone, she would specifically look toward the high table where Sarah sat, sending daggers with every glance.

The music stopped, and the room fell silent for a moment as the musicians changed to another arrangement. When the music began again, Michael was in the center of the floor. "Shall we dance?" he called out. He made a grandiose sweep of his hand, took a young woman by the hand, and began to lead a pavane.

"That would be Sir Ivan's daughter, Miss Adela Oliver." Margaret didn't need to gesture to the beautiful woman who held Michael's hand. Sarah watched them for a moment before seeking out the Moylans again. Catalina and the rest of her group pulled back to stand along the wall. Only then did the floor begin to clear, and more people began to pair off to follow in the dance.

Michael seemed so refined as he stepped out, graceful and charming. Sarah shifted in her seat, afraid to even anticipate what was in store for her. She didn't want to dance, but it would be expected of her. She tentatively glanced around, but no one seemed to want to approach her. Her stomach dropped. Normally she wouldn't fret about not having any takers, but to be the guest of honor and not to have a single offer would be the ultimate humiliation.

Someone did catch her eye though. He was a slightly older gentleman but handsome. He glanced at her but seemed hesitant. Sarah smiled at him invitingly, willing him to come over. *Please,* she pleaded silently. *Let him come over.*

Her plea worked, and the man slowly began to walk toward her. Sarah double-checked her posture and smiled politely as he bowed to her. "Your

Highness. Lady Antonellis," he said acknowledging both her and Margaret. Sarah's smile brightened with gratitude as he straightened. Her lips were already parted, her acceptance lingering on the end of her tongue. But to her dismay, the gentleman's eyes lifted and settled not on her but on Margaret. Sarah's cheeks flushed with embarrassment. He wasn't asking *her* to dance, but Margaret.

She wanted to slump down in her chair and disappear, but she somehow remained poised. Margaret started to refuse the man's offer, but Sarah cut her off. "Go," she whispered.

"But I mustn't leave you here alone."

Sarah gave her a nudge. "Go. I'm sure I can manage a few minutes by myself." Margaret finally nodded and left to join the others on the dance floor just as the pavane gave way to a lively galliard. A lump grew in her throat, but she forced herself to look through the crowd for a hopeful prospect. By the time the galliard had moved into yet another dance, she found the weight of her smile almost impossible to maintain. Had she completely misplaced her alluring charm tonight? She tried to swallow the lump, but it was firmly wedged in her throat. Again, her thoughts turned to Luther. She would have given anything to have him there with her. He wouldn't have hesitated in standing up with her. She tried to imagine him holding her hand like he had when they were in the stable. She certainly needed some of his strength now. How could she be in such a crowded room and still feel so alone?

Members of the royal family are not to reveal their emotions, she told herself, trying not to crumple under the weight of her humiliation As the dance went on, she noticed more and more people watching her, and the whispers were becoming audible. Michael drew close to a single, young gentleman and leaned over to whisper in his ear before continuing on with the dance. It was easy to guess what he had said. The unsuspecting young man glanced nervously at Michael then up at her before quickly dropping his gaze. He stepped back and melted into the crowd. Unable to bear the humiliation any longer, Sarah dropped her head and discreetly pressed her handkerchief to the corner of her eye to remove the moisture.

"I am not a dancer, by any means, but I would be honored to take a turn with you."

Sarah recognized the voice immediately, and a smile of relief pulled up the edges of her mouth. She looked up to where Tobias towered above her. Of all the men in the room, she hadn't expected him to be the one to come to her aid. She was sure that dancing was something he was in the habit of avoiding, and the look on his face confirmed it. He held his arm out for her awkwardly and glanced to where the other dancers were weaving around the floor.

"You're very kind," she said, "but you don't have to do this."

"I know. But I want to." Tobias jutted his chin in a gesture to those around them. "These men are fools to let the political ramifications get in their way of taking a turn with the most beautiful woman here."

He led her through the crowd where they took up their position in line and started moving in sync with the other dancers. Although Tobias knew the steps, his execution was rough and awkward. As the promenade brought them closer together, he continued to explain, "Most people are afraid to approach you while the Moylans are here. Their family is powerful, and too many people are afraid of what will happen if they appear to be supporting you or Michael."

"What power do the Moylans hold in order to dictate people's actions during a simple dance?"

"They have various techniques to persuade people. No one here wants a group of the Moylans to show up on their doorstep to pressure them. Many here do business with the family. They don't want to risk losing profitable customers like the Moylans simply by speaking to you at a banquet."

Sarah nodded grimly. If it hadn't been for her uncle, no one would have asked her to dance tonight. Suddenly Tobias's awkward movements appeared more graceful to her.

The notes faded away, and the crowd began aligning themselves for the next frolic. Tobias bowed to her. "I apologize, but as you just witnessed, dancing is not one of my better skills." He directed her to the edge of the crowd when a woman in front of them abruptly turned around. Sarah recognized the jade-green dress.

It was evident Catalina Moylan was quite irritated at coming face-to-face with them. Protocol demanded that the woman acknowledge Sarah, but her face hardened with stubborn determination, and she stood unmoving. Sarah could feel every eye in the room on them, and she held her breath, praying that Catalina would at least offer the obligatory curtsy for royalty. But each torturous second that passed spoke volumes of the dissent among the Kyrnidian people. Tobias rocked on the balls of his feet as he glared at Mrs. Moylan. At last Catalina offered the slightest nod of her head. Several gasps erupted around the room. The bow of her head, however slight, was not directed to her but to Tobias.

"Now if only I could get them to respect me as they do you," Sarah whispered as they moved off the floor.

"If I had my way, I would've run that woman through right there." His hand moved to the hilt of his sword. "I earned respect the easy way—in battle. Your brother could use a little more of it though, and I don't see how he can get it by indulging in these silly frivolities."

"I heard that." Michael appeared by their side. "And believe it or not, Uncle, we want the same thing for Kyrnidan, and any measure of sophistication I can lend to our country will be a benefit, including these so-called silly frivolities."

"You keep telling me that." Tobias rocked on his heels. "I try to keep my sword in check, but these other things you insist on—reading and music lessons—I don't see how they'll help our country."

"They will." Michael excused himself and moved back into the crowd.

"Is he trying to get you to take music lessons?" Sarah tried not to smirk.

Her uncle grunted. "It's worse than that. He's required it. And not just me. All the young men coming into the army. They're also required to have an hour of academics before they train each day."

"I think it's a noble pursuit to educate one's people."

"I might consent to the idea of reading and some basic mathematics. Those do come in handy once in a while, but the rest—music, dance, banquets, science, and art? They're all silly frivolities."

Sarah patted her uncle's arm. "It's culture, and it's not considered silly in other countries, but a sign of refinement and education."

"I am astounded at the similarities you share with your brother." Tobias reached down and fingered the decorative chain that hung around Sarah's waist, lifting it so he could examine the unicorn dangling from the end. "Do you know why this magnificent creature represents Kyrnidan?"

"No," she admitted.

"Unicorns represent strength and majesty. Power. Our country needs to embody *those* ideals if we are to succeed. Our country needs a strong monarchy. *That* is a sign of our refinement, and I believe Michael can achieve it. He just needs some direction."

Sarah regarded her uncle with a touch of surprise. The sense of pride coming from him was deeper than she had expected. His thick, accented voice was bound with conviction, and his eyes flashed with passion. "I agree," she said. "Michael *can* do it."

CHAPTER 14

"It's not too hard for me to comprehend why Sir Durrant didn't talk to you. He's been in a terribly foul mood of late—but his son?" Michael shook his head and paced in front of the massive shelves that filled the cramped bookroom. "Chandler, at least, should've had the gumption to speak to you, and I can hardly believe he refused me when I asked him to take a turn with you!" Michael stopped at a corner table and looked at the old tome laying there. He slapped it shut, sending a puff of dust up from the pages.

Sarah shifted her little brother to her hip as she walked across the room to a small chest of toys. "Michael, it's over with. Let's forget the whole thing."

"Forget it? Their treatment of you last night was completely inexcusable. I tried to maintain my composure, but let me assure you, I have never been so appalled in my life."

Sarah waved a carved wooden horse in front of Nathaniel until he grabbed it with his little hand. He gurgled some nonsense words then put the toy to his mouth. It was easier to tune out Michael's complaints when playing with Nathaniel, but going to her mother's room might be even more effective. She had already spent most of the morning there; she liked the peaceful atmosphere. Her mother still wasn't coherent enough to know exactly who she was, but there were moments when she'd open her eyes and hold Sarah's hand.

Sarah looked up as her father entered the room. It appeared he would be joining them—until Tobias stepped into the doorway behind him. Her father's face creased with a frown, and his shoulders seemed to sag. Tobias sought out Nathaniel with a smile then gave Sarah a playful wink before he and her father left the room together.

"Michael, I've been meaning to ask you something," Sarah said.

"What?" He didn't look at her. His head was down as he tugged on the pair of gloves which had been tucked beneath his belt.

"It's about Father and Tobias. I've only seen them together on a few occasions, but it seems that they're . . ." She paused, trying to come up with the right words. "Unhappy with each other. Is there something that has caused a breach between them? In their youth perhaps?"

Only then did Michael look up. "I am not aware of any bad blood between them. As with any family, they've had their disagreements, but I've been told they worked well together in their youth. They oversaw many campaigns together and were quite successful as you already know."

"Yes, I heard about the battles. I understand that's how Father became king."

"Father did more than win battles. He conceived and developed many of the renowned tactics we use in training today. He also made improvements to the entire Kyrnidian army in his youth."

Sarah noted the pride in Michael's voice which caused a smile to tug at the corners of her mouth, but she was still unsatisfied with his answer. "Perhaps Tobias was jealous of being in Father's shadow," she suggested tentatively.

Michael's expression hardened. "That's absurd. Tobias doesn't have the slightest measure of jealousy in him. He is absolutely loyal to Father."

"I know he means well, but there was a time when Tobias wasn't entirely loyal or he wouldn't have threatened to kill the firstborn if it were a girl." Sarah knew it was stretching, but she had nothing else to go on and really wanted to figure out why she felt disharmony between the brothers.

Michael's voice turned cold. "Tobias made that heedless threat two decades ago. He had no idea Apollo would take such extreme measures. Uncle felt terrible when it all came to light. Now that you're back in Kyrnidan, has he done anything which makes you believe that those were his true sentiments?"

"No, of course not. He has been a perfect gentleman, and I am quite fond of him. I can say with all sincerity that I do not hold any malice toward him."

"Nor does Father. He forgave Tobias of that long ago."

Sarah nodded, but she could tell that she'd upset her brother.

"I need to go," Michael said as he turned toward the door. "I'm meeting with the constable to discuss the facilities in the guardhouse."

Sarah sat Nathaniel on the rug then hurried over to Michael and placed a hand on his shoulder. "I'm sorry, Michael. I thought there might be a rift between them, and I only wanted to know the cause."

"Are you sure you're not imagining this? Is it possible you arrived here with preconceived expectations? Perhaps we have fallen under your scrutiny, and Father and Tobias simply have not measured up to your notions."

Sarah pulled away. "Do you think I'm that judgmental? I, myself, detest having to meet other's expectations; I would not impose that on anyone else."

Michael shrugged. "Come, Sarah, even unconsciously, we all judge each other. Perhaps you should go somewhere and ponder what exactly your motives are. Perhaps then we can talk about it."

* * *

Sarah knew the perfect place to ponder Michael's words. She entered the stables and stepped out of the way as two young servants led a matching pair of bay steeds out the wide doors.

"Your Highness." Both boys bowed, but the older one addressed her. "We are readying Lord and Lady Moreno's carriage. We'll be with you in a few minutes to assist you."

The Morenos. The name sounded familiar. She'd met them at the banquet but couldn't place faces with the name. They must have stayed the night at the castle. "I don't need assistance, thank you. I've just come to groom Pearl and to give her some oats."

"Very well, Your Highness. We'll return shortly if you do need anything."

Sarah walked down the row to Pearl's stall. "How are you today, girl?" She rubbed the horse's soft white muzzle, and Pearl nickered quietly. "Sorry, I forgot to bring an apple, but how about some oats and a good brushing? Perhaps you can tell me if I'm being overly judgmental."

Pearl didn't respond with so much as a nicker. Sarah walked to the end stall where the bags of oats were stored and grabbed a feed bag. She leaned over to fill it when there was a soft shuffle on the floor behind her. Probably one of the stable boys returning to assist her.

"Sarah."

The hair on her arms stood on end, and panic surged through her. She knew that voice. Dropping the feed bag, she used the oats as a step and launched herself over the back wall of the stall. Her skirt caught in a crack and tore, but she yanked it over with her and turned to face the man.

"Chad!" Did the quaver in her voice show? A sick smile slid across his unshaven face, accentuating the maniacal look in his gaunt eyes. "How did you get past the guards at the gates?" She took a step back as he moved toward the stall she had just vacated.

"I still have connections. I will *always* have connections. Shall we go now?" He motioned toward the door with a slight bow, as a gentleman would when asking to escort a lady onto a dance floor.

Fear buried icy fingers into her heart. "I am not going anywhere with you."

"Oh, you are. I am taking you back to Calibre. And I am *really* going to enjoy the trip back." He gripped the top of the stall and leaned toward her. "I am going to take from you what you denied me when we were together."

A sickening feeling churned in Sarah's stomach. Chad had dabbled with women before, and it was no secret what exactly he was implying. She trembled and glanced at the doors—her only chance of escape. She was judging the distance when she saw movement out of the corner of her eye. She looked back just as Chad leapt over the short-planked wall.

She stumbled backwards, turning toward the doors. The sound of Chad's heavy boots spurred her on. She ran but was jerked back when he grabbed her arm. His fingers latched around her in a vice-like grip. "You'll come back to Calibre with me." He shook her. "And after I've had my fun, I'm going to throw your broken, lifeless body at my dear cousin's feet."

She couldn't stop trembling, but she wasn't about to let Chad take her so easily. Just as she was about to kick him with the sharp heel of her shoe, she was stunned by the sound of a thump and subsequent ringing of metal.

Chad fell to his hands and knees, moaning, manure and straw embedded into the back of his shaggy hair. Sarah looked up just in time to see Margaret swing a shovel and once again whack him on the head. He collapsed to the floor in silence. They both watched him for a moment. He seemed unconscious now.

Margaret walked around him and nudged him with the toe of her shoe. "I saw him following you. Is this Chad?"

Sarah nodded then froze when she saw movement. Chad moaned then pulled his hands under him and began to push himself onto his hands and knees.

"Run!" Margaret tightened her grip on the shovel. "Call the guard!" Sarah didn't need to be told twice. She hiked her skirts up and ran as fast as her trembling legs would allow. Just as she reached the stable doors, she heard another satisfying thwack of the shovel.

How long would Margaret be able to keep him down? She slowed as she rounded the corner and headed to the courtyard.

"Don't slow down!" Margaret was right on her heels. "And don't look at me like I'm abandoning my post. I'm not about to stay in there with a madman!"

* * *

Sarah sat in a high-back chair staring at an untouched cup of chamomile tea. She jumped to her feet when Margaret and Apollo walked into the sitting room.

"Did they apprehend him?"

"No." Margaret reached for her hands. "He was gone when the guards arrived. No sign of him."

"It can't be!" Sarah's hands tightened into fists, and she stomped a foot on the ground. "He was right there. You knocked him down with the shovel. How could he get away?"

Margaret leaned toward Apollo and whispered, "He had a very thick skull."

"He always did." Sarah replied. "But you can't mean to say he got up—after you hit him three times—and managed to escape.

The look of concern on Apollo's face deepened. "The guards searched the area, and when he wasn't found, they did a thorough search of all the castle grounds."

"He did say he had connections. Does that mean someone helped him inside the castle grounds and then helped him escape?"

"We don't know." Margaret picked up the cup of tea and tried to hand it to Sarah.

Sarah turned away. "Now what?"

Apollo put a hand on her shoulder and made sure she was looking at him before he spoke. "You will have a guard with you at all times when you are out. There will be guards posted at your door as well."

"Where's Luther? Isn't he supposed to be my guard? Isn't he supposed to keep Chad from getting close to me? So where is he?"

Margaret looked at Apollo. "I believe he's with His Highness. They are overseeing the extended search. I'll have him come here as soon as he is located."

"Don't bother. I'll find him myself." Sarah stormed to the door and flung it open, startling the two armed guards on the other side.

"Your Highness," one said. She didn't reply. Instead she ran down the hallway, determined to make him work to keep up with her.

Sarah made her way around the castle grounds with the annoying sound of leather and armor hounding her every step. Eventually she stopped and faced her two militant shadows. "I don't need you following me."

"His Majesty says otherwise, Your Highness."

"And I have the authority to give orders myself. And I request you keep your distance." The men moved away but kept her within eyesight. She still couldn't locate Luther, though several people admitted to seeing him around. She spotted a young boy heading toward the armory and caught up with him.

"Do you know where Mr. Luther Tandy is?"

The boy was in a hurry and attempted to bow to her as he trotted along. "No, Your Highness."

"Will you help me find him?"

"I'm fetching a poleax right now."

Sarah put on her most charming, kind smile. "But I would really appreciate your help."

"I'm fetching a poleax."

Enough was enough. Sarah reached the armory first. She opened the door just wide enough to cram herself in then closed and locked it behind her.

The boy pounded from the outside. "Please, I need to get in there. If I don't fetch Sir Alder another poleax, he'll give me a lashing."

Sarah pressed her back against the heavy wooden door. "I will let you in as soon as you fetch Mr. Luther Tandy for me." A moment later, she heard the boy grumble and hurry away.

She slid down the door and sat on the flagstone floor to wait. The room was dark and menacing. Thick chains used to lift heavy armor hung from the ceiling, and the floor was dominated by oversized wooden racks filled with a variety of weapons. Like the solders of Kyrnidan, they were sharpened to perfection, organized, and standing at attention, ready for battle. The tang of metal and the smell of oil assaulted her nose. She buried her head in her hands and hoped Luther would come soon.

She longed to hear his voice—something that sounded like home, without the Kyrnidian accent. She wanted something warm and familiar, something comforting to close the distance between her and this strange country.

Nearly twenty minutes passed before the door shifted behind her as someone tried to open it. "Sarah . . . Your Highness, are you in there?"

Sarah released her tension with a long breath. She stood and opened the door. Luther's face was soft with concern. She almost wished he would wrap his arms around her to comfort her. She needed the reassurance.

"Why on earth did you lock yourself in here? What's going on?"

"It was the only way I could get the lad to go find you."

The boy had already grabbed the poleax and frowned at her as he ran out.

"I was told that Chad—" She broke off, unable to finish. Luther stepped next to her and lowered his head, dramatically narrowing the space between them. He didn't touch her or put an arm around her, but she could feel his closeness. The air around him felt warm and protecting. She soaked in the feeling, trying to pull strength from it.

"You were told that Chad has escaped?" Luther asked.

Anger bubbled up inside her. "Yes. How could that happen? How did he get on castle grounds, and how could he escape?"

Luther's chest rose as he drew in a long breath. "The tight security measures which were in place for the banquet had reverted to standard procedure this morning. That allowed Chad to get through the gates. We have significantly elevated the security since then, and we will continue to maintain it. From now on, those coming in or going out will be meticulously checked by the guards."

"But he got in once. He might be able to again."

Luther shook his head. "We suspect he came in this morning with a group of purveyors bringing bundles of sticks for the kitchen fires. Margaret probably didn't knock him unconscious, and he must've slipped out the gates the same way he came in before the guards got there. There were a lot of people coming and going this morning, and the Kyrnidian guards had never seen him before, so they didn't recognize him. I admit, I didn't expect him to come all this way; otherwise, we would've been on the watch for him."

Sarah dropped her head. She should have told Luther she thought she'd seen Chad back at the inn when they were traveling. But even she had found it difficult to believe he had followed her all the way to Kyrnidan.

"We now have Calibrean guards posted on the gates," Luther continued. "They will watch for him, and no one will come through unless the Kyrnidian guards personally recognize them."

Sarah turned away, not wanting him to see her disappointment and worry. She appreciated the added security, but he had not heard Chad's threat, and she couldn't bring herself to tell him. It was too humiliating that anyone would have such appalling intentions toward her.

"I know what you need." Luther placed a hand gently on her shoulder. She didn't move. She couldn't imagine anything that would make her feel better.

"Would you like to take Pearl out for a ride?"

Sarah lifted her head. Riding. In the past it had been the one reprieve that allowed her to escape from all her troubles. "Can we do that?" she asked. "Is it safe?"

"Of course we can. I'll clear it with Prince Michael." He patted her shoulder. "And yes, it's safe. We have soldiers scouring the entire countryside. Chad's most likely heading back for Calibre as we speak." Luther softly cupped her chin in his hand and lifted it so she would look at him. He must have seen her uncertainty. "It's all right, Sarah. I'll be right there by your side. I'll protect you. And if it makes you feel better, we'll take a couple of guards for added security."

Sarah let her tension go with a long exhale. She could already feel her spirits lifting, but she tried not to let it show. Luther must have seen through her false expression because there was a knowing satisfaction in the way his lips pulled into a smile.

"You'll enjoy this ride," he said. "I know the perfect place to take you."

CHAPTER 15

SARAH WAS LULLED INTO A sense of contentment by Pearl's rhythmic movements as she and Luther rode side by side through the rugged Kyrnidian landscape. Two of Luther's handpicked guards flanked them on either side. Even with the added security, Sarah had darted nervous looks at every person she saw until they moved to a remote location where the only thing in view was the beautiful scenery. They passed a striking landmark where the bedrock jutted up from the earth, like giant fish jumping out of a lake, frozen in time.

Pearl gave a small whinny and tossed her head as if she were making sure Sarah was taking in the beautiful sight. "I know; I see it." Sarah reached down and patted the horse's snow-white neck. Pearl snorted her response.

They rode into a wooded area on a well-beaten trail and were in the thick of the foliage when Sarah heard the soft roar of cascading water. When they emerged on the other side of the small forest, she found herself looking down from their rocky perch as mist billowed up toward them in soft clouds. The scene before her was breathtaking.

The waterfall spilled out below them, and beyond the mist, a crystal blue pool awaited them at the bottom. Laughter drifted up to them, and Sarah spotted a group of kids swimming and playing on the grassy edges of the pool. She scrutinized each one, making sure Chad wasn't among them. She knew he wouldn't be but checked anyway. While she was eyeing the children, Luther gave instructions to the guards. One was to remain at the top of the trail with the horses while the other one went down ahead of them to make sure the area was secure.

Sarah dismounted, anxious to explore the small glen below. There was nothing down there that would be a danger to her, she was certain. A few minutes later, the guard called to them from the bottom of the glen, his words muffled by the sound of the waterfall. He smiled and waved, urging them to come down.

The trail was steep and rocky, too treacherous for a horse, so Sarah willingly handed Pearl's reins over to the other guard. The horse didn't seem to mind until she turned away and reached out to take Luther's hand. Suddenly Pearl snorted and stomped her hooves. Sarah turned back and stroked the horse's neck. "What's wrong, girl?"

The horse snorted again, and Sarah wondered if she detected a note of warning in the sound. Most likely it was her own imagination. Her nerves had not quite settled yet. "It's all right," she coaxed, just as much for her benefit as for Pearl's. "There's nothing down there. Luther will take care of me." The words startled her as she said them. Luther *would* take care of her. She didn't need to worry anymore. He was there with her.

Pearl seemed to settle and even dropped her head to sniff at the grass growing along the trail. "I'll take right good care of 'er, Your Highness," the guard said. "Go on down."

Sarah patted Pearl on the shoulder and turned to go. It wasn't until she took Luther's hand to navigate down the steep, rocky trail that another sharp whinny rang out. She looked back to see her horse watching her closely. She knew the horse would sense if there was any real danger, but Pearl didn't seem to be overly anxious. Whatever the irritation was, Sarah was certain that it wasn't Chad. She looked back at Luther then down to their hands, which were clutched together. Could Pearl be jealous of Luther's attention? Luther was only helping her down the rocky trail, something she didn't dare attempt on her own, especially in these absurd shoes of hers.

Sarah pulled her hand away from Luther's to see what would happen. Pearl instantly relaxed and dropped her head. When she took Luther's hand again, Pearl tossed her head and stomped a foot on the ground. "Silly horse." Sarah rolled her eyes and took a tighter hold of Luther's hand as he guided her down the steep incline.

"What was that about?" Luther questioned.

"I haven't been paying much attention to Pearl lately, and I suspect she's a little jealous."

Luther chuckled, and Sarah's lips slowly pulled into a smile. It *was* silly. She wasn't in danger of being completely enticed away by Mr. Luther Tandy. At least she hoped not. At that moment, Luther reached up to steady her, and Sarah was suddenly aware of the feel of his hand on her. She tried not to think about the feelings it stirred inside her, but her smile dissolved. She needed to be careful around him.

She negotiated her way over a series of small boulders and felt his grip tighten when her foot slipped. "I miss sensible shoes," she mumbled.

Luther laughed out loud, and Sarah flushed when she realized she enjoyed the sound. She needed to watch her footing around him. She was all too aware that a little misstep, even figuratively speaking, would send her tumbling in a direction she didn't want to go.

Once they reached the bottom, Sarah drew in a deep, refreshing breath of moist air. The guard wasn't far away. He stood alert and ready, swinging his head back and forth as if anticipating trouble. Sarah wished he would relax a little. The only other people around were the children. There were four of them, three girls and one boy. They stopped to look curiously at her for a moment before returning to their splashing game.

Luther had already pulled off his boots and stockings and had stepped into the blue-green water that pooled beneath the cascading falls. He waved a hand, beckoning for her to join him.

There was a large, sun-baked rock that seemed particularly inviting. It lay near the edge of the pool, the water lapping one side of it, and would be the perfect place to sit and dangle her toes in the water. She hesitated and suddenly wished she'd brought Margaret along. Up until now, Sarah had liked Kyrnidan's less restrictive customs regarding their women. She wasn't required to have a female companion escorting her everywhere she went, but this time it made her uneasy. In the secluded little cove, she would have liked Margaret to be there to advise her on what was appropriate or not.

"You can't really expect me to wade with you. It's not proper," she called to Luther.

"It may not be proper in Calibre. But as far as I know, it's perfectly acceptable in Kyrnidan—as long as you maintain your modesty."

Sarah rolled her eyes. Her modesty would not be an issue. Even the young girls playing in the pool were perfectly discreet in their under-dresses.

"You don't know what you're missing." Luther pulled his leggings up to his knees and stepped farther into the water. One of the girls splashed him then ran to the other side of the pool, giggling.

He turned around, and Sarah laughed when she saw his tunic dotted with water and his face moist from the spray. He held a finger up, signaling that he would get back to her in a minute, and then, with a playful yell, he charged around the edge of the bank. A chorus of excited screams came from the children as they scattered to get away from their new playmate.

Sarah sat down on the grass and discreetly removed her heeled shoes. The grass felt wonderful on her feet, even through her stockings. She looked up as Luther cornered two of the children and was using both hands to splash them. The other two waded into the water behind him, and then Luther was suddenly getting the worst of it from both sides. With a cry, he held up his hands in defeat and retreated. As he emerged from the pool, he flashed her a grin, causing a small tingle in her stomach. She dropped her gaze and began to pull at the grass, silently berating herself as she tried to squelch the feeling. She shouldn't enjoy watching him like she did.

Seconds later he walked over to where she sat. Water tracked down his chin and dropped onto his soaked tunic. "I was ambushed." He dropped down to lie on the grass next to her. She tried not to look at him, afraid of the feelings it might bring.

"You like it, don't you?"

Sarah had to look at him now, confusion clouding her face. "I like what?"

"The glen. The waterfall." He pushed himself up onto an elbow and nodded toward the pool. "Tobias took me on a ride around the area so I could get familiar with the location, and we came past here. I thought you would enjoy seeing it."

"Oh, I do. This is a beautiful country. The rocky outcroppings, the forests, it's all so different from back home."

"I could call this place home," Luther said. He rolled onto his back and stared at the tree-lined sky.

"You would leave Calibre? Forever? But you've served the royal family for so long; and what of your other ties to Calibre?"

He propped himself up again and looked at her. "Ties are just that—ties. They limit you. Wouldn't you like to be liberated? Free to live your life where and how you want?"

Sarah met his gaze. "Yes, in a way. I would like to be free, but not from my relationships, only from the expectations others put on me. However, they go hand in hand."

"The weight of those unwanted expectations is mostly your own doing." His mouth twitched into the partial smile she liked. It always appeared at the strangest times, and she couldn't tell if he was disappointed in her.

"What do you mean?"

"There are those who expect you to live up to their idea of a royal princess, but you weren't raised for that. You could choose not to accept their expectations and just be who you are."

Sarah looked at him for a long moment. "If I did that, I would have to renounce my title."

"Not entirely. You'll always be Prince Michel's sister. You'll always be the king and queen's daughter. But you need not be Kyrnidan's firstborn royal princess."

Sarah looked back at the grass. Luther's words were always so blunt, seeming harsh at times, but isn't that what she wanted—honesty? After all, her only purpose in coming to Kyrnidan had been to see her family, not to get involved with the monarchy.

"Maybe I'm wrong," Luther went on. "Perhaps you should be their princess and heir."

Sarah shook her head. "No. Michael is the sole heir. He'll advance Kyrnidan to new heights. I've never been a part of it, and I don't need to be now . . ." She let the words trail off, somehow feeling hollow and misplaced. It seemed as though she *was* ready to abdicate her position.

She frowned. More than a year ago, Alex struggled with the expectations put upon him. He had almost abdicated his throne, but in the end, he had been able to live up to everyone's ideals. If she couldn't do the same, it would prove she truly was unworthy to be his bride.

"Is something wrong?" Luther asked. He furrowed his brow with a touch of concern.

She hesitated, but he clearly expected an answer. She wasn't about to discuss her feelings about Alex with him, but there were so many other things wrong in her life right now, she merely needed to pick one to satisfy him with a response.

"I was just thinking about the banquet last night. It was horrible."

"I heard it was quite a fancy affair with all the best in attendance."

"You weren't there," she said before she could stop herself.

"Did you want me there?"

Sarah paused, reminding herself to tread carefully. The children's laughter drew her attention. They were splashing around in the water again, and she could tell they wanted Luther to join them. Children never had such complicated issues to deal with. Perhaps it was their honesty that kept things simplified for them. Perhaps if she were honest, things wouldn't be so confusing. Finally she took a breath. "I admit there was a time during the banquet when I wished you were there. I wanted someone brave enough to dance with me."

Luther repositioned himself so that he was sitting next to her, their shoulders almost touching. "You mean to tell me that no one danced with you?"

"No, I did have a dance. My uncle, thankfully, took a turn with me."

"Tobias?"

"I'm pretty certain it was him. I know it wasn't his dog. I would have noticed the difference." Luther leaned over, playfully nudging her shoulder so she would stop teasing him. "Of course it was Tobias," she said. "I have only one uncle."

"And did he dance well?"

"It was a nice dance, and I very much appreciated his efforts."

Luther stuck out his bottom lip in a thoughtful manner and nodded in understanding. "What if I were to promise to attend the next banquet and make it a point to dance with you?"

She looked down and straightened her skirt, once again reminding herself to tread carefully. He nudged her to encourage an answer. She stalled longer and placed her hands on the grass behind her and leaned back. He mimicked her movement, placing his hand so close to hers that their fingers touched. She could feel the warmth of his skin, and for a moment, it jumbled her thoughts.

She looked over at him. He had a content look on his face, and she liked the way the breeze played with his hair. "Well?" he asked. For the briefest moment, she focused on the soft curve of his lips when he spoke. She shrugged, forcing herself to look away.

She was watching the children when she felt his hand move to partially cover hers. Something stirred inside her stomach again.

"You don't have to answer." He leaned over to press his shoulder up against hers. "I'll just make you the promise. I will be there for the next banquet, and I *will* dance with you."

Sarah couldn't bring herself to respond for fear of taking that misstep she was trying so hard to avoid. Luckily she was spared the trouble when a sprinkling of water sprayed across them, followed by the familiar chorus of giggles. Luther jumped to his feet with a battle cry, and the children squealed as they ran in the opposite direction.

It wasn't Luther but the guard who chased after them shaking his finger and telling them to leave the princess alone. Luther extended his hand to her, offering to help her up. It was time for them to go, and staying any longer might be too tempting. She took his hand and let him pull her up. His hand lingered for a moment longer than it should have. Then he leaned in close to her. His lips almost touched her cheek as he whispered in her ear.

"Sarah, I want you to think about something. This is a new land, and it can be a new start—for us, together. I just want you to know I'm here and willing." He moved back and watched her curiously for a moment then smiled. He turned and walked to the water's edge and stepped in. After a moment, he looked back over his shoulder at her and motioned for her to join him.

Sarah's heart was pounding. She closed her eyes and listened to the cascade of the water. She could almost picture each little droplet letting go and falling—carefree. Suddenly the water, and Luther, seemed more inviting than ever before.

CHAPTER 16

"Do you want to talk about it?"

Sarah looked up at Margaret with a bewildered expression. "Talk about what?"

Margaret peered at her carefully. "I don't quite know. It's just that you've been quiet ever since that outing yesterday. I thought the ride would have lifted your spirits."

"Oh, it did." It wasn't a lie. Sarah had enjoyed the ride immensely.

"It doesn't seem like it." Margaret put down her needlework. "His Highness even agreed to dispense with the guards per your request and that didn't even lighten your mood."

"He only dispensed with the guards who followed me inside the castle. He still wants me to have one if I go outside. That isn't much freedom to celebrate."

"All right." Margaret put her hands on her hips. "I know something's been on your mind since the ride yesterday. Now out with it."

Thoughts of Luther swirled in Sarah's mind, and she suddenly felt warm. "It's nothing. Perhaps I enjoyed the outing too much." Sarah didn't elaborate. She wasn't ready to discuss Luther. She needed to keep those things within her own heart until she could sort them out for herself.

"I see." Margaret picked up her needlework again. "You had a taste of fresh air, experienced the wonders of Kyrnidan, and now you're stuck here in the castle again. Well, you just need to speak up. Would you like me to arrange for another ride? Mr. Tandy would be able to handle the added security and—"

"No." Sarah was surprised at how tempting the offer was, which was exactly why she should refuse it.

"Perhaps something else then? How about a visit with your mother?"

"That would be perfect," Sarah said. Anything to keep her mind off of Luther and the offer he had made her yesterday.

Although Sarah had made the walk down the hallway multiple times a day, it was never easy. Despite all the visits she'd had with her mother, the queen still hadn't been lucid enough to be completely aware of her presence. As Sarah approached the door to her mother's chamber, the usual cluster of people hovered nearby. There were always two guards, at least one doctor, and a few maids—Sarah suspected they were flirting with the guards. She was surprised to find an addition to the group today. Apollo. He stood silently apart from the rest.

"Apollo, I didn't expect to see you here."

"I'm here more often than Her Majesty's physicians would like, I'm afraid." There was a bit of sadness in his tone.

"If you don't mind my asking, why do you come?"

"You may ask me whatever you would like at any time, Your Highness." His open invitation was not lost on Sarah. "I have some matters of reconciliation I desire to address with Her Majesty."

It wouldn't be hard to guess what exactly those matters were. After all, Apollo's decision so many years ago had certainly caused an estrangement. Sarah turned her attention to another man with whom she'd become acquainted. "Mr. Bartolome, how is my mother today?"

"Still gravely ill; however, there seems to be some improvement. She is conscious and speaking clearly."

Sarah's heart leapt. "Does she know I'm here?"

"She does, Your Highness. She knows of your arrival in Kyrnidan, and she's anxious to speak with you."

"Thank you."

As she turned toward the heavy door of her mother's room, she heard Mr. Bartolome address Apollo in a rather cool tone. "I'm afraid, sir, you will have to continue to wait."

Apollo's gentle response surprised her a bit. "My years have taught me to be patient. I will be here for as long as it takes."

Inside, Sarah noticed that the room was devoid of its usual band of servants—with the exception of Grace. They exchanged glances. *I know you're watching me*, Sarah thought. She approached her mother's bed and felt the servant's eyes continue to follow her.

The queen appeared to be sleeping. Her skin was still pallid and thin, like fine porcelain, and her long, blonde hair was showing a considerable amount of silver. As if sensing Sarah's presence, her mother turned her head and opened her eyes. It took only a moment for recognition to brighten her face.

"Sarah," she whispered. Her voice was hoarse from lack of use. She pulled a thin hand from underneath the blanket and reached out to touch her daughter. "Sarah."

"Yes, Mother. I'm here." Sarah's own whisper was hoarse from an unexpected wave of emotion. Tears spilled down her cheeks and dampened the coverlet on the bed as she leaned forward and kissed her mother's delicate hand.

"I always knew . . ." Her mother had to pause for a breath. "I felt something was missing after Michael's birth." Another pause for breath. "I have always loved you."

Sarah couldn't speak; she just held her mother's hand and softly cried. Sarah had spent countless hours trying to analyze her feelings—worrying about having another set of parents and if she had enough love in her heart to accept the queen as her mother. Now all the doubt and apprehension vaporized. "I love you," she finally managed to say.

"I owe Miranda a great debt." The statement surprised Sarah, and she looked into her mother's eyes. "I harbor no ill feelings toward her." She paused again. "Or Apollo."

Sarah had to strangle the gasp that nearly escaped her lips. She could understand her not harboring ill feelings toward Miranda. After all, Miranda had cared for Sarah, nurtured, and loved her. But Apollo? How could the queen be so forgiving of him? This man had abducted her daughter. Granted, he had done it because of the threats, but there were other options. It had been her parents' right to decide how to handle it, and he had taken that agency away from them. Sarah shook her head unable to understand how her mother could give him even the slightest amount of reprieve. She opened her mouth to ask, but her mother spoke first.

"My dearest love, please forgive me. I am so very tired."

"Of course," Sarah managed to whisper. The brief conversation had obviously fatigued her. "Mother?" Sarah asked.

"Yes, my darling?"

Sarah opened her mouth but couldn't formulate the words, knowing the conversation would tax her mother even more. She would ask later, when the queen had more strength. "I love you."

With shaking hands Sarah poured some water into a small glass and helped her mother take a few sips; then she sat for a long time, holding her frail hand as she drifted back to sleep. Several more minutes passed, and then Sarah softly kissed her mother's cheek and wished her farewell until their next visit.

"Your Highness." A soft voice sounded behind her as she approached the door to leave.

"Yes?" Sarah didn't turn around. She had almost forgotten that Grace was in the room.

"If I may . . ." The servant seemed to be gathering herself to say something important. But at the moment, Sarah wanted to be alone with her thoughts.

"You know of the prophecy?" Grace asked.

Now was not the time to discuss such foolishness, and Sarah had a curt reply at the ready. "Yes, and I—"

"It's you!" Grace said, cutting her off, her voice full of conviction. "It's you! You are the one whom the prophecy spoke of."

Sarah would have laughed except for the desperate look in Grace's eyes. "Is that why you've been watching me?" Grace nodded, but Sarah just shook her head, opened the door, and walked out. "I fear you are greatly mistaken."

Grace followed her down the hallway. Once they were away from the group clustered at her mother's door, the maid grabbed her arm. Stunned, Sarah turned to look at the woman.

The maid glanced around quickly before leaning in and whispering, "I know. I know what the high priest said." She dropped her voice so low it was almost inaudible. "I was there." Grace looked around again before peering into Sarah's face with a look of relief and desperation.

Sarah stared at her. She had wanted to find someone who had actually heard the high priest give the prophecy—but not Grace. She needed a councilman, someone of influence who could convince others that the prophecy was completely erroneous. The last thing she needed was someone who'd heard it and believed it referred to her. That is, if Grace really *had* heard it. Sarah had learned the hard way that many servants lied in order to gain favors. More than likely, Grace was up to something. She might have been around that day, but they wouldn't have let her into the council room while the high priest was giving revelation.

It was a long moment before Sarah spoke. "I believe you are sadly mistaken. I know my place, and it is not to fulfill a prophecy meant for my brother."

"Don't discount yourself so readily." Grace let her words trail into silence when they both noticed Apollo standing nearby. He was looking out one of the narrow windows but had apparently overheard their conversation and raised an eyebrow as if awaiting Sarah's reply.

"May I remind you I am here for the sole purpose of seeing family." Sarah looked at both of them. "I resent being drawn into people's political machinations."

Apollo stepped closer to them. "But you are involved. You have been since the day you were born."

Grace seemed heartened by Apollo as an unlikely ally, and she pressed again. "Please, Kyrnidan needs you. Won't you consider . . ."

"No," Sarah said, decidedly. "Please, do not importune me any longer."

The distant chatter coming from the group lingering outside the queen's chamber died down. Sarah looked. Her mother's premiere physician, Mr. Martin, stood with the door open as he collaborated with Mr. Bartolome.

Apollo excused himself and approached the group. "Mr. Martin," he called.

The physician paused in the open doorway and looked over his shoulder. He promptly shook his head and closed the door with a definitive *thunk* just as Apollo reached it.

Sarah felt a pang of guilt. She had been shutting Apollo out just like the doctors had.

She took one last look at Grace and turned to walk down the hallway. "I'm sorry. I'm not the person you want me to be."

CHAPTER 17

"This is not a good idea," Sarah said as she followed Michael down the corridor. "There's a reason I've declined your requests over the last week."

He didn't stop or even turn to look at her but continued walking toward the council room. "You need *only* to listen."

Her brother couldn't possibly understand her anxiety. Political matters were *his* specialty, not hers. She didn't want to get involved, even if it was only to sit in attendance. It didn't matter that she and Michael practically shared the same birthright; her aspirations were completely opposite of his. Michael seemed to be at his best when it came to matters of state. He was always jumping in with both feet, and she was struggling to keep out. Michael pushed open the door to the council room and gestured for her to enter. Something stirred inside her. Despite her disinterest, a part of her wanted to go in, if only to watch her brother's administrative skills.

Sarah stepped over the threshold and realized it was not going to be a friendly environment. She tightened her grip on her skirt and forced herself to walk in. The heavy wooden door closed behind her, cutting off her chance to back out. As she entered the room, everyone stopped what they were doing and stared at her. They weren't the type of looks that said, "*We're happy to have you join us.*"

There were ten men sitting around the long polished table, and she could see the same thought run through each of their minds: *What is she doing here?* And at that moment, she was asking herself the same thing.

"I invited my sister to listen in on these proceedings," Michael announced as he took his place at the head of the table. "As you know, the Moylans have been using her presence in Kyrnidan to escalate their cause; therefore, I thought it best to include her today."

Sarah looked at her father and Tobias, who both presided at the head of the table as well, but their expressions remained indifferent. It was clear that the conducting of this particular meeting had been deferred to Michael. She suspected that, due to the king's age, a lot of responsibilities had been deferred to his son. The rest of the men at the table stood as Michael introduced each one to her, including Sir Henry, whom she already knew. Afterward, she was invited to take a seat with them.

Still clutching her skirt, she moved toward the empty chair next to her father, but the toe of her ornamental shoe caught on the rug and she stumbled forward. Her face burned hot. Perhaps her blunder wasn't that noticeable. She hoped. She felt the weight of every eye upon her. Mortified, she quickly composed herself and took her seat. Sir Henry was scrawling furiously on a piece of parchment—most likely documenting her awkward entrance.

She tried to keep the color from her cheeks by turning her attention back to her brother. He began the proceedings by relaying the grim statistics about the recruiting Robert Moylan was doing. She listened as name after name was read, listing those in the kingdom who were thought to have sided with the Moylans. The next item of business was equally depressing: the scheduled rally was far more publicized than first expected. The councilmen added their own information and weighed in with opinions forecasting the possible outcomes. Sarah sat completely silent. She was the only weed in this well-maintained garden. Each of these men had purpose, knowing exactly what to add to the conversation and when to add it.

The man named Mark tapped a finger against his lips then looked at Michael. "I think you should enforce your position."

There was a long silence in the room before anyone spoke. "I agree," Tobias said. He leaned back in his chair and traced his mustache with his fingers.

Enforce his position? What does that mean? Sarah didn't dare ask.

Another man nodded his head in agreement. *Luke,* Sarah recalled his name, remembering that both he and Mark were reminiscent of two of Christ's apostles—at least in name. Beyond that she suspected there were few similarities. There was another pause, after which three other men voiced their agreement.

Sir Henry scribbled something onto his parchment then looked up. "To what extent are we talking?"

Tobias and Mark looked at each other before Mark spoke. "Just enough to subdue the Moylans."

"Our army here at the castle would be more than adequate," Tobias added.

Sarah stiffened. Were they talking about attacking their own people? Was that what they meant by *enforcing Michael's position*? She looked around at the other men but stopped when her eyes fell upon her father. He was looking at Tobias with an air of warning. There was a hint of regret in the king's eyes, something deep and painful that passed between them. Again Sarah wondered what secrets they were hiding.

"We'll explore the possibility of every option," Michael said. "We will only utilize the army as a last resort."

"We should consider it," Luke pressed. "Many families will sway to support us if the Moylans are out of the way."

"If we do enforce your position, we need to do it soon," someone else added. "Set the army against the Moylans before they have the chance to further the dissent. Before their rally."

"Thank you. The suggestion has been noted." Michael's voice was tight.

"We don't need to eliminate all of them," Mark put in. "We can create just enough chaos to prevent them from organizing."

Sarah glanced around the room, her mind churning. She couldn't believe what she was hearing. She held her breath and waited for someone to oppose the idea. They'd been trying for years to avoid a revolution, and now they were contemplating starting it.

The men continued to discuss the most appropriate time to move against the Moylan family and the perceived benefits. Sarah pinched the bridge of her nose and closed her eyes. *Someone should say something.* She waited, but nobody seemed to want to counter the proposal. She could speak up herself. No. She wasn't supposed to get involved. She pressed her back into the chair and slid down in her seat. The discussion went on around her as the men tried to determine what an acceptable loss of life would be. Sarah felt ill. How long could she listen to this? Somewhere deep inside her, she did want to help, and right now she couldn't suppress the building urge. She opened her mouth to speak. Suddenly the room felt hot, and her heart began to pound.

Intertwining her trembling fingers, she placed them on her lap beneath the table then leaned forward and cleared her throat. "It may not be my place to make suggestions; however"—she took a breath—"the Moylans' decision to revolt against the monarchy will be justified if those in the government take on tyrannical methods of enforcement."

The men stared at her. She had actually shocked them into silence. Unable to withstand the stillness of the room, she continued. "It seems to me that setting the army against them will only fuel their cause. It is my understanding they oppose the monarchy for the preservation of the old policies. They're not rising up out of jealousy or because of an inequality of wealth or power, which means they don't oppose the entire system. I believe a more diplomatic resolution can be found."

She had done it again—complete and utter shock.

* * *

Sarah watched the men filter out of the room. By the end of the meeting, her words had at least delayed any attack on the Moylan family. For a few minutes, she had caught a glimpse of what it was like to make a difference—to shape action by contributing her own ideas. It felt good. Perhaps she could have some positive influence as a princess after all—she could get involved. Just a little. As she stood and walked out, she glanced back at her father. He had a pleased look on his face.

Out in the corridor, Michael pulled his hat off and ran his hand along the brim. When Sarah caught up with him, he reached out, taking her arm to stop her.

She smiled at him. She was satisfied with the results of the meeting and was sure her brother was too, but his grip on her was tighter than necessary.

"I thought you only wanted to listen." He let go of her arm. "I wasn't expecting you to give your opinion."

Sarah was taken aback. "I . . . I couldn't help it. I couldn't stay silent while the council offered ill-fitted advice."

"Those men are trusted advisors. They know the situation far better than you. And might I remind you—Tobias has nothing but the best intentions, which are in complete support of my leadership. If he agrees with an idea, then I have faith it will benefit in the long run."

"I know Tobias wants to better your situation, but that doesn't discount the fact that the advice was still dire. Do you really believe attacking your own subjects will *benefit* you?"

Michael held her gaze. "I will always try for a diplomatic solution first, but if the negotiations fail, we will have lost everything. The opportunity to use force will have passed by. The Moylan's influence will know no bounds after they have their gathering, and it will be impossible to quell a full revolution."

"You are talking about killing your own people. You've already prepared for your coronation; don't forget that you'll be promising to serve these people as a righteous ruler. How can you do that when you consider such an act? Will you continue to eliminate everyone who opposes you?"

"I don't think you realize what's at stake. There were riots in the village yesterday. We've had them before, but they are becoming more frequent." Michael's face dropped as he struggled to control his emotions. "Father has already sent Sybil away with Nathaniel."

"What?" Sarah gasped. "What do you mean?"

"As I said before—you do not comprehend the situation. We've tried to get things under control through diplomacy but to no avail, and now when we could implement a stronger measure to resolve the situation, you would have us lose the opportunity. Did you not hear the report of the weapons and men the Moylans have been acquiring? An assault may be inevitable. Father understands how dire the situation is, and that is why he sent Nathaniel away. At least our little brother will be safe when the Moylans have enough supporters to overthrow us."

Nathaniel was gone. Sarah's face tightened. An attack on the castle had always been a possibility, although she thought it remote, but now it seemed imminent.

"The negotiations are still the right thing to do," she said, blinking back tears.

Michael put his large, feathered hat on and adjusted the brim. "Is it right to let them slip back into the old ways? To let them run Kyrnidan into the ground in poverty?" Michael shook his head, and his frown deepened. "I know I can do great things for this country, Sarah." He held his hands out in desperation. "I know what this country is capable of becoming. But it can only happen if we move forward."

"Yes, but at what price?"

"I've always been aware there would be a cost in exchange for the betterment of my people. I guess the difference between us is that I am willing to pay it—with my own life if necessary. You see, Kyrnidan is *my* country and these are *my* people."

Sarah took a step back. "Are you saying I lack feelings for this country? That they are not *my* people?"

Michael shrugged. "I'm not sure Kyrnidan is where you're supposed to be right now. Maybe the best thing would be for you to leave."

CHAPTER 18

It took three attempts before Sarah could get any words to come out, but Michael had already disappeared down the corridor.

Her chest grew tight. How was she supposed to do anything? They put her into this position and buried her under their expectations, yet they didn't want her involved. Her brother said she had a right to be in the council meeting, but had she no rights beyond sitting there?

Sarah made her way to a nearby seat and slumped down. She could still feel the anger exuding from Michael, could still picture his expression—his cutting gaze and his set, rigid jaw. She hoped she had not just severed their relationship. She had never intended on driving a wedge between them. Tears threatened, and as she tried to blink them away, she saw movement in a corner doorway.

It was Grace. The last thing Sarah wanted was to be confronted by someone who thought she should get more involved.

"Princess, may I have a word?" Grace hurried toward her.

Sarah shook her head, her thoughts still on Michael's harsh rebuke. She stood, holding a hand up to warn Grace not to follow her, then ran down the corridor.

Margaret wasn't in the room when Sarah got there. Which was good. She walked over to a small chest sitting on a table next to her bed and opened the hidden compartment in the back. A fat pouch of money was tucked inside. If she was frugal, it would be enough to get her back to Calibre. She wouldn't need an entire caravan to accompany her this time; she didn't intend on traveling like a princess. Just a single trunk and no good-byes. Just pack a few belongings and slip away like—

She rubbed her hands on her skirt. Was she so cowardly that she would run away? She didn't want to be. She paced around the room. The need to get away still mounted inside her. Michael didn't want her here, and she didn't want to become a pawn in the Moylans' political game. But running away—she couldn't live with that either.

She walked to the chest and closed the hidden compartment. Maybe she could just leave for a few hours. Go for a ride on Pearl, just to sort out her thoughts and give her and Michael a chance to calm down.

Once outside, Sarah headed for the stables. She hadn't brought a guard with her like she was supposed to, and she wasn't quite sure why. Maybe it was just her way to rebel against Michael. She was still safe enough. At least the added security at the castle gates was enough to justify her reasoning. She slipped into the outbuilding undetected and made her way to Pearl's stall. She didn't have Michael's permission to go out riding, and she wasn't about to go ask. She was persuasive enough though and was positive she could convince the gate guards to let her go—if she agreed to stay close to the castle and let one of them come with her.

She stroked Pearl's forehead and leaned her head against the horse's white neck. Pearl nickered softly as if trying to comfort her. "You think we can get out of here?" The mare pressed her head into Sarah's palm as if to answer her question.

Sarah reached for the bridle hanging next to the stall when a shaft of light jutted its way across the floor, and Luther stepped in. He paused before closing the door behind him. She noticed that his green tunic complemented her own emerald gown.

"I thought I'd find you here," he said. "I was told to check on you."

Sarah looked away. "Am I that closely watched?"

"More than you know." Luther approached then raised a hand as if he were about to brush her hair from her face. He caught himself and dropped his arm awkwardly. "Tell me what's going on. Tobias said you were trying to fulfill the prophecy."

Sarah rounded on him. "I am *not* trying to fulfill any prophecy."

"Then what *is* going on? He said the entire council is up in arms."

"I was invited to sit in on their meeting, and I offered my opinion."

Luther looked hurt. "You're getting involved? I thought you said you didn't want to—"

"I don't . . ."

He moved his hand and slipped his fingers around hers. His touch was reassuring so she softened and allowed it. "What else did Tobias say?"

"Only that you're not the firstborn son."

Sarah dropped her head, but he softly tilted her chin up. His dark eyes, partly hid behind wisps of his sandy-brown hair, were full of concern. "Listen to me, Sarah. This could be dangerous. I don't want you to do anything to make these people think you're meddling in their affairs. I have seen similar situations turn fatal very quickly."

"Do you really think offering my opinion might compromise my safety?"

"It could." He looked intently at her. "But not if we leave."

Sarah couldn't admit she had actually contemplated the same thing. "Where would we go?"

"It doesn't matter where. And we don't have to come back if you don't want to."

Sarah felt a jolt run through her. He had hinted at this very proposal the other day when they were at the waterfall. She searched his face for any revealing emotion. "Are you asking me to run away with you?"

"I don't think I need to answer that. My wants are quite apparent. I'm only waiting for you to pin down your elusive wishes."

Sarah let out a long, slow breath. She pulled her hand out of his and stepped away from him. The thought of leaving Kyrnidan still tempted her, but running away with Luther would have entirely different consequences. It would insinuate a commitment to him. She briefly closed her eyes before looking back at him. "I don't know . . . Can you make things any better?"

Within two large strides he was beside her. He wrapped his arms around her, pulling her to him. She didn't pull away, and that both surprised and bothered her. It felt good to be in his arms. She searched his eyes and could tell he wanted to soothe away her problems. Slowly he dropped his gaze to her lips then bent down and warmly covered her mouth with his.

The kiss was firm and loving, and for a moment, she wanted to fall deeply into his embrace hoping it would release her from the torment that plagued her. Then a sinking feeling engulfed her. *This isn't right.* She pulled back, "Please, Luther. I can't—"

He pulled her closer, and his mouth covered hers again, smothering her protest. His lips were warm and coaxing, but it was not the same as with Alex.

Alex . . .

Sarah turned her head, pulling away from the kiss. She pressed the back of her hand to her lips where she could still feel the warmth left behind from Luther's mouth. How could she kiss one man while part of her heart still belonged to another? Everything about Alex seemed so distant. She tried to picture his face, but the memory was dull and out of focus as if a vast chasm separated them. *There was a time it was good with him.*

Luther leaned back and looked at her. "What's wrong?"

"We shouldn't have done that. You are my personal guard and my friend; I can't do this. I can't leave with you when . . ." Her voice faltered as guilt and uncertainty engulfed her. "There are so many things I need to consider."

"Is your relationship with Prince Alexander one of those things?"

"Yes. I am still engaged to him." The words were heavy, tainted with her disgrace of allowing Luther's kiss.

Luther took a step back. "I thought that situation had changed, considering everything that's happened here."

Sarah dropped her head. That assessment was tragically sad, yet more close to the truth than she could admit. "I am uncertain about my feelings toward Alex, but I have not corresponded with him to end our engagement, so for now, it is still in effect. However, that is but one of my dilemmas. There are other things to consider."

"Then tell me—What else is stopping you? What is here for you? You came and tried, but it's not working out. Whether you consider yourself still engaged or not, I can still take you to safety."

"You don't understand. I can't just leave with you."

"So, you won't go?" His voice was tinted with a bitter edge.

It seemed as if she was driving everyone away. "It's not that. Do you understand the implications I would face if we ran off together? Besides, I can't leave right now. I can't run away. My parents and Michael—I don't want it to end this way. I need to make things right."

Luther stared at her for a long, silent moment before turning and striding toward the door. "All right," he called over his shoulder. "When you get tired of fighting for something you're not even a part of, come and find me."

CHAPTER 19

SARAH WRAPPED HER ARMS AROUND herself and squeezed her eyes shut. She had expected to feel callousness against Luther's cutting words, but she was more susceptible to his accusations than she wanted to be. Did that mean she really did care for him after all?

She had given up on going for a ride on Pearl. Even that wouldn't be enough to sort out her emotions. When she walked out of the stables, Luther was nowhere to be seen. Actually, she couldn't see anybody. The courtyard was strangely empty. She'd never seen it like this. Even after the restrictions were put in place with the castle gates, there had still been some activity in the courtyard. Of course, the other side of the keep was always busier, as that's where the soldiers trained, but this side should hardly be devoid of people. Along with the stables, there were kennels, a poultry yard, sheep pen, and falcon house—all of which should have been attended to by servants and milking maids.

She turned around, her eyes searching for someone—anyone, but the entire compound was completely and eerily desolate. Where had everyone gone? Her stomach clenched with dread. Something was wrong.

A hen clucked noisily and beat its wings against the pen. Sarah jumped at the sound. The empty courtyard amplified the smallest noise. Even the dog scratching at the ground inside its kennel put Sarah on edge. She started to walk toward the castle, consciously pacing her steps, trying to suppress the fear to run. *It's nothing*, she told herself.

She focused on the castle door and had almost reached it when she glimpsed movement out of the corner of her eye. She stopped and looked to the edge of the keep. The foreboding wall cast a shadow over her, but nothing moved. She stood still, watching. Something had moved, she was sure of it. Someone was just around the corner. The uneasy feeling grew, nagging her to get inside the castle, but she hesitated. She had seen something and part of her wanted to find out what. It was only a few steps to the corner, but she couldn't will her feet to move.

The uneasy feeling intensified. Instantly she made her decision. She wouldn't take the risk. She needed to get inside.

She turned to run up the castle stairs when heavy boots pounded the ground behind her. She had hesitated too long. She turned, but a large sack was thrown over her head, enveloping her down to her waist. The rough, woven material stank of greasy wool. The musky odor gagged her, and she nearly vomited before she could get out a scream.

She groped from inside the bag trying to pull it off, but the man grabbed her, his arms tightening like clasps, forcing the air from her lungs and bringing tears to her eyes. "Chad!" she gasped. She wasn't sure it was him, but who else could it be? He hoisted her over his shoulder. She kicked, trying to get him to drop her, but he was too strong. With rattling momentum, she was thrown over the withers of a large horse.

She writhed, trying to take in air, but raw panic threatened to close off her throat. Still, she managed to scream. "Stop! Help me!" The words were sucked away with another jarring blow as he hit her, pinning her in front of his saddle, and the horse began to gallop.

"Stop!" she tried again, but the plea was raspy and weak. With each pounding stride, her screams became nonexistent. Her breath came in ragged gasps between the jolting bounce of the horse, and she couldn't stop the tears from coming.

Pain shot through her repeatedly as she slammed against the horse, but she continued to struggle, trying to push herself off. She couldn't let Chad take her—couldn't let him do to her what he had threatened. She tried to quiet her cries, mounting what energy she had left. Taking a deep breath, she pushed up and kicked at the same time. Finally her elaborate footwear was good for something. The toe of her pointed shoe sunk deep into the muscle of the horse's foreleg. The animal whinnied and jumped to the side. It was enough. Chad lost his grip, and she fell, hitting the ground hard. A hoof caught her as the horse sprang forward, and the momentum violently flipped her over. Her leg exploded with pain. She rolled to a stop and laid still. She didn't want to move, but even then she could hear the pounding hoof beats turning around. Chad was coming back for her.

"No," she cried. She struggled to her feet, yanking at the sack still covering her head. The pain in her leg intensified, but she knew it wasn't broken when it supported her weight. She almost had the sack off when he grabbed her from behind. She let out another scream, but his crushing grip choked it off. Tears ran down her face and her legs buckled. Chad had no problem lifting her weight. He lifted her as if her were going to throw her over his shoulder. Then all at once he set her down, but he kept a tight hold on her. Between her gasps for air, she heard the thundering beats of another horse.

"Help!" Her voice went shrill. "Help me!" She flailed trying to get out of his grasp and extricate herself from the sack; then, unexpectedly, she was flung to the ground.

Sarah curled into a ball, trying to protect herself from another attack, but when it didn't come, she pulled the sack off and stumbled to her feet. Her leg was throbbing now, but she ignored the pain. She heard the sharp clang of swords and turned, catching a foggy glimpse of the two men fighting in the forest. She felt faint, and everything seemed to move around her. She tried to focus, tried to wipe the tears from her eyes. But all she could see of the men was a sickening swirl of bodies and weapons. Someone had heard her scream though. Someone had come to help. Trying to get her bearings, she looked around. Relief flooded over her as she spotted the castle beyond the grove. She needed to get there—to safety. She took a step forward and had to steady herself against a tree. Everything seemed unreal, like a dark, disjointed dream.

She had to move, but her legs didn't want to work. Stiff with tension, she forced herself forward. Her strides were slow and choppy at best. Her mind was still foggy with panic, but something clicked when she saw the two horses standing nearby. The sharp clang of swords revived her fear. She clamped her jaw shut, and with determination, she struggled the short distance to the closest horse.

The lanky animal shied away from her before she was able to catch hold of its reins. "Whoa, boy," she soothed. Her voice sounded raw and unnatural. She pulled the horse to her then managed to coax her sore, trembling leg into the stirrup, and using all her strength, she climbed into the saddle. With tears blurring her vision, she glanced back at the two men. They had moved farther into the trees. Holding onto the reins with shaking fingers, she pulled the horse around and headed for the castle.

CHAPTER 20

THE KNOCK ON SARAH'S CHAMBER door aggravated her already pounding headache. She wasn't in the mood for more visitors. Both her father and Michael had questioned her quite thoroughly while the physician had tended to her injuries. He confirmed her leg wasn't broken—despite it being swollen and bruised. It was wrapped with a comfrey poultice, and she was given a sleeping draft, which she was now beginning to feel the effects of.

The knock came again. "Should I turn them away?" Margaret asked.

"See who it is," Sarah said. Perhaps this person brought news. Tobias and a group of soldiers had ridden out, and she wanted to know if Chad had been apprehended—if she'd been able to send help to her rescuer in time.

"Your Highness." Sarah opened her eyes. Margaret was standing at her side. "It's Mr. Tandy."

Sarah gingerly shifted her position on her bed and winced. "Let him in."

Margaret led Luther into the room. "Don't take long," she warned. "She's just been given a draft and needs to rest."

"I just want to make sure she's all right."

Sarah looked up as Luther approached the bed. His appearance was shocking. His hair was tousled, and his right cheek was swollen with the telltale signs of an emerging bruise. It took a few moments before she was able to say anything. "You . . . you were the one who came to help me."

Luther used the back of his hand to wipe at the dried blood on the edge of his lip. "I heard you scream."

She held his gaze. The irritation she'd felt toward him earlier melted away.

She didn't know what to say. She wanted to express her appreciation, but she couldn't seem to formulate the words. She pulled her arm out from under the heavy covers and softly slipped her fingers into his. Then, taking a handkerchief from her bedside table, she tenderly dabbed at the clotting blood on his knuckles as she whispered a simple, "Thank you."

"Has that fiend been taken into custody?" Margaret asked.

Luther took a moment before answering. "He's dead."

A jolt shot through Sarah, causing her body to go numb. "Dead?" Sarah could hardly say the word. Not that she cared for Chad, but she hadn't wished him dead. She wasn't like him. She valued human life. "He's dead?" she said again. "Chad's dead?"

Luther shook his head. "It wasn't Chad. I don't know who it was. I didn't recognize him. I suspect he was a hired thug because he was packing a small sack of gold."

Sarah let out a long breath. It hadn't been Chad. Although he could still be the one behind the attack. She looked back up at Luther. She wanted to pull him down by her side and run her fingers through his rumpled hair, wipe the smudges from his cheek, and kiss the pain away from his injured lip.

Another knock at the door made her headache throb again. Before Margaret could answer it, Michael let himself in. Luther dropped Sarah's hand and stepped away from the bed.

"I know you want to rest." Michael walked over to her. "So please forgive my intrusion. I'll only be a minute."

Sarah kept her eyes on Luther, wishing he hadn't moved away.

"No doubt Mr. Tandy has informed you that the assailant is dead."

Sarah nodded.

"The maligner has been identified."

Luther's head jerked up.

Michael let out a soft sigh and continued. "This treason has hit closer to home than any of us thought possible." He paused as he moved closer to Sarah and took her hand. "I'm sorry, Sarah. Your assailant was a guard here at the castle."

Sarah's mouth opened, but there were no words to respond. She'd expected Chad or another enemy—someone who openly hated her. But a guard within their own walls?

Michael's brow was furrowed, the grief evident on his face. "You said no one was in the courtyard when you were abducted." It wasn't a question, but Sarah nodded anyway. "We have checked with the servants who should've been working there at the time. They all claim to have been given orders by either the marshal or house steward which took them to other areas of the castle during the time of the attack. However the marshal and steward insist they never gave any such orders."

"Surely we can find who's behind this without too much difficulty," Sarah said. "They had to get their orders from someone."

"It was all relayed by word of mouth by a new servant girl." He gave her hand a consoling squeeze before letting it go. "Unfortunately, she is not to be found. We have searched the castle grounds extensively to no avail. Our only conclusion is—she has fled." Michael rubbed the back of his neck as he continued. "We believe the guard, your attacker, is the one who arranged it, but we have reason to believe he was working under the direction of someone else."

Sarah clutched the edge of her blanket. "Someone here at the castle?" She didn't want to be accusatory of Michael's domain, but treason had already infiltrated.

"It hasn't been ruled out. But it is still more likely an outside source. We must explore every possibility though. Has anyone expressed hostility toward you aside from Chadwick Hill?"

Sarah could think of a couple of other possibilities. The Moylans and those who were with them at the banquet. However, they were using her to further their cause. She knew they disliked her, but it wouldn't make sense for them to harm her. Then there was the maid, Grace. She'd acted suspicious at every encounter, but the woman believed Sarah was meant to fulfill the prophecy, so it wasn't likely her. Sarah's headache was getting worse, and racking her brain was making her nauseous. The thought that it still might be Chad crossed her mind, but Michael had already named him as a possibility. Finally she just shook her head. "Other than Chad, I can think of no one who would truly want to hurt me."

Sarah laid her head back and closed her eyes. Michael blew out a long breath. "Don't worry. We *will* find out who's behind this." He patted her hand gently. "Get some rest. Keep me advised on her recovery," he said to Margaret before walking out the door.

"I should go clean up," Luther told her after Michael had gone. She reached out for his hand one more time and smiled when he stepped forward and took it.

"Please stay for just a little longer. Just until I fall asleep?" Sarah's eyes were already drooping, and her words were drawn out and sounded distorted in her ears. She didn't want to admit that she was still scared, and she felt secure as long as he was by her side. She gave his fingers a light squeeze as she began to relax. When she closed her eyes, her mind was filled with images of Luther fighting a man with no face, then there was Grace peeking at her from behind the trees, and then there was Chad.

CHAPTER 21

MARGARET PLACED THE TRAY CONTAINING some bread and a bowl of broth on the side table. "One of the kitchen maids brought you some food."

Sarah sat expressionless in her bed, not responding.

Margaret nudged her. "Come, you must eat something."

"No."

"Would you like me to have the physician bring another sleeping draft?"

"No." Sarah stared at the wall. The first draft had not worked well. She had slept fitfully for only a couple of hours, and when she awoke she felt as though the seasons had changed. A definite shift had occurred in her mind. There was a heaviness in her chest, and her stomach felt hollow, as if every feeling had been removed. She wanted to see Luther. She needed to talk to him. She wasn't certain of her feelings for him, but she knew he cared deeply for her, and perhaps that was enough. At least he had offered her another option, and right now it was the only direction that made sense.

"Try to eat something," Margaret coaxed. "You have such a grave expression; the food will help lift your melancholy."

"Margaret," Sarah said without blinking, "please start packing my belongings."

Margaret gasped. "You . . . you plan on leaving?"

"There's nothing left for me here. I've seen my family. I have nothing to offer these people."

"You would return to Calibre with no other explanation?"

She didn't answer. She didn't want to admit that she wasn't planning on going back to Calibre. She couldn't—not like this—defeated and unworthy. Her heart ached, and the hollow feeling deepened. She had nothing left to give to either country, nothing to offer Alex. She felt as though she had endured a long and complicated dance; now it was over, her energy spent, and she simply could not go on. She would've had nowhere to go if Luther hadn't given her another choice. She would take his offer and go with him, abdicating her position. The attack on her earlier had made her realize that it really was the best plan.

Margaret was standing with her hands on her hips. "Have you forgotten who you are?"

Sarah lifted her head. "I don't think anyone knows who I am. In Calibre, I've tried to get involved as they wished, but it has all come to naught. All I have accomplished is to become fodder for prattling old biddies. Here in Kyrnidan, I have tried not to get involved—just as they wished—and I have failed miserably at that as well. My interference at the council meeting very nearly cost me my relationship with my brother and landed me in bad graces with my uncle. I don't fit into the politics here, and it nearly cost me my life." Sarah felt her despair radiating out, pulling at Margaret, and bringing her down. "I have no desire to die for a cause that I shouldn't even be involved in." She didn't specify, but her statement applied to both countries.

Margaret walked to the corner table where her satchel lay. She picked it up, pulled out a handkerchief, and dabbed her eyes before sneaking a drink from her hidden bottle. "What do you plan to do?" she asked as she laid her satchel back on the table.

Sarah remained quiet, unwilling to admit her plans. "Please, pack my belongings." Her voice sounded flat and distant.

Margaret stood motionless until a knock sounded at the door. "Should I admit them?"

"Only if it's Luther. I will see no one but him."

Sarah couldn't make out what was said at the door, but when Margaret returned to her bedside, her friend was flushed and bewildered.

"Is it Luther?"

Margaret shook her head.

"Then turn them away. I told you—I will see no one but him."

"But, Your Highness . . ." she whispered. "It's your fiancé, Prince Alexander."

Sarah's face fell slack, and she looked at the door, which remained opened a crack. She climbed from her bed, wincing at the pain, and began pacing in short, limping strides. "No, it can't be."

Margaret nodded, wide eyed. "It is."

"I don't believe it." She hobbled to the door, pulled it open, then suddenly slammed it. Leaning against it, she stared at Margaret.

"Oh dear, dear, dear." Margaret hurried over to the door and pushed Sarah out of the way so she could open it wide enough to stick her head out. "She's going to need a minute, Your Highness. Please . . . wait."

With the door shut again, Margaret grabbed hold of Sarah's arms. "What are you doing?"

"I can't see him." Sarah shook her head, her body starting to tremble. "Not now. I can't bear to face him."

"What are you talking about?"

Sarah pulled away and limped over to the table where Margaret's satchel lay. "I can't do this." She grabbed the bag and pulled out the little bottle. She remembered how her stepfather had used heavy liquor to dull his senses. That's what she wanted. She needed to drown her problems away, to not feel how disappointing she was to those around her. Desperately, she pulled at the cork until it popped open.

Margaret rushed over to her, but Sarah had already put the bottle to her lips and was taking a deep draw. At once, Sarah's eyes widened, and she spewed the liquid across the room.

"This is . . ." she stumbled over the words as she stared at the bottle. "This is . . . tea!"

Margaret pulled the small container away from her and corked it. "Of course it is! What else would it be?"

"But I thought it was—But you were always so secretive about it."

Margaret held the bottle to her chest protectively and dropped her eyes. "You weren't supposed to know." Her cheeks flushed with embarrassment.

"Margaret, it's not as if you were hiding distilled spirits—it's tea for heaven's sake."

"It's not proper for a lady to have an addiction of any kind, and a woman of upper-class, like myself—it's shameful. It's an awful, obsessive habit. Try not to think too badly of me."

"The only thing offensive about it is—ugh—the taste." Sarah wiped the bitter liquid away from her mouth.

"It's Lady's Mantle," Margaret explained as if that would rectify Sarah's opinion.

"Lady's Mantle is to treat feminine problems." Sarah threw her hands up in exasperation. "I have *male* problems. What am I supposed to do?"

"You're supposed to talk to your fiancé." Margaret pointed to the door. "I don't think I can."

Margaret tightened her grip on the bottle as if she needed to guard it from Sarah. "Of course you can! Were you expecting to find your strength in this bottle? Your courage is in here." Margaret tapped a finger on Sarah's chest. "Now prepare yourself, dear. I'm going to open that door, and you are going to face him."

Margaret walked to the door then paused. She whipped the cork out of her little bottle and took a quick swig. Looking back at Sarah, she took a deep breath then pulled the door open.

CHAPTER 22

ALEX WALKED INTO THE ROOM, and Sarah's pulse quickened at the sight of him. His raven-black hair hung carelessly in his eyes, giving him a boyish look, but his firm jawline and set eyes bespoke his maturity and concern. She felt her breath catching, but she steeled herself and feigned a smile, hoping he wouldn't see her tormented feelings.

His dark green doublet, tainted with dust from his journey, was overhung with an ornamental chain that rested on his chest, indicating his status. The royal emblem only added to her pain. It represented everything they could have had together, yet it was so tragically out of her reach. He was so wonderful and surpassed her in every way. She would never be able to match him.

"Sarah." He spoke her name with tenderness and pulled her into an embrace, wrapping his arms tightly around her.

She dropped her head to his chest and sighed heavily as he kissed the top of her head. He loved her and that only added to her guilt and confusion. Oh, why had he come? Why did he have to love someone so unequal to himself? Why did she have to love him back? She closed her eyes, dreading what she now faced. She had determined to go with Luther, but she didn't know if she had the strength to follow through now that Alex was here.

"I arrived about twenty minutes ago," he said. "Your brother explained what happened. Are you all right?"

She nodded, even though she was nowhere near all right. It had been so very long since she had seen him, and so much had happened. Perhaps too much.

She trembled, still unable to meet his gaze. Alex pulled away. "Are you certain you're fine? Can we have some peppermint tea brought up? It will help restore your strength."

At this Margaret made an odd coughing sound. It was an expert attempt to cover up a snort. Now that Margaret's tea preference was known, Sarah would never hear the end of it. She threw Margaret a quelling look, which quieted the woman.

"I'll go ask the physician what he recommends," Margaret said and then left the room.

Despite the lenient rules of chaperoning, Margaret wouldn't leave them alone very long. As soon as the door was shut, Sarah looked up into Alex's eyes. All at once she remembered the familiarity of his gaze. But what would he see in her? She dropped her head. "I don't understand," she said. "Why are you here?"

"Michael notified me about Chad's attack on you. I'm so sorry. We should've been more cautious. I had already extended my search for Chad beyond the borders of Calibre. My greatest fear was that he had followed you to Kyrnidan." Alex's face twisted with remorse. "But I hoped he wouldn't go to such extremes. I was devastated when I received the letter from your brother detailing what had happened. As soon as I heard, I put together a group of soldiers and departed for Kyrnidan. I wish I would've arrived sooner. Maybe then you wouldn't have gone through this most recent ordeal." He wrapped his arms tighter around her and held her. After a few minutes, Sarah pulled out of his embrace. She longed to stay in his arms, but it didn't feel right—not when minutes ago she had decided to leave with Luther. She sat down on the edge of her bed, unable to look at him.

"Sarah, are you all right? You don't seem well, and it's no surprise after the terrible episode you had today. Perhaps you should rest." He knelt on one knee in front of her and tipped his head so he could look at her face. "We can talk later if you'd like."

"No. I'm all right. You really didn't need to come all this way."

"Of course I would come. I was concerned about you. I needed to make sure you were all right. I needed to see you for myself. I left with no other thought, so . . ." His expression turned to uncertainty. "I missed the council meeting. They voted on our marriage proposition." His voice had grown quiet. "The result was not wholly unexpected since I wasn't there to plead our case. Our opposition took advantage of the situation. But I assure you the council will review it again when we have both returned to Calibre."

Sarah didn't say anything. It would be too painful for her to admit that the council's decision was probably for the best. Perhaps they had been right all along—she and Alex weren't a congenial match. She looked down and noticed how perfectly their fingers intertwined and how comfortable his touch was. She softly rubbed the back of his hand with her thumb. Oh how she would miss the little things about him. "Finish telling me about Chad. Have you learned anything else regarding him?"

"We don't have any information on his whereabouts. However, it is a good possibility that he is fleeing back to Calibre. I set up a network, so if he makes contact with any of his old connections, we'll know about it. We also looked for any sign of him on our journey here.

"Several nights ago we stopped at a tavern, and I offered a small reward to anyone who had information regarding Chad. The proprietor spoke up."

"And what did he tell you?"

"Chad was in the tavern several days ago and met with a man—not one of the locals that frequents the establishment—but a stranger. The man offered Chad money in exchange for information about you."

Sarah furrowed her brow. "About me? You said he wasn't a local—someone from Calibre?" It was more politics. It was probably someone who opposed her marrying Alex and was trying to find something that would malign her reputation even more.

Alex shook his head. "The man wasn't a local, but he did have a thick accent."

Sarah let the information sink in. "Someone from Kyrnidan?"

Alex nodded. "Chad spent considerable time in conversation with the man. The proprietor overheard enough to learn that the man belonged to a group of Kyrnidians who don't want you in their country. He stated that your life might be forfeit soon." Alex's voice faltered, and he pulled her into a hug. "After I heard everything the proprietor had to say, I left and rode ahead of my soldiers so I could get here as soon as possible."

"So is Chad working with this group of Kyrnidians?"

"I don't think so—at least from my experience with Chad, I don't think he'd conspire with others. That would require some cooperation, some subservience on his part to share the power and decision making. That's not Chad's nature. I believe they share similar intentions, and that is all."

"So the attempted abduction today was not planned by Chad but was issued by this group of unknown Kyrnidians?"

"That's what we believe. Although your brother said he wouldn't completely rule out the possibility of it being someone from the Moylan group."

Sarah felt numb. Did any of this really matter? Chad, the Moylans, or this unknown group of Kyrnidians—they all hated her.

Alex squeezed her hand. "We'll get to the bottom of this, Sarah. We're trying to learn more about this concealed Kyrnidian group. Our first step is to identify the man who met with Chad. Unfortunately we don't have a name. We do have a description, but it's vague."

"It doesn't sound like we know much of anything."

"We know that someone doesn't want you here and will apparently go to great lengths to accomplish their ends."

Alex put his other hand on top of hers. "Sarah, your life is in danger here. We're lucky Luther was able to save you this afternoon, but I can't stand by and have you risk your life here. I want you to come back to Calibre with me."

Sarah lifted her eyes until she met his gaze. This was a way out for her, but she couldn't take it. Tears slipped from her eyes and fell to her lap. Why did he make it so hard? She had not been his equal before she came to Kyrnidan, and she was even less so now. She and Alex were on completely different paths. She was not the person he had fallen in love with. If she went with him now, things would appear to get better, but eventually he would realize she didn't meet his expectations. She couldn't drag this out— it wouldn't be fair to him. The words were painful to say and caused more tears to fall, but she finally got them out. "I'm not going back with you."

CHAPTER 23

SARAH STOOD OUTSIDE THE LARGE, heavy door and flatly refused to go in. She felt as if she were standing at the gates of purgatory. The torment that awaited her inside was so terrible she couldn't bring herself to face it.

"Go on," Margaret said. She had pushed, prodded, and had practically dragged Sarah down the castle's corridors to get her there but still looked remarkably composed. The woman ran a hand over a few loose strands of hair and appeared as proper as ever. "They're waiting for you." When Sarah didn't move, Margaret crossed her arms and began tapping a foot. "I just don't understand. I thought you welcomed this opportunity."

"About as much as I would welcome the opportunity to clean the cesspool."

Margaret put her hands on her hips and stepped forward, forcing Sarah to press herself against the door. "Forgive me for being so bold, but Sarah, you are being childish. What is it going to take? Would you like a drink of tea?" She patted the bag that hid her little bottle.

Sarah stuck out her jaw with stubborn determination. "I don't think your satchel is big enough to hold the one thing that will make me go into that room."

"And what would that be?"

"The entire Kyrnidian army."

"But I've got the next best thing." A sly smile spread across Margaret's face as she pointed to herself. "Me." She wrapped her arm around Sarah's waist with such strength that Sarah was taken by surprise. Then with one hand she pulled the door open and, with unnatural force, pushed Sarah inside.

"Here she is, Your Highness, just as you requested." Margaret bowed her head toward Michael, pushed Sarah forward, and quickly backed out before closing the door.

Sarah lifted her chin and poised herself before walking over to stand next to her brother. Apollo was leaning over a table inspecting what looked like a list of names. She wasn't happy with his presence, but it caused only mild discomfort compared to the other two men in the room.

Alex and Luther stood next to the window in quiet conversation. Both men—in the same room together—and they were both darting glances in her direction. Beads of sweat formed on Sarah's brow. This was all wrong. She wanted to run over and push them apart, to send them to different rooms, anything so she didn't have to see them both together.

This meeting was supposed to be about her safety while in Kyrnidan, but what if Alex and Luther's discussion expanded to include a few more personal matters? A knot of anxiety settled in her stomach. She studied their intense expressions, looking for any traces of anger or jealousy on either part, but they were unreadable.

Michael placed a hand on her arm and nodded toward Luther. "Inasmuch as Mr. Tandy is in charge of your safety, we have included him in this meeting. And I hope you don't mind that I've asked Apollo to sit in as well."

Sarah let out a wary sigh. Apollo was without rank, and she didn't see the need for him to get involved with her protection. Michael must have perceived her thoughts because he hurried on with an explanation.

"I have met few men who possess discernment as keen as Apollo's, and it is to our benefit he's agreed to advise us."

Sarah nodded without complaint. There wasn't much she could do to oppose or even ask for an alternate consultant. Her father, along with Tobias and the other councilmen, were currently busy scrutinizing the servants and staff, making sure there were no other dissenters in their midst.

Sarah moved to the table and sat down. She hoped the others would take the hint—she wanted to get this over with. Luther sat down and looked at her passively. Even when Alex pulled his chair next to her, Luther's expression remained unchanged. Sarah felt like she was about to come apart at the seams. There should have been some emotion in Luther's demeanor, some glint in his eyes that showed he disapproved of her closeness to Alex, but there was nothing.

"Sarah, I understand Prince Alexander has requested for you to return to Calibre with him," Michael said as he took his place at the head of the table. "However he says that you will not go at this time."

Sarah confirmed it with a dip of her chin. She'd heard the disappointment in her brother's voice. He still wanted her to leave—to return to Calibre. But she wasn't ready to face that option.

"Well then," Michael continued, "we must do what is necessary to ensure your safety for the remainder of your stay."

Luther leaned forward, and for the briefest moment, his eyes locked with hers. She tried to hold his gaze, but he looked away. He was calm and poised, but she wondered if—beneath it all—he was thinking of *his* solution to keeping her safe. Taking her away, just the two of them.

"Of course, the most urgent matter of security will be the banquet tonight," Michael said.

Alex gripped the edge of the table, nearly coming out of his chair. "I assumed you would cancel the banquet in light of what happened to Sarah yesterday."

Michael frowned. "I have already discussed this with my father, and we are in agreement—we will continue on as planned."

"But this is unacceptable." Alex's chair scraped harshly against the flagstone floor as he stood up. "I will not allow you to expose Sarah and risk her safety at a public event."

Luther joined in now. "As you know, my men and I will be present. I, myself, will be at her side as her personal guard for the entirety of the evening. I *will* ensure her safety."

Sarah wondered if his statement was intended to remind her of his promise that he was going to be dancing with her at the banquet.

Alex shook his head and leveled his eyes back on Michael. "No. It's still too risky. You must cancel the banquet or at least reschedule."

Michael rose slowly, and the tension in the room thickened. "A nice suggestion—coming from our esteemed visiting dignitary. Need I remind you that you already agreed to be our guest of honor?"

"It has been nearly a year since I agreed—"

"So time weakens your promises?" Michael's voice grew louder. "You gave your word—assured me, in fact—that you would sit as guest of honor the next time you came to Kyrnidan. You know the importance. We must exhibit our connections with other monarchies."

"I hardly expected to arrive under these circumstances. Do you not realize the danger this puts Sarah in?"

"We are a nation with a great military history and prowess; I think we excel at calculating risks! By refusing to attend the banquet, you not only deny me, *but my people*!" Michael thumped his fist on the table to accentuate his last three words.

Sarah closed her eyes. With so much posturing between the two princes, she wouldn't be entirely surprised if it came to blows. The bitter mood was palpable.

"If I may," Apollo spoke. Sarah had almost forgotten he was in the room. He leaned forward in his chair, his eyes steadfast and reassuring. Alex and Michael exchanged cold glances as they took their seats.

"Your Highness," Apollo spoke to Alex. "I am certain you will understand. Consider, if you will, how you would handle the same situation if it arose in your own country—heaven forbid," he added hastily. "This series of closely scheduled banquets is the stratagem Prince Michael has employed to combat the uprising. You see, he invites influential citizens and thus subtly exposes his people to the new government. They are offered a chance to witness the sovereignty firsthand, to see the sophistication of it, and to mingle with those who are in office as well as with visiting dignitaries. They begin to see what the future can hold for this country, and fears of the unknown are dispelled. At the same time, it gives us the opportunity to see where public opinion is swaying. This particular banquet can hardly be put off. As we speak, the Moylans are gathering a mass of people at their estate, and this is the last banquet scheduled before they hold their rally. This will be the last opportunity to counter their assembly. Prince Michael *must* use this event to secure as much support as possible."

Alex let out a long breath then placed a finger over his lips in a thoughtful manner. A minute went by in silence. It was obvious he was carefully considering Apollo's words. "All right," he finally said. "I will not oppose the banquet, but I insist on a vast increase of security, especially where Sarah is concerned."

Luther shifted in his chair. He was good at making his thoughts with his unyielding expression.

Apollo cleared his throat and slid the list of names he had previously been looking at into the middle of the table. "This is the list of those who will be in attendance. I have adjusted it."

Michael pulled the sheet toward him and looked over it. More than a few names had been visibly crossed off. He nodded several times in approval then tapped his finger on one particular name that had been blotted out. "You think Sir Clint Garlynn is a threat?"

Apollo gave a half shrug. "No, not exactly, but I've never liked him. He is the shadiest of characters. You did say I was at liberty to adjust the list as I saw fit." Apollo leaned over and pointed at several other names. "These with the marks next to them, I believe should be allowed to attend for obvious political reasons; however, we should not discount them as threats. They are not to be trusted, and you should post a guard to each one—discreetly, of course.

Michael nodded his agreement then looked at Alex to see if he had an opinion. Alex nodded, but there was a tightness to it as though he were holding back from saying something.

Sarah tuned out the men as they continued to discuss the added measures of security on her behalf. Alex kept watching her. Had he noticed the looks that had passed between her and Luther?

At last the final details were settled on, and Sarah stood and excused herself. Her hopes of slipping quietly from the room were shattered when both Alex and Luther decided to escort her. She walked to the door, sandwiched between the two men.

"I thank you for your services," Alex told Luther. There was no threat or malice in his tone, just honest sincerity.

Luther gave a passive nod. "It's my pleasure to protect the princess."

Sarah continued to walk down the hall, keeping her eyes forward, unwilling to look at either man. Outwardly she remained calm, giving no hint at the turmoil that swirled within her. Deep down her emotions writhed. Did Luther serve her out of duty or for the pleasure? And what if his protection meant taking her away from Alex? Could she live with that?

CHAPTER 24

"I . . . I DON'T UNDERSTAND." MARGARET stood looking aghast. "You don't really mean that."

Sarah crossed the room to look at herself in the mirror. This was already hard enough, and she didn't want Margaret to argue the point. Looking at her reflection, she reached up and fingered the beads that had been expertly woven into her hair. "I do mean it. I know we've spent a lot of time getting ready, but I can't do this. My decision is final—I am not going to the banquet tonight."

Margaret shook a finger at her. "Oh yes you are. They're waiting for us; now come along."

Sarah furrowed her brow with determination. "I'm not going. Make my excuses. Tell them I'm tired of their politics and refuse to be their puppet." It wasn't wholly a lie. She did detest the political pandering, but that was slight in comparison to facing Alex and Luther together again.

"Oh, don't be so improper. You endured the same obligations in Calibre before you came here—why so adamant now?"

Sarah didn't answer. She simply couldn't explain the turbulence she felt every time she thought about going down to the banquet. If she were placed in a situation with both men again, she would have to make a decision between them, and she couldn't do that. She was emotionally involved with both of them now. And until she sorted it out, she couldn't be with either one, let alone both of them.

Margaret walked over and placed a hand gently on her shoulder. "All right, I'll make an excuse. I'll tell them you have a headache or something, but only if you explain what's really going on. What's really preventing you from attending?"

Sarah's stomach rolled, the turmoil bubbling up until she couldn't control it anymore. "Luther kissed me," she blurted. She cupped a hand over her mouth and stepped back, bracing herself for the reaction.

Margaret gawked at her in disbelief. The room filled with interminable silence.

"Please say something—"

Margaret held a hand up cutting her off. "You let Luther kiss you?" She turned away, shaking her head. "That did not just go in my ears." She began pacing the floor. "Oh dear. Luther, Prince Alexander—that *is* cause for a headache." She looked at Sarah. Her hard judgmental expression melted into one of sympathy. "Oh dear! Do you love Luther? And what of your engagement?"

"I don't know." Sarah pressed her hand to her heart as if the gesture would help subdue the pain she felt. "I love Alex, but there are . . . complications. I don't know if I love Luther, but there is something. I have feelings for him, and in a way, I feel we are better matched."

Margaret slumped down in a nearby chair and let out a heavy breath. The moment of silence stretched out as she fanned herself. At last she looked up and shook her head. "I can't tell you what to do. I have no great words of wisdom, and I admit I cannot offer much comfort either."

"I don't expect you to sort it out for me. Just understand that I cannot go down and face both of them together—not until I can figure out where my heart lies."

Margaret nodded. "I will make your excuses. Would you like me to come and sit with you after I tell them?"

"No, thank you. I saw the way that gentleman, Mr. Montero, looked at you during the last banquet. Stay and enjoy yourself."

Margaret flushed at the mention of Mr. Montero's name, but she quickly recovered. "Are you certain about this? I don't want you sitting up here alone, stewing over this . . . this . . . *headache*."

"I'm certain. I'll be fine here. I need to be alone. It'll give me time to sort through things, and no one can do that but me."

Margaret looked relieved, but for added measure she pulled her bottle out and took a long draw. She no longer tried to hide it from Sarah but still insisted that any compulsive habit was improper for a lady and had asked Sarah to keep her secret.

"All right." Margaret stood and looked at herself in the mirror. "I'll be on my way then." She turned and embraced Sarah. "I am sorry, my dear. If you feel lonely at any time, please, send for me, and I'll come straightaway."

Alone in her room, Sarah slumped down in a chair and nervously bounced her knee. She hadn't even begun to sort things when she was up again, pacing the room. There was no solution. She rubbed the back of her neck then walked to the side table and stared blankly at the needlepoint Margaret had been working on. The stitched picture depicted a royal maiden in a blue-violet gown bending over to put her hand in the water of a fountain. Absorbed with the unsolvable situation with Luther and Alex, Sarah absentmindedly tugged at a loose strand sticking out from the canvas material. Before she could stop, the gold thread unraveled. Sarah gasped. A moment ago, there had been a gold crown encircling the maiden's head. It was gone now. The thread must've been tied to another strand because some of the woman's hair was missing too.

"You dolt," Sarah chided. Margaret would be furious to find her work of art desecrated. But what was worse—Sarah still had a desire to keep pulling the thread—to unravel it until nothing was left. She threw the stitch work across the room onto her bed. This wasn't like her. She grabbed a cushion and began wringing it with her hands. She wasn't handling this Alex-Luther situation very well at all. She needed to get away before she lay waste to the whole room.

Avoiding as many people as she could, Sarah made her way through the corridors until she came to the base of the grand staircase. Hesitating, she listened to the sounds coming from the great hall. A few people lingered in the doorway. She drew in the aroma of savory beef and spiced vegetables. *They must be about to serve the meal.* She debated about going in, but seeing Alex and Luther would only make things worse.

Leaving the sounds of the festivities behind her, she climbed the steps. As the second floor came into view, she paused and looked around. The upper landing was vacant, so she moved to sit on one of the benches along the wall. The high, vaulted ceiling and massive tapestries made it a place where she could contemplate with little distraction. This hall was where she had first met her father. There had been several people here then, but now it was eerily silent. She could no longer hear the noise from the great hall, and she stared at the image woven into the largest tapestry across from her as she tried to focus her thoughts.

She needed to determine what she was going to do—whether she was going to leave with Luther or not—and she needed to make the decision tonight. "Oh, what am I to do?" she whispered to herself. Her words drifted off quietly as footsteps sounded in the corridor. Shortly thereafter, Apollo's figure emerged at the top of the stairs.

"Do you mind if I join you?"

She preferred the solitude but couldn't bring herself to outright refuse him, so she simply nodded. He took a seat next to her. "I no longer hold a rank of distinction or importance; therefore, I'm not required to attend the banquet, but you—you should be enjoying the festivities."

Sarah angled away from him. "I'm not feeling quite well. I have a headache." It was a minimal response, but it was all she was going to offer. She went back to staring at the tapestry, hoping he would soon take his leave.

"Ah," he said, following her line of sight. "Lovely, isn't it? Of all the tapestries in the castle, this one is actually my favorite."

Sarah didn't respond. The tapestry was beautiful, one of many that featured an image of a unicorn, but this particular work of art had a serene feel to it that was rather comforting. It depicted a young maiden sitting in a grove of trees with a unicorn lying next to her, its head resting peacefully on her lap.

"The unicorn is a symbol of purity and grace," Apollo said. "Something that can only be captured by the innocent and pure." He turned and looked at her, his eyes intense and sharp. "I believe there's a reason you are drawn to this tapestry. I believe you recognize something of yourself woven into the very threads of that image." He paused, and when he went on, his voice had a fervor that indicated his conviction. "The gentle and pensive maiden has the power to tame the unicorn."

Though quite subtle, she understood his meaning. She was the maiden who was to tame the unicorn. Apollo thought she was the prophesied one that would unite the people of Kyrnidan.

Unwilling to meet his gaze, she directed her eyes to the young maiden in the tapestry. The peaceful expression on the girl's face tore at her heart. She longed to be able to bring that kind of serenity to the people, but she had promised herself over and over again that she wouldn't get involved. Her only reason for coming was to see her family, although her heart ached for something more. If she were brave, she would not run away, and if it were in her power to unite the people of Kyrnidan, she would. Sarah had not conceded it out loud, but even as a silent confession, it pained her. There was nothing she could do. She was in no position to do anything for the people of Kyrnidan.

Tracing a hand along the decorated chain around her waist, Sarah took the small unicorn figure into her hand. She tenderly ran a finger over it then yanked on it, breaking it free from the pearl and topaz belt.

She held it out to Apollo. When he hesitated she pressed the unicorn into the palm of his hand. "Take it. I'm not the maiden in the tapestry. There's nothing I can do."

Slowly he closed his fingers around the small figure. The pain she had grown accustomed to seeing in his eyes deepened, but this time it echoed her own feelings.

"If you'll excuse me. I think it's time I retire for the evening." Sarah stood, but Apollo didn't look at her. He kept his gaze on his hand where he clutched the unicorn. Meeting no comment, she walked away.

In a dark, secluded corridor, she stopped and leaned heavily against the cool, stone wall. The profusion of emotions heaving inside her was nearly unbearable. Where did she fit—in Kyrnidan or Calibre, with Alex or Luther? Adding to her confusion was the weight of everyone's expectations of her and the prophecy—she felt like a volcano about to erupt. She took several calming breaths. "One thing at a time." As words came out, she recognized the application. She could handle one thing at a time. She still didn't know if she could commit to leaving with Luther or not, but in the meantime, there were other issues she could deal with. And she knew the first thing she was going to confront.

Pushing herself off the wall, she strode down the corridor with determination.

* * *

Having met no guards along the way, Sarah paused outside Tobias's chamber door. He was, of course, at the banquet, but there was still a possibility a servant might see her. She looked around then slid the heavy metal latch on the door. The metal squeaked as it moved. Sarah cringed, darting another quick look around, hoping no one was in hearing distance. There was definitely some room for improvement when it came to the castle's maintenance. With the latch moved, she pushed the door open just wide enough to slip into the dark room.

She didn't want to wrap her mind around the problem with Alex and Luther, but she could face the prophecy head on. If she was going to dispel the expectations surrounding it, she needed to learn all she could about it, and this was the one place she knew to start.

The shutters in Tobias's room were partially closed, with only the faintest light from the moon shining through. Sarah made her way to a shadowy table and lit the candle she found there. The small flicker dimly illuminated the chamber, casting shadows that danced around her, and for the first time, she took in the surroundings of her uncle's room. Her breath caught in her throat.

Tobias's chamber, though clean, was dramatically filled to overflowing. Paintings, armor, weapons, and tapestries of every size took up every inch of space on the walls from the ceiling to the floor. The copious collection had a startling effect, and Sarah spent several moments taking it all in. Her eyes darted from piece to piece, and slowly continuity emerged: unicorns, banners of red and blue, weapons, armor, flags bearing the royal crest, and various paintings—including a large portrait of Michael. It all depicted Tobias's patriotism and loyalty to Kyrnidan.

The vast assortment, despite its patriotic theme, seemed inappropriate. There was a frantic extremity to it all, a zealous intensity. Seeing the depths of Tobias's passion displayed so compulsively here in his most private quarters was more than disturbing. It almost scared her. This was a glimpse into her uncle's soul, and it revealed something manic.

Pushing aside the uncomfortable feeling, Sarah remembered her intentions for coming and set about looking for the particular tapestry she wanted to see. There were nearly a dozen throughout the room, but at length she found the one she was looking for at a place of prominence. It hung above his bed, surrounded by other items of great significance in his distorted collection and ringed in by the heavy bed curtains that hung on either side.

At first glance she thought the unicorn featured in the hanging was being hunted by a large group of armed men, but upon deeper inspection, she realized that the army surrounding it was actually being led by the unicorn. Draped in a royal cape, the creature commanded the soldiers. A shield depicting the familiar Kyrnidian crest was placed above the scene, and next to it were the words of the infamous prophecy.

Tobias had said that the exact words were sewn into the tapestry. She read them now and committed them to memory. *It shall be the son, the firstborn in the new monarchy, who shall quiet the fears and unite the nation again.*

Sarah pondered the unsettling phrase. Any way she looked at it, it was wrong. She was the firstborn under the new monarchy, yet it decisively did not refer to her, nor did it to Michael because he was not the firstborn. Yet enough people had placed their hopes in it that it was dividing the country.

Despite the eerie feeling the room exuded, Sarah pulled a chair out from Tobias's table and sat down. It was sinister the way everyone pushed their beliefs in this ill-worded declaration and protected the high priest from his blunder. Even Tobias made his opinion perfectly clear. He loved and lived by the prophecy, so why did he hide the tapestry here in his room, away from public view? "Because of its obvious mistake," she answered herself. She looked over at it again. Even in its place of prominence, it was obscured by the clutter surrounding it . . . hiding it.

A feeling of dread settled over her. Tobias was the extreme. He had gone beyond the fathomable by threatening to kill the firstborn if it were a girl. For what—to protect the high priest's facade? To ensure the people would continue to put their faith in their spiritual leader? He couldn't risk the chance that the prophecy was wrong, so he was going to force it to come true by covering up the mistakes. Sarah's hands grew clammy. What other extremes was Tobias capable of?

The candle flickered as Sarah let out a long breath, and she watched the distorted shadows dance on the cluttered walls. The encumbered room was even more unsettling now. She stood, anxious to leave, and with a sudden urgency to tell someone about her concerns. Alex or Luther. Which one should she speak to? Her fingers trembled as she snuffed out the candle, and the darkness surrounded her.

CHAPTER 25

SARAH STOOD IN THE SERVANT'S entrance to the great hall, hesitant to look inside. She wrung her hands, trying to decide who to seek out. Luther was in charge of her security, and wasn't this a matter of security? She took a step toward the door and then stopped. It was more than that. Her decision right now would signify who she really wanted to be with. She needed to choose between Alex and Luther, and whichever one she chose, she would put her full trust in.

The guests had finished their dinner, and the quiet chatter of mingling people drifted out to her against the backdrop of soft music. She put a hand on the doorframe and leaned forward.

"What are you doing here?" Margaret bustled through the door way, forcing her to step back.

Sarah shrugged. "I'm trying to decide."

Margaret's eyebrows seemed to motion toward the great hall. "Between the two headaches?"

"Yes. But one headache isn't standing out over the other. What am I to do?"

"Hmmm." Margaret cupped her chin in a thoughtful manner. "Let's start with Prince Alexander. What do you like about him?"

"Well, he fell in love with me before he even knew I was a princess."

"That's a good sign."

"I admire the way he shoulders his responsibilities. He's strong-willed and confident and always seemed to know the best way to handle things." Sarah paused, raising her eyes to the ceiling as she thought. "He naturally assumes the mantle of leadership and is never daunted by the heavy load it places on him. He knows who he is and what he needs to do."

"All right, dear," Margaret cut her off. "This is starting to sound like a list of what it is about him that makes him a great leader."

Sarah had to agree, but those were the things she admired in Alex. It was also a list of the qualities *she* longed for but still found herself lacking in.

Margaret shifted her weight onto her hip. "Now what about Luther?"

"He's physical and daring," Sarah started.

Margaret nodded. "That he is."

"I do love his impulsive nature. He lives for adventure." Sarah chose not to say anything about Luther's plot to take her away. The idea scared her, but that's also what made it alluring. He was so confident that it would work, and maybe it would. "Luther is fearless," Sarah continued.

Margaret shook her head. "This sounds like a list from a bar maid describing a rogue from some fantasy adventure—all handsome, brave, and venturesome. Perhaps you should look a little deeper."

Sarah let out a groan. "This isn't working. There are things I love about both men. I'm going in there, and I'm going to talk to both of them."

Margaret positioned herself in the doorway using her ample pale-green gown to block the way. "Are you sure you want to do that?"

"Actually, I do. I have something important to discuss with them." Sarah couldn't choose between them right now, so she would just have to tell both of them about her concerns about Tobias.

Sarah pushed past Margaret and stepped into the great hall. Although this was the same room where the previous banquet had been held, there was an entirely different atmosphere to this event.

She had to give her brother credit for his planning. While the last gathering had been bright and delightful, this one had a different effect altogether. It was suave and elegant. The entire room had a heavenly appearance and gave the impression of dignified sophistication. Low hanging chandeliers softly illuminated the twisted columns of shaped greenery and reflected off shimmering ball gowns. She wondered if the decor was another subtle tactic Michael was using to sway the people. By putting them in an atmosphere that reflected what he wanted them to emulate, they were more likely to act accordingly.

Sarah looked from one person to the next, their movements made fluid by the sweet melody being played in the background. It was tempting to get caught up in the exquisiteness of the moment. She gave herself a mental shake, recalling the unnatural atmosphere of Tobias's room and his extreme tendencies.

At last she spotted the men. Alex was accompanying her brother in greeting guests and Luther followed behind. She watched them for a minute, and something stirred inside her. Slowly and unexpectedly her feelings were coming into focus. Alex and Luther. Suddenly she knew which one she wanted to be with—which one she needed. She nearly laughed out loud as she realized it was the way they walked across the floor that made her decision clear. The stark comparison of the two men's movements sharpened the blurry lines of her devotion.

Her heart gave a sigh at the sudden acknowledgment, and she fixed her eyes on Alex. He moved confidently through the crowd, his eyes sparkling behind his raven-dark hair, while Luther lumbered two steps behind, burly and moody.

Alex was the one she truly loved. She had loved him from the beginning—before their lives were complicated by royal matters. Despite what had attracted her to Luther, her heart still belonged to Alex. Luther may have professed feelings for her, but he didn't encourage her to be a better person. He had tried to convince her to settle for less than she really was. She didn't want to spend the rest of her life lumbering two steps behind her full potential. She would not run away with Luther. Instead she would stay and do what she could to help her country and meet the expectations put upon her. She would have the ability to do that as long as she was with Alex. He was the one who encouraged her to live up to her birthright.

From the doorway, she watched him make his way through the crowd. She felt the familiar desire to emulate him—to walk tall with certainty. That ambition still seemed daunting, and there was still the fear of being unable to measure up. She didn't know if she would ever fully convince her critics that she was worthy to be by Alex's side, but at the very least, she could fight for it. After all, she did have Kyrnidian roots, and if anyone were fighters—they were.

Sarah felt light as she stepped farther into the room, and as if Alex had felt her presence, he looked over and met her gaze. It was one of many things that she loved about him; one look and he understood. He made his way through the crowd toward her, and they slipped out the door together.

Margaret sidled up next to her. "If this is the headache you choose, I approve. He suits you better anyway." She gave a wink then sauntered back into the hall and disappeared in the bustle of people.

Alex stared after her. "What was that about?"

"Nothing." Sarah's heart quivered at his closeness, and she yearned to go somewhere more private—where they could talk, where she could confess her love for him all over again. She started to lead him up the corridor, but he put a hand on her arm, stopping her.

"Sarah, has your headache abated? I was told that you were resting."

All at once the evening's events came rushing back, pulling her with them. "I confess I have not been resting."

His eyes narrowed with a hint of frustration.

Sarah intended on telling him everything that had transpired that night, but she would start with her concerns about her uncle. "I talked with Apollo," she started to explain. "He's subtly been hinting that I am the one who will unite the people of Kyrnidan, so I went into Tobias's room to see the words of the prophecy myself, since they're sewn into a tapestry he keeps there."

Alex's frustration dissolved into disappointment and concern. "Sarah, what are you getting yourself into?"

The look on his face brought her up short. This wasn't going at all like she'd planned. Only moments ago, she had glimpsed into her heart and deciphered her baffled feelings about Alex. She had realized what he meant to her, and she had every intention of showing her appreciation and gratitude for their relationship, but now he looked at her as if they were drifting apart.

"Sarah, I love you." He took her hand. "But you don't realize the depths of the conflicts in this country. Please do not involve yourself. Have you already dismissed what happened yesterday? There's someone out there who means to harm you. They've gone to great lengths in gathering information about you, and they were almost successful in having you abducted from castle grounds." He paused as his eyes pleaded with hers. "You need to be very careful. Whatever this is you're trying to figure out—just leave it to Michael."

Sarah pressed her lips together in a tight line. Perhaps telling him about this wasn't a good idea. She didn't want to be put under lock and key for her own protection.

Alex placed a hand on her cheek. "Listen to me. Your brother will sort all of this out. There is no need to concern yourself with such issues."

This was not the direction she wanted to go. Alex could feel the pull Kyrnidan had on her, and he wanted her to resist. But it was too late. She loved him, and she was determined to be with him, but to do that, she had to resolve some things here—at least the things that affected her directly, like the prophecy.

"I agree with you," she said. "But shouldn't we follow through on any leads that may direct us to a resolution? Perhaps it will help us discover who is trying to get at me."

"Did you glean any such information on your adventure tonight?"

"Only that Tobias is not who I thought him to be."

Alex gave her a firm look. "What exactly do you mean?"

"He's obsessive. If you could only see his chamber; it's not normal." She let the sentence dangle for a moment. "I didn't find anything that would convict him of any maliciousness, but something is not right about him. Come with me, and I'll show you."

She tugged on his hand, but he pulled out of her grip. "I'm not going to sneak into Tobias's chamber uninvited."

Sarah's hopes crumbled. She didn't know what she was getting at, but her uncle's unhealthy compulsions were something that should be taken into consideration, shouldn't they?

"It's not that I disbelieve you," Alex said, lowering his voice. He put a hand around her waist and directed her farther from the doors. She suspected he didn't want to risk the chance of anyone overhearing their conversation. When he removed his hand, she felt the loss of his touch more severely than she expected.

"It could be completely possible that something is amiss with Tobias," Alex said. "We've witnessed firsthand in Calibre how a relative can crave power and do unspeakable things to get it."

"Yes." Sarah knew he was referring to Chad, and she supposed it made sense. Tobias did have an obsession for the monarchy. Alex lifted his eyes, and his expression indicated that he took her concern seriously, but then he turned and walked away.

"Wait," she called. "Where are you going?"

"If that's the case, then we must confront Michael. Wait here."

Sarah began pacing the floor, wondering how she would broach the subject with her brother.

"What is this all about?" Michael said minutes later when he joined her in the hallway. His brows were knit together in a grim expression. "Truly you do not think that Tobias is capable of treachery."

Sarah cringed. This is exactly why she hadn't approached Michael in the first place, and she hadn't expected Alex to convey her suspicions without her being there to explain them properly. "I'm sorry, Michael. It's just that—"

"No need to be sorry," Alex said, cutting her off and then pointed at Michael. "It's something that needs to be taken into consideration."

Michael pulled off his flamboyant hat and ran a hand through his sun-kissed hair. "I know the torment your cousin Chad caused you. And I'm sure you would have liked someone to forewarn you that he was trying to maneuver himself onto the throne, but you know nothing about Tobias."

Alex's face darkened. "With the recent abduction attempt and the impending uprising, I would think you would scrutinize everyone capable of organizing such efforts."

"And in such volatile situations, the last thing we need is for people to be blindly accused." Michael folded his arms across his chest and looked hard at both of them. "You know nothing of Tobias, neither one of you. If there is anyone who would sacrifice everything for our cause, for the monarchy, for our family, or for me—it's Tobias. He has done as much to prepare me for the throne as has father. How can you even conceive that he craves power and position?"

"It's more than conceivable," Sarah said. "He's captivated by it." She stopped short of explaining why she suspected as much. She didn't want Michael to know she had been in their uncle's room and seen his obsessive collection.

"I can't believe you're doing this." Michael raised his hands in exasperation. "Can you not see he is our family's greatest supporter? He wants only what is best for us." Sarah opened her mouth to speak, but Michael held up a hand, stopping her. "If only others were as loyal."

Her brother's insinuation was painful, and her retort slipped away unsaid.

"Now enough of this business. Are you going to come and join us?" Michael gestured toward the great hall.

A long moment of silence stretched between them, and Sarah looked at Alex hoping to find some encouragement or at least comfort. He just shook his head. "I've had enough. You may go in, but I think I am ready to retire." Sarah stared at him, baffled. Was that it? He was giving up and going to bed?

Alex turned toward Michael and offered a slight nod of his head. "I feel you're trying to hold off the inevitable, my friend." Sarah wondered at the endearment tacked onto the end of the sentence. They had been friends, but now there was tension between them. Tension that she had caused. "Your country is on the very pivot of change. I pray it goes in your favor. If there's anything in my power to help, you need only to ask." Alex paused and looked back and forth between her and Michael before continuing. "Otherwise, I will be leaving in the morning."

A gasp rose in Sarah's throat, but she managed to contain it. She didn't want him to leave so soon. Her brother didn't react at all to his declaration other than a tight nod. Alex turned to Sarah and put a hand on her arm. "Sarah, in consideration of your safety, I expect you will be ready to accompany me home."

CHAPTER 26

"Blast it!"

Sarah usually wasn't so cavalier in her choice of words, but if ever there was a situation that called for expressive grammar, this was it. The explosive phrase was followed with a twinge of guilt, reminding her of why she seldom cursed. She wasn't good at it, and it always made her feel worse afterwards. Less ladylike. She darted her eyes around to make sure no one had heard. Alex had retired to his room, and Michael had gone back to attending the guests in the great hall, so she was sure she was alone.

"Excuse me, Your Highness."

Of all the rotten luck. Sarah spun around to see who might have witnessed her coarse expression. Standing behind her was a young lady dressed in a fitted, pale-yellow gown with most of her red hair tucked beneath a starched wimple. It only took her a moment to place the girl. She was the steward's daughter, although Sarah couldn't recall her name.

"Mr. Luther Tandy asked that I give this to you." The young lady curtsied as she held out a folded piece of paper. Sarah took the note and opened it. *Meet me outside by the stables at half past the hour. West doors.*

Quickly refolding it to hide the words, Sarah looked up at the young lady. "Did you happen to read this?"

The girl dropped her eyes and shook her head. "No. Mr. Tandy just handed it to me a few minutes ago. He simply said to give it to you and to tell you it was from him."

"Is that the truth?" Sarah wasn't convinced. Staff were known to read written correspondences, and she didn't want rumors flying around about a covert meeting in the stables.

The girl's cheeks burned pink, and she dropped her head even lower. "I can't read. Please don't tell His Highness, Prince Michael. I know he has stressed that we all must learn." Sarah dismissed her, making a mental note to tutor the girl herself when she had the time. That is, if she had any more time. Alex expected her to leave in the morning.

Alone again, Sarah opened the note and reread the message. Luther hadn't put his name to it. That was thoughtful. If it had been intercepted by someone else, it could prove to be a great deal more than just an awkward situation. It was nearly half past the hour now. She suspected that Luther was probably on his way to the stables now. This would be the perfect opportunity to inform him privately that she had recommitted herself to her relationship with Alex. He deserved that decency at least.

She walked toward the west doors as the note directed. There were no guards.

"Of course," she mumbled. Luther had helped coordinate the security for tonight. It would have been easy for him to dismiss the guards from the entrance for a short time. She stared at the doors and tensed. The gates had been closed, and the only ones allowed entrance were the ones on the guest list, but Chad was still out there somewhere, and he was clever. Sarah crossed her arms. Was she simply using Chad as an excuse not to go talk to Luther? He was going to be upset to learn that she had chosen Alex. But that did not discount his right to know. She couldn't simply go about avoiding him, especially since he was in charge of her security.

She took a deep breath, resigning herself to get it over with. She would be safe enough. There may have been no guards at the door, but this was the busy side of the castle. There would be enough people around, and that in itself would be enough to deter Chad. Pushing open the heavy door, she stepped out into the night and solemnly promised herself to keep the meeting as brief as possible.

Sarah looked around cautiously. She didn't like this side of the castle. This was where the army trained, and as a woman, she felt out of place there. She cast a glance toward the barracks. Several men stood milling around, but no one made any effort to stop her. She hurried, wanting to make short work out of getting to the stables. She was just nearing the corner tower when a door to one of the guardhouses across the compound opened. Two men emerged. The lanterns from the room behind them backlit their frames and cast a glow around their bodies as they stood in the open doorway.

Tobias was one of them, and it took her a second to recognize the other man—Luke. She had met him in the council meeting. Apparently, all business matters weren't put on hold during the banquet, and the two men were too engrossed in their conversation to notice Sarah as she edged along the dark shadows of the castle wall.

"It'll work," Tobias said. "We have one more council meeting scheduled before the Moylans' gathering. We will convince young Michael of this necessary action by then."

Luke nodded vigorously in agreement. "It shouldn't be too hard to persuade His Highness; after all, our supporters are not rallying together as we had hoped."

"After tonight's banquet, when Michael sees the supporters we have gained are inconsequential compared to what we need, he'll see that there is no other way."

There was a pause as if there was nothing more to be said; then Luke's posture sagged. "I suppose we must go back and join the rest of high society. Or perhaps we could . . ."

"What?" Tobias asked. It seemed he too was hoping for another distraction to keep him away from the *silly frivolities*.

"We received our first shipment of swords from the guild in Farellden. Would you like to inspect them?"

Sarah couldn't see the expression on Tobias's face, but she was certain he was smiling. The two men strode across the opposite side of the compound toward the armory without so much as looking at her. She didn't like the idea that they were going to pressure Michael again, but she had faith he wouldn't give up on his diplomacy.

"When are you going to give me a copy of the attack plan?" Luke asked.

Sarah had already slowed her pace so as not to draw attention to herself, but she stopped abruptly when she heard the question. They already had a plan of attack written up? Kingdoms ran on efficiency, but wasn't this a little too presumptuous? Especially when it regarded killing their own people?

"I have it in my chamber," Tobias said. "I'll get it for you when we're done here."

Sarah stared at the backs of the two men as they blended into the darkness. *In his chamber?* She had just been in Tobias's room less than an hour ago. She racked her mind trying to recall if she'd seen anything that resembled attack plans. Had there been papers on his table? She couldn't remember. She was so taken aback with everything else in the room that she would have overlooked any papers.

She looked in the directions of the stables. Luther was waiting for her. Her palms grew moist, and she pressed them against her skirt. She couldn't believe what she was actually contemplating. It was a dangerous idea, but she was going to do it anyway. After all, she'd been the one who opposed an attack against the Moylans in the first place. She wasn't going to give up a chance to find out the extent of the council's scheme to attack them.

Tobias and Luke were now in the armory. She took a deep breath and darted back toward the west door. She had snuck into her uncle's room once that night, and she could do it again—if she hurried.

CHAPTER 27

IT WAS DARK INSIDE THE room. More so than it had been earlier, or so it seemed. Sarah's heart pounded as she hurried to the table. She didn't have much time. She lit the candle with shaking hands and lifted the light high in the air, casting an eerie glow over the room. She tried not to look at the walls and the deluge of items that smothered its surface.

She scanned the table. It was well organized with only a few personal items, no papers. There was a small writing desk in the corner, and she hurried over to it, nearly breathless. Setting the candle down to free her hands, she quickly searched through a small stack of papers. One was a personal missive detailing a list of miscellaneous things to do. Another was a letter about a section of land to be gifted and compensation for some soldiers. She rifled through the rest of the pages finding more letters and a few blank pages. She pulled open the drawer in the desk and fumbled through its contents but found nothing that resembled attack plans. As every second went by, she felt the pressing need to hurry. The plans had to be there somewhere. She spun around and surveyed the room again. *The trunk next to the bed.*

Bringing the candle with her, she rushed over and dropped to her knees in front of the heavy wooden trunk. She reached for the lid when the door latch squeaked. Sarah's breath caught in her throat. She had no time to get out. Instinct took over and, in a flurry of speed, she snuffed out the candle and did the only thing she could think of—she rolled under the bed.

The door opened, and Sarah was painfully aware of the rustling sound her dress made as she crowded herself beneath the rope-strung mattress. At least there was room enough to hide under the bed, unlike the one in Judge Savell's chamber.

The room darkened as the door was shut and footsteps crossed the floor toward the table. He would not find the candle there. She had left it on the floor next to the trunk. A long, silent moment went by, and Sarah tried to regulate her breathing with an open mouth so as not to make a sound. Grit and dust from the floor stuck to her sweaty palms as they lay open, pressed against the flagstones beneath her. The thick stagnant air caked in her mouth. Suddenly the room flooded with a low light. *Tobias must have found another candle.*

The footsteps moved but not in any particular direction. It seemed as if he was turning around in circles. Did he know someone was in the room? Was he looking for her? The footsteps moved again, closer to the bed this time. He stepped close enough for her to see his boots. It wasn't Tobias. At least she didn't think so. She hadn't paid that much attention to Tobias's feet, but she was sure they would be larger than the ones she was looking at. Perhaps it was Luke. Tobias could have sent him in to get the attack plans.

She closed her eyes and wished the man would get what he came for and go away. She couldn't stand to be under the bed much longer. Her arms were squeezed up under her and were beginning to ache. Slowly, she slid her hands out to get some relief. They moved across the dirty floor, across lint, loose threads, and a stray button until she found some reprieve in her aching elbows.

As soon as she had shifted into a more comfortable position, the latch on the door squeaked again. Sarah assumed the man was leaving, but all at once his candle hissed out. With two quick steps, the man was standing next to the bed, against the wall.

Sarah wrinkled her brow as she peered through the darkness. The man in the room was an intruder like she was. He was hiding behind the bed curtains. Why didn't she think of that? Whoever he was, he was much more proficient at this than she was. He was completely hidden with plenty of room to move if needed. If worst came to worst, he at least could make a break for the door. She, on the other hand, was cramped in the nether regions of a bug graveyard. She knew because her hand just found a dead moth. If someone found her, all they would have to do is sit on the bed, and she would be helplessly pinned with no chance to escape. How did she always get herself into these situations?

She was trying to figure out how she would explain herself if she were to get caught when she realized that the new occupant had moved into the room. This, no doubt, was Tobias. His heavy, confident steps moved with purpose. He left the door open, giving the room enough light from the hallway that he didn't need to light a candle. His long strides took him right to the trunk by the bed.

Please don't let him find the candle, she prayed. She heard the hinges creak as he opened the trunk's lid, and then came the rustle of papers followed by a *thunk* as the lid dropped back into place. *The attack plans.* Sarah groaned inwardly as the heavy footfalls strode back across the floor. The door was closed, taking the light with it, and a heavy silence filled the room.

Sarah shook her head in dismay. This had all been a waste of time. She heard the scrape of footsteps as the man emerged from his hiding place next to the bed. She wondered if he had been looking for the attack plans as well. She hoped so. He would leave quickly if he had, and then she could get out of there.

No such luck. The candle was lit again, and for the first time, she realized part of her gown was sticking out from under the bed. The man must not have noticed. His footsteps moved past and walked around the room. Just as she gave a silent sigh of relief, he turned and approached the bed again. Her heart began to pound. Quietly she tried to move. Her hand slid across the floor, reaching for her gown when she heard the slick metallic sound of his sword being drawn from his scabbard. She was too late. The tip of his blade came down, pinning her wayward skirt to the floor.

"Time to come out, Sarah."

She closed her eyes in humiliation. She recognized the voice but didn't dare move.

"Come on. I know you're under there. I recognize your dress." He poked at the fabric with the tip of his sword.

There was nothing left to do but crawl out and face him, yet she still didn't want to. She was getting used to the dust and cobwebs and could happily stay there with them for quite some time.

"Are you going to come out, or do I have to drag you out?"

Sarah moaned. Enough was enough. She hadn't been the only one hiding, and he had some explaining to do too. She shimmied out from under the bed and climbed to her feet. She was sure she looked a mess with spiderwebs stuck to her hair and a powdering of dust and grime clinging to her gown, but she didn't bother brushing herself off.

"What are *you* doing here, Alex?" A smile played at the edge of his lips. He must have been amused to catch her like this. "You said you wouldn't go sneaking around Tobias's room uninvited."

His smile disappeared. "I was invited. You invited me. I just didn't want to bring you with me."

"Well, it seems I'm here anyway." She stuck out her finger and tapped it against his chest. "And it appears my timing was better than yours. You were only in here for a minute before Tobias showed up." She glanced toward the door. "We should go now, in case he comes back."

"It should be safe enough now." The candlelight illuminated his calm expression. "Tobias and your brother should be occupied for the next half hour in the council room. They had a sort of informal meeting planned with Sir Durrant. Apparently, the man used to be one of the benefactors that contributed to several of your brother's improvement projects but recently cut his funding. Michael and Tobias were going to talk to him before the last dance set started. I just didn't expect your uncle to dart in here just before his meeting." Alex's expression was serious now. "This is dangerous, Sarah. What were you doing in here again?"

Sarah pulled some lint from her hair. "If you must know—I came to look at those papers Tobias took. And I would have had them if you hadn't snuck in here when you did."

Alex scrutinized her for a moment. "What were the papers?"

"Notes from a seamstress detailing the latest fashion trends in Kyrnidan. I want to look my best for the next banquet." A smile pulled at his lips again. She liked it. She normally didn't try to be funny, but it was better than offering him the truth. He wouldn't be happy to know she was getting involved.

"Come, Sarah, you're not that vain. What was really on the papers?" When she hesitated, his muscles tightened. "Must I go ask Tobias myself?"

She didn't like keeping the truth from him any more than she liked displeasing him with the answer. "If you must know, they were attack plans for eliminating the Moylans."

His expression changed again. "Sarah! Why would you risk yourself for such a thing?"

"Risk myself? Don't you think it more important that we try to put a stop to this insane scheme to kill the Moylans?"

Alex shook his head in disbelief. "It doesn't matter. The attack plans are nothing new. Michael told me about the options that were proposed at the last council meeting. The attack on the Moylans might be outlined on paper, but it will never be approved."

"But Tobias said they're not gaining back their supporters as expected. Even I know they're running out of time and options."

"Michael won't settle things that way."

In exasperation, Sarah flicked her gaze upward and turned away from him. It was only a moment before he wrapped his arms around her. "What do you want, Sarah?" he asked.

She pulled away. "I want someone to listen to me so I don't feel like I am beating my head against a wall. I want someone to agree that my concerns are valid."

He held his arms out. "Well, I do agree with you on one thing."

"What?"

"Something isn't right about Tobias. This isn't normal." He waved a hand around the room.

Sarah couldn't help but look once more at the bizarre collection. It was hard to ignore the fact that not a single part of the walls was showing, and even when she forced herself not to look at it, she could feel it, a barrage of items surrounding them and closing in on them.

Alex shook his head as he looked around. "Tapestries, paintings, flags, armor, tunics, scraps of material, plaques—anything and everything that represents the monarchy is in here. It all feels . . . wrong. Like things did with Chad. It seems to me that Tobias can't wait to maneuver himself onto the throne. He's completely obsessed."

Sarah rocked her weight onto one hip and dipped her head in agreement. She was glad he shared her concern, but it was painful to admit there was such treachery afoot. It was more than hard when they'd faced that with Chad, and she had hoped to never see such betrayal again.

"I see the indications now. He's doing exactly what my cousin did," Alex continued. "Gaining favorable opinions with other leaders, active in the council, directing the army . . ." He let his words trail off. "If you want to rule a nation, the first step is to rule the army, and Tobias has that."

"So what can we do?"

Alex shrugged. "I'm afraid this subterfuge must run its course between Tobias and Michael. You tried to warn me about Chad, but I simply couldn't believe that my own cousin was trying to take the throne from me. Michael will never believe anything we say about Tobias."

"We have to do something."

"Until there's proof, there's nothing that can be done, and gathering that evidence may take months. I can't afford to stay that long. I'm still leaving tomorrow."

Sarah felt as if the air had been knocked from her. "So you'll leave and do nothing to help my brother?"

"No. I'll do what I can, but I'm not staying here. I do have a few connections in Kyrnidan. I'll hire some men to look into matters regarding Tobias. They're good at what they do, and they can gather the evidence needed. When they have proof of his treason, then I'll come back and help make the case against him."

It wouldn't stop Tobias from wanting to harm the Moylans, but Sarah was grateful Alex was willing to do something.

"You know," Alex looked at her, "we have no initial proof against him. Right now this is all speculation, and Tobias could very well be innocent."

"I know."

He reached out and pulled a dusty particle from her hair. "I shouldn't have demanded that you accompany me home tomorrow. But I'm asking you: please come home with me."

Sarah didn't answer.

"What's holding you here?"

What *was* holding her there? She loved him and wanted to be with him. He understood her, and she wanted to focus on strengthening that bond. Calibre was where she needed to build her relationships and her life. But she still felt some reservation at the thought of leaving Kyrnidan. It almost felt as if she would be leaving things undone—loose ends.

Alex reached out and touched her fingers. He didn't hold her hand but lightly pressed against her. "Michael told me about the council meeting." He moved his eyes from her hand up to meet her gaze. "I know you want to help—to be an advocate for the Moylans. You're only doing what comes natural, but what else is there you can possibly do?"

"I'm not sure."

Alex raised his brow. "But there are things you can do in Calibre."

It was true. Her attempts to establish herself as their princess in Kyrnidan hadn't gone well. She needed put forth the same efforts in Calibre.

"All right," she finally agreed. "I'll tell my family that I'll be leaving with you on the morrow."

Sarah didn't realize how tense Alex had been until his expression flooded with relief and he let out an audible breath. He took her in his arms and pulled her against him. She felt his lips against her forehead, and when she looked up, he covered her mouth with his. She responded warmly. This was what she'd been missing, and she felt it all coming back to her. She didn't pull away or hide behind the insecurities but gave herself to the moment, accepting his love.

"Thank you," Alex whispered in her ear. "I want you to be with me." He pulled back and looked at her. "I was afraid I was losing you. That you were being pulled into some kind of political charade." He nestled his face against her hair as he tightened his embrace. "I was so afraid you would choose to stay here."

"No. I choose you."

CHAPTER 28

PULLING HER SKIRTS UP SO she could run, Sarah dashed outside and down the stairs into the sun-lit courtyard. Her heart pounded as she saw the small barred wagon and several guards who were pushing a shackled man into the cage-like enclosure.

"Is it true?" she asked as she ran up to where Alex and Michael stood. The lock snapped shut, and the figure inside the wagon crouched down and wrapped his fingers around the bars. "Is it really Chad?"

Michael nodded. "I have to say, I'm surprised he tried to get in again. He should have known we'd be better prepared."

The guard standing behind the wagon moved to the side, and Sarah could clearly see Chad's face. He looked harder than when she'd seen him last—meaner. His lips pulled up into a leering smile, and she quickly diverted her gaze to her brother. "Tell me what happened."

"He tried to sneak in again, this time posing as a merchant. He'd just gotten inside the gates when he was recognized."

"What will happen now?"

"Chad is Calibrean. It will be for Alex to decide."

"I won't risk him escaping again." Alex glanced over at his cousin, and disappointment filled his eyes. "He will be taken straightaway to the harbor in Tagmar, where he'll be shipped to a penal colony."

Sarah looked back at Chad. It was sad that it had come to this. "May I speak with him?"

Alex placed a hand on her arm. "Are you certain you want to?"

She nodded then slowly walked over to the barred wagon.

Chad maintained his menacing smile and chuckled as she drew near. "I heard you're going back to Calibre today."

"That's not your concern."

His grin widened, and he leaned in close to the bars. "I was right. I'm still right about everything." He leaned back and made himself comfortable in a corner. "In a way I feel sorry for you."

"You're the one in shackles," Sarah said.

He laughed again. "Am I? But you're going to go back to Calibre and will forever be shackled to your failure here." He tapped a finger on his chin thoughtfully. "Or you can stay here and die."

Sarah wrapped her hands around the bars of the wagon and leaned closer. "You know who's threatening me. I know you met with a man in the tavern—someone from the group of Kyrnidians who oppose me. Tell me who you met with. Who are they, Chad? If you have a shred of decency left in you—tell me who."

He looked at her for a moment, unmoving. "I did meet with someone . . ." Sarah held her breath as Chad paused. He scooted closer to her, his shackles scraping across the wooden planks of the wagon; then he put his cheek against the bars next to where she stood. When he spoke, his voice was barely a whisper, and she had to lean in to hear him. "Why tell you what you already know?"

Sarah leaned back and stared at him. Was it someone that she knew personally? Suddenly there was a hand on her shoulder, gently pulling her away. It was Michael. "We've already asked him." He glared at Chad. "He won't tell us anything." Michael waved to the driver, and the wagon lurched forward. Sarah watched Chad until the gates were closed.

"It's time for me to bid you farewell." Michael wrapped his arms around Sarah. "I have a meeting to attend to right now. They're waiting for me in the council room as we speak."

"You won't be able to see me off?" Sarah asked.

"I'm sorry. If this meeting wasn't so crucial, I would. Robert Moylan arrived this morning, and I hope we can find a resolution to this standoff."

Sarah couldn't withhold her surprise. Margaret had told her that Robert wouldn't set foot in the castle nor anywhere else her family was. "Robert Moylan is really here?"

Michael nodded. "He's waiting inside. If you were staying, I'd allow you to attend the meeting, but I will not interfere with your plans."

My plans, Sarah thought. Michael kissed her on the cheek and bid farewell to her before quickly striding toward the castle. She looked between Michael and Alex. What were her plans? It had been *her* intention to have a diplomatic solution to the problems with the Moylans.

She walked over to where the bustling servants were loading the carriage. Alex led his black Friesian horse over to join the group.

"Are you ready?" he asked.

Sarah clapped her hands together, pleading. "Please, Alex." Her voice trembled. "Michael informed me that the council is about to meet. This session will undoubtedly determine how they'll deal with the Moylan family. Robert Moylan is here himself. This is all so sudden; please understand. It was my suggestion to try diplomacy first. I need to be here."

Alex pinched the bridge of his nose and shook his head in disbelief. "Sarah, I am leaving. Are you going to come with me?"

"Please." She reached out to him. "I can't go. And I don't want you to go either. Alex, you must understand—you are everything to me." She stumbled over the words, unable to make them come out properly. "I know things have been stressed between us, and I'm confused about so many things, but I do know that I love you. Please don't go."

There was a long moment of silence as he looked at her. "I love you too, Sarah, but I can't do this. I need you—all of you. You can't advocate for both countries." He turned his head and looked off into the distance. When he looked at her again, she was blinking back tears. "Maybe this is good for us. Perhaps we need more time away from each other, so you can decide where you really want to be."

It tore at her to see Alex's faith in their relationship fading. With trembling fingers, she took his hand. "I know where I want to be. I want to be with you. But I need to see this out." She felt like she was in a sink hole. She could see dry ground, but she was in too deep to climb out. "I am so sorry. I'll make it up to you, I promise. Please stay—just until after this meeting. I just need to know the outcome, and then we can go."

She held her breath and waited for his reply. At last he nodded, and she fell into his arms. She pressed her head against his chest, resolving to do whatever it took to get back what they once had. She would not let him slip away.

"Meet me in the chapel after your meeting," he said as he stroked her hair. "I'll be waiting for you."

Sarah nodded, her head still on his chest. She could hear his heart beating—slow, steady, and sad.

* * *

Sarah was the first one to leave the council room. She saw the tall figure atop the grand staircase and ran after him, taking the steps two at a time. "Apollo," she called breathlessly.

"Your Highness." He bowed. "I was told that you were leaving." His eyes still held the mournful characteristic that deepened whenever he looked at her.

"I'm not leaving yet. Soon, but I must talk to you first."

He directed her over to the bench they had shared the night before. "I knew you were related to the Moylans in some way—distantly, I thought. But Robert Moylan came to the council meeting today—your own brother." Sarah looked at him for a minute, marveling at the resemblance between him and Robert. She waited for an explanation, but when Apollo remained silent, she prodded him. "How is it that you remain in service to the Delacor family while your own brother despises us to the point that he would do whatever is in his power to ruin us and the monarchy?"

"I take it the meeting didn't go well."

Sarah glanced toward the tapestry and met the hand-woven eyes of the pensive maiden who held the unicorn in her lap. "Nothing was agreed or settled on. And Robert Moylan . . ." Her words faltered. "I have never met anyone who despises me so much." She lowered her voice to a whisper. "Do you know—is your brother over the group of Kyrnidians—the ones who tried to have me captured?" From his treatment of her in the council room, she was sure he was the one.

Apollo shook his head. "No. It could not be him."

"Are you certain?"

"Yes. You alone are not the target for his hatred but the Delacor family as a whole, and as much as he may scorn you, he wants you to remain a visible influence."

Sarah thought about that for a moment. Her *visible influence* was a tool the Moylans had been using quite successfully to weaken Michael's hold on the monarchy. It was understandable that they wanted her to stay in the public eye. Her political position was tearing her family apart, and that's exactly what they wanted.

"Why does your brother regard my family with so much disdain? What spurred this animosity?"

Apollo hesitated. "Let's just say that my family did not take kindly to my public humiliation after my betrayal was made public."

"You're referring to when your plot to hide me was discovered?"

Apollo nodded. His face suddenly seemed older. "After your father found out what I had done, my title was stripped forthwith and my execution called for. My trial was a humiliating process . . . for me and my family. Robert never got over it."

"You must have proved well during your trial. You were not executed."

"In part, the reason for my survival is attributed to the tremendous sway my family holds." He paused. "That, and I like to think that your father and I were once truly friends."

"But you were exonerated after I was found. Did that not heal the rift between our families?"

"By then it was too late. I was freed but never restored to my former position. And my brother is not so forgiving. His resentment has now grown to include me as well. We seldom speak to each other. I cannot condone his hatred for the crown; after all, Their Majesties' treatment of me was fair. I deserved the penalty I received. However, the Moylan family name was irrefutably damaged. My brother cannot understand why I remained loyal to the king."

Apollo directed his eyes toward the tapestry. "The new government had already created a division among the people, and after my family's public degradation, Robert chose his side. Since then, he's been leading the revolt against the Delacors and their monarchy."

He met Sarah's gaze, and she finally understood where his pain came from. "But you—you chose to stay with my family."

"How could I choose otherwise? I did the right thing nineteen years ago. The prophecy threatened your life, and I saved you. It didn't come without cost, but I'm willing to take those consequences."

Sarah's mind tried to wrap around what he was saying. It wasn't just Tobias's threat he had protected her from. It was the prophecy in general. There would have been others who would have tried to kill her if she had stayed in the country, marked as the firstborn. The words ran through her mind again. *It shall be the son, the firstborn in the new monarchy, who shall quiet the fears and unite the nation again.*

"Who heard that particular prophecy given?" she asked. "Tobias told me that several people witnessed the high priest give it. Do you know who they were?"

Apollo looked at her curiously. "Yes. But why do you want to know?"

"Because I want to help. Everyone in Kyrnidan has their beliefs tied to these prophecies, and order cannot be restored until the people see leadership from the one prophesied to unite them—the firstborn son in the new monarchy. And since I exist, that isn't going to happen. Either the prophecy is wrong, or I was never supposed to be born." Sarah had chosen her words carefully and waited to see if Apollo would accept that the revelation was wrong.

Apollo shook his head. "I know it appears that the prophecy is wrong. It must be hard for you to put your faith in something you know little about."

"Appears to be? It *is* wrong. There's no other explanation." Sarah didn't try to hide her exasperation. She was tired of everyone smoothing over such a blatant inaccuracy. "Can't you see? The high priest was nothing but a charlatan."

"Is that so?" Apollo's words were soft. She had expected more of a response—surprise, confusion, even anger—but he was utterly calm. "Have you ever wondered why so many people believe so strongly in the prophecies?" he asked.

"Of course. I can't comprehend why anyone would be misguided into believing something so clearly wrong."

Apollo nodded. "It must be like a nation of people telling you the sky is red when you can clearly see that it's blue."

"Precisely."

There was a rare twinkle in his eye, and Sarah suddenly felt like she had fallen into a trap. He took a deep breath and said, "My dear, have you seen the Kyrnidian sky at dusk when the sun slips below the rocky cliffs?"

Sarah didn't answer. She *had* been tricked.

"It is a red sky." Apollo stated plainly. He reached out and patted her hand. "Your Highness, has anyone ever described to you the high priest's demeanor?"

"No."

"Ahhhh," he said, as if he had just put his finger on the problem. "The high priest was the most honest man I've ever had the privilege to be acquainted with. He spent most of his life in service to the poorest of this country. He was humble—a man who sought neither fortune nor reputation. He was someone you could put your trust in. And he always got it right."

"Then how is it that this revelation is wrong?"

"Perhaps it's not. Sir Cuthbert was the one who recorded the exact words, but he never engraved the plate for that particular prophecy, so what we have is only by word of mouth. I, like many others, believe in the high priest, and he gave a prophecy that someone would reunite the nation. Our faith is in that."

"But we have the exact words. They may not be engraved on a plate, but there were other witnesses that confirmed it."

Apollo raised an eyebrow. "Viable witnesses? My trust is in the high priest, not the councilmen who reiterate his words. They have other motives."

Sarah stared at him as she absorbed this new concept. "Are you saying that the exact wordage may have been changed?"

"It *is* possible. Without Cuthbert's plate, it's all hearsay, and people interpret it how they think it should be."

Sarah was now even more desperate to talk to someone who had heard the original prophecy. She didn't need them to admit the high priest's blunder, but to see if they would admit a discrepancy in how they remembered the wordage.

"Apollo, tell me who was in the room when the prophecy was given."

He looked thoughtful for a moment and then said, "Besides Simon Cuthbert, there was Sir Mark Dinary and Luke Warrens, whom I believe you have already sat with in council."

Sarah was taken aback. They were the two men pressing the council to use force against the Moylans. She knew she would get nowhere talking with either of them. "Was there no one else?"

Apollo looked back at the tapestry, his eyes tracing the maiden. When Sarah placed her hand over his, he finally looked back at her. "I am sorry I took you from your family, Your Highness. I'm sorry I took you from your country. And I am sorry I sent Miranda away from here—away from me."

He paused, trying to swallow his emotions. He dropped his head, but she could feel his anguish and torment. For the first time, she wanted to comfort him. She wanted to tell him that she understood now, that it was all right. Her throat grew tight. She picked up his hand and leaned forward, pressing her cheek against it.

Apollo cleared his throat causing her to straighten and meet his gaze. "But if I was faced with the choice again—I would choose the exact same path."

Sarah slowly nodded. There was no doubt his choices had caused pain for many people, but she had no regrets. Her life now included her real parents, whom she would forever love. But Miranda would always be her mother. The last several weeks had opened her heart to the depths of Miranda's love. Her mother had sacrificed her whole life. She had left home, friends, family, and all she held dear for Sarah. She had left Sarah a heritage, an undeniable legacy of devout loyalty and love. It was something she could draw strength from.

Sarah averted her eyes to the floor. She had done a poor job in living up to her mother's example. What had she been loyal to? Lately she had been doing everything halfheartedly. She had let herself slip away from Alex, and she had made only meager attempts to fulfill any role here in Kyrnidan. But all that was about to change.

Again she looked at the tapestry and the maiden with the unicorn. If she looked hard enough, maybe she could see herself in the image. "Apollo," she said, "I need to know—was there anyone else who heard the prophecy?"

He looked at her for a moment before answering.

"Tobias."

CHAPTER 29

SARAH SAT RIGID AND UNMOVING. Why hadn't Tobias told her that he'd heard the prophecy firsthand? An uneasy feeling stirred in the pit of her stomach. There were only three men still alive that had heard the prophecy, and it seemed they were completely in accord with each other.

"Was there no one else who heard the high priest?"

Apollo shook his head. "Not that I am aware of."

Footsteps sounded on the stairs, and Margaret's figure appeared on the landing. Sarah tried not to look at her friend's face. Margaret's eyes were still red-rimmed from her long bout of crying after Sara had reported her pending departure.

"The maid was right," Margaret said as she walked over to them. "She told me I would find you up here."

"Who?" Sarah asked. "Grace? Has she been spying on me again?"

"No. It was Rose. She saw you come up here."

"Grace," Sarah said thoughtfully.

"No. Rose. Do you need to clean your ears out?"

"No. Grace. She heard the prophecy." Sarah looked at Apollo. "I don't know if she was telling the truth, but as I left my mother's room the other day, Grace told me she'd been there when the prophecy was given."

Apollo raised an eyebrow. "It's possible. Grace has been here in the castle since she was a young girl. She could have overheard it."

"But I don't know if I should even trust her. She's spied on me continuously, and it's not inconceivable that she's doing it at someone else's request."

Apollo shook his head. "I've known Grace since the day she came to work here. She's trustworthy. She wouldn't be your mother's maid if she wasn't."

"What are you talking about?" Margaret asked.

"I'll explain later," Sarah said as she stood and hurried toward the stairs.

"Where are you going?" Margaret called.

"To find Grace, of course."

* * *

Sarah didn't have to wait and was admitted at once into her mother's chamber. As she entered, a silent admiration fell over her. Her father sat in the tall wooden chair next to the bed. His stately appearance and majestic bearing was softened as he leaned over and whispered softly in his wife's ear, all the while holding her hand. The queen, though still visibly weak, was sitting up with a smile lightly touching her lips.

Her father straightened as she approached the bed, and his face fell. "You have come to say good-bye."

Sarah opened her mouth to speak, but the king stood up and cleared his throat as if he had more to say. She knew it was best not to interrupt, so she waited.

"I have not told you, Sarah, but thank you for what you've done here. Thank you for sitting in on the council meetings and for trying to promote a peaceful resolution. I'm sorry things didn't work out the way you expected, but more so, I'm sorry to see you leave Kyrnidan."

Sarah stepped forward. Finally she could feel the bond forming between her and her father. "I appreciate your kind words. I, too, would be sorry if I left so soon; therefore, I will not be going today."

His eyes lightened, and he reached out, placing a hand on her shoulder.

Sarah marveled at the gesture, feeling surprisingly stronger, able to bear the weight—weight that she was choosing to take on.

"How long will you stay?" he asked.

She paused before answering, taking the time to determine what she needed to do. "I will wait until the issue is resolved with the Moylan family."

She thought she saw a flash of surprise in his eyes which then settled into satisfaction. "Do I sense a little of myself in you?" he asked.

Sarah smiled. "That would be my stubborn side." She glanced at her mother, whose pale face brightened. "I have a few notions that I would like to look further into myself." She looked back at her father. "Do you mind?"

His thick brows tightened together. "What kind of notions?"

"The prophecy about the firstborn. I believe there's a discrepancy that, if resolved, might help reunite the supporters of the monarchy."

The king rubbed his chin as he considered the idea. "What exactly will this entail?"

"I need to speak with Grace, Mother's maid."

"Is that all?"

"It is for now."

He rubbed his chin as if he were contemplating the idea. "I see no harm in that, but I haven't seen Grace today." He turned to his wife. "Do you know where she might be?"

"I believe Mr. Martin sent her to the market. He gave her a list of herbs and tinctures to pick up from the apothecary for him. She has a friend that works there, so I suspect she'll be there for quite some time. She does like to visit."

The king looked back to Sarah. "Very well. Look into it if you must, but keep in mind that your safety is still our utmost priority. You may go into the village to find Grace, but I insist you be escorted by my private guards. You must keep them with you at all times. They know the area and the people."

Sarah nodded. The idea that there was still someone after her was never far from her mind.

* * *

Sarah took a deep breath as she walked down the stairs to the courtyard. Alex was no longer waiting for her in the chapel but was giving last minute instructions to the servants. Seeing him pulled at her heart, but she straightened her shoulders and steeled herself. She passed Luther without acknowledging him and walked over to Alex.

Alex's expression fell when he saw her. "Sarah."

She reached out and took his hand. Not meeting his gaze.

"You are not coming, are you?"

She swallowed the lump in her throat and ran her thumb across his hand, not daring to look at him, afraid that her resolve would weaken if she did. At last she shook her head. "No," she whispered. She felt him tense, but it did not dissuade her. She needed to stay in order to straighten out the confusion regarding the prophecy, but more than that, she needed to stay to prove to herself that she was deserving of her position. Until then, she would always feel unworthy of him.

Alex took her chin and tilted it up until she was forced to look at him. "Are you sure about this?"

"This is where I need to be right now. I can't pretend that I don't want to get involved anymore. I do want to—I need to."

He let go of her chin and looked away. His eyes were dull and distant. He would not be asking her to go with him again, and that thought made her ache.

"Please stay with me," she pleaded.

Alex shook his head firmly. "No. We have the same obligations, but mine are in Calibre."

Sarah's breath was about to collapse, the gnawing ache almost unbearable. "Please don't fault me for choosing this. I need to do this. I need to see this through."

"I don't fault you, but I can't help but think your obligations will perpetually keep you here."

A single tear made its way down her cheek. She had finally found a way to be worthy of him, but that solution could very well keep her in Kyrnidan indefinitely.

Her thoughts were interrupted when Luther came over to them. "Excuse me, Your Highnesses. The caravan is ready to depart and must leave now in order to make it to Quartermain by nightfall."

Luther's voice was tight, and Sarah could feel his anger radiating out like heat waves. Her dismissal of the secret meeting in the stables the night before was likely the source of his foul mood. She had only planned to go in order to tell him that she had chosen Alex. She hoped that her choice was apparent now—she and Alex were together. There was no need to elaborate on something so obvious, and she certainly wouldn't apologize for her decision.

Alex stepped away and pulled on his riding gloves. "I must go." He didn't look at her. He called to the driver of a small carriage—the one that carried her personal trunks and handmaids—and gave him instructions that they would be staying behind.

She let her tears fall as she went to him. He took her in his arms and pulled her to him. "I want nothing more than your happiness." He buried his face in her neck. "And if that includes taking care of things here, for your own people, then so be it." *Her* country and *her* people. She pulled back and looked up just as Alex lowered his head. She met his kiss. It was sweet and fervent. She pressed herself into it, no longer allowing her tentative nature to restrict her. She both longed for and dreaded this moment—to be fully embraced in his strong arms and not knowing when she would be again. They both lingered as they found their way through their emotions. As Alex lifted his head, Sarah rose on her toes, letting her mouth cling to his for a few more precious moments, and when she pulled away, she was breathless. If he would have asked her to go with him right then, she would have. Instead he looked at her, and his sharp blue eyes seemed to remind her of who she was.

"I love you," he whispered before he kissed her again. He pulled away sooner than she had expected and quickly mounted his tall black Friesian. The horse shook his head, tossing his long mane. It seemed as if he, too, were aware of the painful parting.

A wave of Alex's hand set the small caravan in motion; he turned in his saddle and offered her one last fleeting smile. Then he looked past her, focusing on someone else. "Take care of her."

Sarah turned to see Luther. With a stony expression, he bowed to Alex. "I will."

CHAPTER 30

SARAH WATCHED AS THE CASTLE gates closed behind Alex and the rest of the convoy, leaving the courtyard dreadfully vacant. Luther stepped closer to her. She didn't take pleasure in his nearness as she once had. It was uncomfortable. It seemed as if his movement implied ownership. She took a step back, looking at him, but was unable to read his expression. It appeared that she would have to make her feelings clear after all. "I have made my decision. I love Alex."

Luther's jaw tightened, and he nodded slowly. "So there's nothing between us? Is that all I was—your personal guard?"

Sarah looked at the ground for a moment before meeting his gaze. "I can't deny I had feelings for you. But it cannot continue. It was only in my insecurities that I mistakenly allowed my attachment to you. I truly do love Alex; therefore, I ask that from now on, you be nothing more than my personal guard."

Luther shook his head. It was slight—almost imperceivable, but it was there nonetheless. He leaned forward, dropping his face close to hers. Then he whispered something. She expected him to confide that he couldn't do as she asked—that he relinquished his position—but his voice was low and unintelligible. She tried to wrap her mind around what he was saying, but the words were in a different language. She grasped at the phrase but was only able to commit the last two words to memory before he pushed past her and stalked away.

"Your Highness." Sarah turned at the sound of Apollo's voice. He strode toward her, his hand resting not entirely casually on his short sword. "Is everything all right?"

"I . . . think so." Sarah looked to where Luther had stormed off.

"What was that about?"

"I'm not certain. He said something in a different language. Something about . . . *dare dolorem*?" She repeated the words she could remember.

Apollo's face hardened. "It's an old language. The literal translation is to give grief or pain. We have an old battle cry that uses those words. In effect it means, 'You command me to give unspeakable grief.' It was used to frighten the enemy. If the army's demands weren't met, they would be forced to cause unspeakable grief."

"Let's hope he was *not* referring to a Kyrnidian battle cry."

Apollo's expression was now one of guarded concern. "Indeed."

Sarah looked again in the direction Luther had gone, but he was nowhere to be seen. Perhaps he was referring to pain and grief she had caused him.

Apollo waved over a group of four men to join them. Two of them were her father's personal guards, and the other two were Wilf and Andres, Calibrean guards whom she knew well. "I understand you're going to the village," Apollo said. "May I accompany you?"

"Yes. I think I would enjoy your company very much."

"Enjoy my company? I never thought I'd hear you say that."

"I'm sorry for that," she said quietly. "I've been unfair to you. However, I'm beginning to see things differently now." She wasn't sure if she would ever condone what he had done, but after the conversations they had shared, she was beginning to see Apollo in a new light.

"No need to be sorry. My past is what it is—but thank you for trying to understand. Shall we go now?"

"Shouldn't we wait for Luther?" Wilf asked.

"No," Sarah said. "We'll go now." She took Apollo's offered arm. *How different things have become*, she thought.

* * *

Sarah inhaled deeply, taking in the smell of roasted meats, spices, leather, and tantalizing baked treats—the things that made the marketplace so fascinating. The entire assembly was more rustic than back home in Calibre. There were fewer established shops and more of the cramped wooden stalls. Brightly colored fabrics were stretched across the tops of the booths, and underneath, goods and products were elaborately displayed.

More unlike Calibre was the unusual number of vendors selling all types of weapons and armor. Not surprisingly, the men—every one of them—carried a weapon. Most of them wore a sword at their side, but she spotted a few with bows, their quiver of arrows slung across their backs. A burly man with a thick red beard shopped at a nearby poultry booth. With one hand he held onto his tiny daughter, while his other hand held a battle ax resting casually on his shoulder. Even the young boys carried small weapons. Two youngsters, no older than four or five, sparred in the streets with wooden swords.

"There are still some Kyrnidian customs that might take some time to get used to," Sarah commented to Apollo. She paused at a purveyor of fine knives. Although the workmanship on the tools was superb, none of them were adorned with fine jewels or inlaid with precious metals. These were meant for function rather than decoration. She picked up a knife and noticed its weight and balance.

"Are you the craftsman?" she asked the seller.

"I am, Your Highness." The man's expression was hooded, and Sarah couldn't decide if he were pleased or wary. "You are highly skilled." As she replaced the knife, she turned to Apollo. "Before I return to Calibre, when we have more time to browse, would you please assist me in selecting a knife from this man as a gift for Prince Alexander?"

"Indeed, Your Highness. It would be my pleasure." There was a gratified tone to his voice—something Sarah hadn't noticed before. Perhaps they might become friends after all. Putting aside her former feelings, she found that he was likeable. He had not crumbled under the adversity he faced from his past, and that impressed her.

Apollo took her arm again and directed her toward the apothecary while the guards flanked them on either side, watching protectively. "When do you intend to return to Calibre?" he asked.

"As soon as the issue with Robert Moylan is taken care of."

Apollo frowned. "Soon then. I don't foresee it taking much longer. Things are coming to a head, and I suspect within a week or two, it will all be taken care of—for good or for bad."

"And regardless of the outcome, I must return to Calibre when it's over. I feel my staying here might continue to cause problems. I don't want anyone who is ever unsatisfied with my brother thinking that I might be a good alternate for him. Besides, Calibre is my home."

"And what of the prophecy?" Apollo kept his voice low so their conversation would remain private. "There are a great number of people who expect you to fulfill it."

Sarah knew he was included in that group. "I don't know how or even if I fit into the prophecy, but I'll try to sort that out while I am here. In the end, though, I will go back to Calibre."

Apollo gave a solemn nod but said nothing more. As they continued down the street, Sarah noticed the reactions of the people as they recognized who she was. Some of them stared; a few pointed fingers and whispered. Surprisingly, there were a number of people who curtsied or bowed and offered Sarah a smile. It almost made her feel as if Kyrnidan could truly be her home, but the feeling was tempered by those who scowled and only offered a stiff nod of recognition. "I see that the villagers' opinions of me are as diverse as the nobles'."

"The fact that some of our people disagree about where you fit in should not dissuade you. In truth, what matters most is what you believe your own purpose is—and what God intends for you." Apollo steered her through the doorway of an open shop. "The One who orchestrated all life would not leave us to wander aimlessly. We are all born with a purpose."

The apothecary was dimly lit, and Sarah closed her eyes so they would quickly adjust to the dark. She took a deep breath and was instantly transported back home into the kitchen where she, Miranda, and the servants worked to preserve their own herbs. Miranda had found her purpose and had lived it well. Sarah hoped that she could do the same.

When she opened her eyes, she looked around the cramped, little shop. The guards had not accompanied her inside; instead, they had taken up positions outside the open door. There wasn't space for all of them in the narrow room. It was filled with shelves that held woven baskets of dried herbs. Hanging from the ceiling in large bundles were more herbs and flowers in various stages of dryness. In the corner stood a large table that held an old hanging scale. Grace was standing nearby with a couple other women. Before Sarah could step in that direction, Apollo stopped her.

"Sarah, your birth was not an accident. When I put the mark of the firstborn upon your shoulder, it was not a misstep." He tenderly placed her silver unicorn pendant in her hand. It felt comfortable, heavy, and warm. "Your life wasn't spared so you can ignore your responsibilities. I believe those events were divinely orchestrated so that you might fulfill a higher purpose. Perhaps that purpose has presented itself."

Sarah stared at the unicorn while Apollo's words penetrated her mind and heart. She caught movement out of the corner of her eye and looked up. Grace was standing a couple of feet away. The woman leaned in with an understanding nod. Sarah slid a finger across the polished silver before tenderly placing the unicorn in her satchel. She took Apollo's hand and looked into his eyes. He continued to bear so much on her behalf, and he did so with grace and humility. "I'm still not sure what I can do. But thank you, Apollo. For what you've done for me and for your continued faith in me."

"It was my honor, Your Highness." He bent and kissed the back of her hand.

Sarah was about to turn to address Grace when several shouts rose from outside. She looked at Apollo, panic already rising up her neck. The sound of clashing swords echoed in the distance.

Apollo was first out the door, closely followed by Sarah. Her guards were a short distance away, engaging several men with swords. Women and children scattered away from the fray while other men rushed forward, coming out of booths and shops, with weapons drawn to join the fight. They seemed to know where they wanted to be. Some joined her guards; others picked the opposite side—Kyrnidian against Kyrnidian. One man stumbled backwards. It was Andres, one of the Calibrean guards. He clutched at a wound in his side; blood seeped through his fingers. He turned, his wild eyes sought out Apollo. "They're coming for the princess. They intend to kill her!"

Apollo grabbed Sarah's arm and pulled her back to the door of the shop. He was saying something to her, but Sarah couldn't take her eyes off Andres. The guard cupped his bleeding wound with one hand then charged back into the battle.

CHAPTER 31

SARAH'S STOMACH CLENCHED WITH FEAR. Apollo pushed her back protectively, but she couldn't take her eyes off the battle when another familiar face seemed to jump out at her from the commotion. It was Luther. Her heart skipped a beat. Luther was there. She stared at him in confusion then took a step forward, not believing what she was seeing.

"No!" Grace cried, catching her arm and holding her back.

Sarah recoiled. Luther was there—fighting *against* her guards. He struck another blow to Andres, cutting a deep gash in his arm. Sarah's heart began to pound up into her throat. Luther's eyes were wild with rage. He pulled his sword back; it was stained crimson. He was savage, as if he was out of his mind. A sickening feeling washed over her. He wasn't out of his mind. He was decisive and calculating. Luther was the one after her.

"Run!" Apollo yelled.

The word didn't register. Sarah stood frozen, her heart near exploding as it pounded against her ribs. She still didn't dare believe it, but it was clear Luther was leading the attack. The two Calibrean soldiers along with the Kyrnidian guards were struggling. Their defense would have given way already had the bystanders not joined in. Luther's expression hardened with hatred, and he tried to break through the throng once again. Andres fell to the ground unmoving.

"Run!" Apollo grabbed her arm. Sarah pulled her eyes away from the ruckus to look at him. "Go! I will meet you back at the castle!"

He leveled his eyes on Grace. "Go! Take her. Make sure she's safe. I'll stay long enough to make sure our defense holds, then I will join you."

Apollo took Sarah's hand and gave it a squeeze. It seemed as though things had come to a standstill. His face, all consuming with his ardent expression, swam before her. Luther yelled something to his men, and they surged forward, almost breaking through. Apollo was drawing his sword and turning around. She didn't want him to fight, but there was no other option now, every sword was needed. The flood of emotions threatened to drown her as she tried to cling to his hand—as she tried to take back all those days she had pushed him away.

Shouts echoed in her ears as he pulled out of her grasp and ran toward the battle. Grace yanked on her arm, causing Sarah to almost fall over. She couldn't hear herself yelling. Her cries were lost amongst the sharp sound of clashing blades, yet she still screamed out for Apollo. He had sacrificed his position, his title, his family, and friends to save her life nineteen years ago, and now he was going to risk his life for her.

Out of the corner of her eye, she glimpsed a young boy with his wooden sword, trying to run toward the conflict. His mother caught hold of him. The woman shook a finger at the young lad but smiled proudly at the same time.

Apollo reached the battle now. With sword raised, he charged in just as Luther pushed through the defense. Their steel met with a loud clang.

Even at a distance, the intense hatred in Luther's eyes was evident. It sent a chill down Sarah's spine. He was going to do everything he could to kill her. Had it been him all along? Grace jerked Sarah's arm, and at last she moved. They began to run, but Sarah's mind was still on Luther.

He was trying to kill her. She could hardly comprehend it. Yes, she had disappointed him—hurt him even—but this? Why would he try to kill her? Did he hate her that much? He had openly admitted he didn't think she should rule. He had tried to talk her out of getting involved. He had offered to take her away, and when she refused—she'd been abducted. Her stomach roiled. She had never seen her abductor clearly, but Luther had been there. She recalled the two horses standing amongst the trees. A tall, lanky Kyrnidian breed and Luther's bulky Calibrean mount. Her mind reeled as she remembered when her attacker had thrown her over his horse—wide and stocky—Luther's horse. Bile rose into her throat. Could it be? Had Luther been the one who had tried to steal her away? She nearly vomited as she realized the truth.

She pictured Luther coming into her chamber afterwards, his face bruised and bleeding. Suddenly her heart ached for that Kyrnidian soldier who had heard her cries and had come to help. He had died trying to save her life and had been labeled as the traitor.

Sarah hardly realized she had slowed and that Grace was now pulling her along. Her feet were moving, but her trembling body was numb. Everything around her seemed surreal. At the end of the street, Grace pulled her down a side alley, but Sarah broke away and took one last look at the people who fought to defend her—her countrymen—her people.

CHAPTER 32

GRACE'S INGENUITY IN GETTING THEM to safety impressed Sarah. The servant knew which streets would be empty and even procured a horse at the edge of the village, allowing them to get back to the castle quickly.

The horse raced into the courtyard, his hooves clattering against the cobblestone paving. Sarah nearly knocked Grace from the saddle as she dismounted before the lathered stallion could even come to a complete standstill. Her fancy shoes slipped on the pavers, but she quickly gained her balance, pulled up her skirts, and ran to the stairs just as Michael started down them. His tall, dappled stallion stood nearby, saddled and at the ready, but whatever his plans were, they would just have to wait.

"Sarah, what's wrong?" He grabbed her by the arms to steady her.

"It was Luther! Michael, it was Luther who abducted me. He has a group of men with him, and they attacked us in the village. Grace and I escaped while our guards and Apollo held them off. You need to send men. They've started a battle, and the villagers are fighting too."

Michael let go of her hands and started barking orders to the three soldiers standing guard in the courtyard, telling them to mount up and to ride into the village to subdue the fight.

"No!" Sarah yelled. "It won't be managed by three men. Call out a battalion!"

Michael ran a hand down his face. "There is no battalion!" He waved his other hand, gesturing toward the compound, and Sarah noticed how devoid it was of the usual guards. "They're gone. All of them. Tobias took the entire garrison out for a routine drill, only . . ."

Sarah suddenly felt numb. "Only what?"

"I just received word. They didn't go out to the fields where we usually drill. Instead, they've marched to the Moylan estate."

Her stomach lurched. "The rally?"

"Robert Moylan scheduled it for tomorrow morning. Already there is a large crowd gathered at his manor."

The ground seemed to move under Sarah and she swayed. Why did everything seem to be happening at once? She stumbled to the castle steps to sit down, but the sound of thundering hooves made her pause.

A dark horse carrying two riders came hurtling through the gate. Apollo's tall frame swayed in the saddle and only managed to stay upright by the efforts of Wilf, who struggled to hold onto him.

No! This is all wrong! Sarah ran to the horse as it skittered to a halt. The animal spooked and sidestepped as Apollo was helped to the ground by Michael and Wilf. Apollo slumped forward, but looked up when Sarah touched his arm. She met his gaze, and all time and sound stopped. In less than a heartbeat, she saw the recognition in his eyes. He had risked everything for her, and now he saw her safe in the courtyard. A moment of relief washed across his face as if years of anxiety and torment had disappeared from his worry-creased brow. He let out a soft sigh.

"Luther's gone mad," Wilf choked out.

"Where is he?" Michael demanded as he took the weight of Apollo's body. Apollo was ghostly white. Blood covered his tunic, seeping down his pants and into his shoe from the deep wound in his side. Wilf shook his head. "He escaped. When he noticed the princess was gone, he ran. We weren't able to stop him. Apollo insisted we come back here." He turned to Sarah. "His biggest concern was your safety." He pressed a fist to his mouth as he looked into Apollo's pallid face. "He's badly wounded. I tried to get him here as quickly as I could. Did I make it in time?"

It looked as though Apollo might lose consciousness. Sarah grabbed his hand as he was laid on the ground. His hand was limp and cold. His breath, thin, ever slower.

Michael tenderly laid his hand on Sarah's arm. "There's nothing we can do." His voice trembled. "His wounds are too severe."

"No!" she sobbed still clutching his hand. Michael must be wrong.

But she knew he wasn't. The light was already fading from Apollo's eyes. "Not like this." She began to cry. "Apollo!" She put a hand on his cheek. His skin was cold, and there was no response. She watched his chest, willing it to rise and take a breath. She counted each one until there was nothing.

Michael dropped to his knees and put a hand on Apollo's chest, slipping his fingers under the edge of the bloodstained surcoat. A moment later, he stood up. She saw the look on his face. He didn't need to say anything, but he put a hand on her shoulder and confirmed her fear. "He's gone."

Wilf and Michael stood back, allowing her to grieve over Apollo. The tears came unexpectedly hard, racking Sarah's body with pain. It felt as though her heart would literally burst. This man was the link to her past, to Miranda's past, and she had let that bond slip through her fingers because she had been too uncomfortable to face him. She had openly rejected him, but he had always been loyal to her, always believing she would become who she was meant to be. Sarah's tears flowed freely as she looked at his face. The worry was gone, and for the first time since she'd met him, he looked at peace. She, however, wasn't. She mourned the missed opportunities, she mourned the great man that he was, but most of all, she mourned a friend.

Her knees ached from kneeling on the cobblestone, but she refused to get up. She refused to let go of Apollo's hand. Wilf and Michael were talking behind her. She didn't particularly care about their conversation until she heard Michael ask about Luther.

"I heard his orders to retreat," Wilf said. "He had just struck Apollo down and broke through our defense line, but by then the princess was already gone. Once he realized she was out of his reach, he ran up the street, calling for his men to fall back and join Tobias."

"Blast it!" Michael said. "He must have known where the troops were going, and Tobias, no doubt, will accept them into his ranks."

Sarah tried to tune out her brother as he asked for details about how the fight was dispersed. It wouldn't have taken long to settle the villagers down once Luther and his men were gone. If only she and Grace had left sooner, perhaps Apollo would still be alive. She rubbed her fingertips across the back of his hand then reached up and touched his cheek. There was no warmth left in his skin. She tried to block out the image of Luther striking him down. Instead she focused on how her and Apollo's relationship had grown. There were so many missed opportunities to regret, but there were so many more to be had because of him.

CHAPTER 33

SARAH FELT HEAVY, AS IF she would collapse under her own weight. Michael stood over her, his hand resting on her shoulder. He was talking, but she had to force herself to concentrate to understand what he was saying. A few more men had gathered in the courtyard, and he was giving them orders.

"Go and get Margaret." One of the guards saluted and hurried to the castle door. Sarah's eyes followed him, and she spotted her father near the entrance. His face was rigid, refusing to show any emotion, but his eyes betrayed him. They were glazed with remorse.

Michael turned to another guard and pointed to the castle. "Take Apollo's body inside and have it tended to."

The guard looked baffled. "Inside? You mean to the room in the barracks where we normally tend our dead?"

"No." It was the king who answered. His voice was thick and husky. "Inside the keep. To my own physician."

Two guards brought a litter and gently laid Apollo's body on it. As they stood to leave, a hushed reverence fell over the small assembly. One by one, men came and lined up. Standing at attention, they placed fist over heart with bowed heads. Sarah felt her brother remove his hand from her shoulder. When she looked up, she saw he had taken up the same reverential salute.

She wiped her eyes and watched as Apollo was borne away in solemn respect. As the men turned and followed in procession behind the body, Sarah noticed her father still standing in the shadowed doorway to the castle—his own fist placed resolutely over his heart. His chin began to quiver as he turned to follow the last man in line. As the door closed behind him, his broad shoulders heaved with emotion.

Unable to bring herself to move, Sarah sat for a long time on the cold ground, staring at her hands until Margaret came and pulled her to her feet. The men were coming back into the courtyard now, and stable boys were bringing horses out from the stalls.

"Come, we should get you inside," Margaret coaxed.

Sarah looked around. Grace was gone along with the horse that they had ridden to the castle. "Why would she leave like that?"

"Who, dear?" Margaret asked.

"Grace." Sarah looked around again and spotted her brother. He was already mounted on his gray dappled horse and calling the small group of men to formation. Pulling away from Margaret, she ran up to him. "What are you doing?" She grabbed the bridle of the tall horse. Michael pulled on the reins, but the horse wouldn't move while she controlled the bit. He looked down at her with red-rimmed eyes.

"I'm going to see if I can prevent Tobias from annihilating the Moylans."

Sarah waved a hand to the men in the courtyard. "You scarcely have fifteen men here."

"Yes. It really is an opulent amount considering this is only a matter of negotiation—something I can handle by myself. However, Father insists I take the remaining guards with me."

"I fear Tobias is a greater man to be reckoned with than you believe, and I suspect Father knows that."

Michael gave an impatient grunt. Sarah braced for his retort, but they were interrupted as a soldier galloped through the gates and brought his horse up sharply next to Michael's.

"Your Highness." The man saluted and handed him a letter. "From Tobias." He gave a sharp bow of his head then moved his horse away to give them some privacy.

Michael broke the seal and began reading. His jaw tightened, and he crushed the paper with a growl.

"What is it?" Sarah held her hand out, wanting to read the note for herself, but Michael kept it tight in his fist.

"Tobias has declared that he will act in order to quell the political unrest being escalated by the Moylans." Michael paused as he rubbed his forehead. "He will not wait for diplomacy, and if I know what's good for the country, I should come and prove my mettle by taking command of the army and leading them to victory."

"He wants *you* to lead the attack against the Moylans?" Sarah's voice rose louder than she'd expected, and she quickly looked around to see who had heard. "He wants you to prove your mettle by attacking your own people? But of course you won't—will you?"

A fleeting expression transformed Michael's face, mournful and weary, but he buried it just as quickly and squared his shoulders. Sarah had been told that Michael excelled at fighting—he was, after all, his father's son— but she'd never seen that side of him. He was logical and scientific, and she couldn't imagine him taking up arms against his own people. At the same time, she couldn't ignore the cold chill inside her that said he might have to do just that. His eagerness to lead his people into a promising future would hold little value until he could prove himself in the eyes of his subjects. And what the Kyrnidians would value was a warrior.

Michael turned in his saddle, called the men into formation, then signaled for them to follow. Sarah reached out and touched his leg. "What are you going to do?"

"What I do best—negotiate."

Sarah's stomach tightened into knots as the men rode away. There was one thing she was certain of—Tobias would not negotiate.

CHAPTER 34

"WOULD YOU LIKE A DRINK?" Margaret offered her the small bottle. Sarah declined with a shake of her head. She appreciated her friend's willingness to share the tea, but her stomach had clamped down into a twisted knot, and she couldn't bring herself to drink anything. She picked nervously at one of her nails and turned back to the narrow window where she'd been watching and praying for the last three hours.

The quietness of the courtyard below seemed deceptively out of place. The castle gates remained closed, blocking out the reality of the dangers beyond. Sarah pinched her eyes shut and pressed her hands together as she muttered another prayer for the safety of her brother and his men. She wondered if God was listening. It was a terrifying possibility that Michael already lay dead with the rest of his men outside Tobias's encampment. She straightened her posture and tried to bury her worry. Another minute or two passed before she silently stood and walked away, allowing Margaret to take a turn at the window.

"It will be all right, dear." Margaret's voice was tight despite her efforts to sound comforting. "They'll—" She stopped midsentence with a gasp.

Sarah turned around with a jerk. Margaret was staring out the narrow window, but her hand was frantically waving for Sarah to join her. She ran across the room, and Margaret instantly moved aside, allowing her to look out. A small group of horsemen were filing through the gates into the courtyard. Sarah leaned forward, squeezing her shoulders through the constricted space so she could get a better view. She couldn't believe what she was seeing. They were back. All of them, it appeared, and uninjured. She scanned the group closely. There was one rider out of place. He rode up front next to Michael, and his mount was not the tall, pale Kyrnidian breed, but a bulky, majestic, black Friesian.

"Alex!" Sarah was already spinning around and running for the door. Moments later she was in the courtyard. Alex had scarcely dismounted when she had her arms wrapped around his neck and was up on her toes, pressing a kiss to his mouth. She knew she looked terrible. Her eyes were probably red and swollen from crying, her hair was disheveled, and her clothes were still dusty from the hasty ride back to the castle. But she didn't care.

Alex responded by enfolding her into his strong embrace, holding her tightly to him before pulling away and allowing his eyes to wash over her. "I had the most uneasy feeling come over me when I left." He took her face in his hands. "I changed my mind about returning to Calibre and was on my way back to the castle when I met Michael on his way to Tobias's camp. He told me everything. I was sorry to hear about Apollo. He truly was a great man." Alex paused then motioned to her brother. "Michael said you were safe here at the castle, and once he convinced me that there was no immediate threat to you, I joined him."

Sarah couldn't speak. She just nodded, grateful he would lend his support to her brother.

Alex brushed her cheek with his thumb and searched her eyes. His expression darkened. "Michael also told me about Luther. I should have never entrusted him with your care."

Sarah let out a long exhale. None of this was Alex's fault. "At any point in time, had you any reason to suspect he was so malevolent?"

"No. Unfortunately I concentrated on how well he performed his job, and since he excelled at that—" He broke off and shook his head in frustration. "I should have—"

"There's nothing you could have done. We all trusted him, and—I'm afraid—I was more naive than anyone else." She looked at Alex, her heart filling with remorse for ever allowing those feelings she'd had for Luther. Her cheeks burned crimson when she realized that Alex could read her expression.

"To my humiliation, I was enticed by him." Sarah ducked her head in shame, but Alex slid his fingers under her chin and lifted her face to look at her.

"I had my suspicions," he said softly. "It was difficult to miss the looks that passed between you two during the security meeting. I suspect it was his intention all along to draw you in, and I'm certain he was very persuasive." A long moment of silence passed between them before he continued.

"It's all over now, and I will never question you about it again if you will just tell me where your feelings lie now."

Sarah felt tears pricking at the corners of her eyes. "I admit that a part of me was drawn to Luther. But please understand—my whole heart is with you. And I did not simply choose you after the fact. I made my choice *before* I knew of Luther's treachery. Still, I'm ashamed to acknowledge I entertained his ideas at all. He wanted me to leave with him, and I thought it was an easy way to dismiss all of my problems. It took me some time to sort through things. It was when I refused him that he tried to abduct me."

Alex's jaw tightened. "Had I known then, I would have killed him."

"Everyone overlooked him as a suspect. It was too easy to assume that the abduction was politically motivated by those against the monarchy. I believe that since his first attempt failed, he intended to try once again. Last night he arranged to have me meet him in the stables, but as you know I ended up going to Tobias's room instead." She paused for a moment. "I'm not trying to excuse myself. I allowed myself to have feelings for him, and I shouldn't have. This morning I told him I wanted to be with you; I think that's what triggered the attack in the market."

Alex pulled her closer, wrapping his arms protectively around her. "I'm sorry for what you went through, and I don't fault you for falling into his trap. I didn't encounter him when we went into Tobias's camp, but mark my words—he will be caught."

Sarah shuddered to think they might attempt to go back to Tobias's camp. She looked over at her brother. He was speaking to a soldier. As if sensing her eyes on him, he dismissed the man and walked over to join her and Alex.

The negotiations had not gone well. His rigid stance and rock hard expression said it all, but at least it was better than the fate she feared for him. "Meet me in the council room in ten minutes." And with that, he turned and walked toward the castle without another word.

* * *

The group was small. Only Michael and the king were in the room when Sarah and Alex joined them. Sarah worried about her father. He slumped in his chair as if he had no energy to even move. His red-rimmed eyes stared at nothing. At times she thought a tear might break free and slip down his cheek, but he was too strong-willed to allow that. Nevertheless, his pain was acute and visibly evident. Sarah's throat grew tight as she watched him. Having a brother turned traitor would be almost too much for a man to bear, but her father had also lost Apollo today. Their estranged friendship had never been fully mended. Like her, he would have regrets.

Michael straightened a paper in front of him and then cleared his throat. "Tobias refuses to withdraw his intentions."

"And what exactly are those intentions?" the king asked. His countenance hardened as he shifted his focus to matters at hand.

"The army surrounds the Moylan estate, and they will attack at first light. The majority of those who oppose the monarchy are at the manor, including everyone who has openly campaigned against us. Tobias made it clear—he'll not leave until they are eliminated." The room fell silent, and the king rubbed his temples as if deep in thought.

After a minute, Michael spoke again. "Tobias—a true patriot." His voice hung heavy with sarcasm. "Always ready to defend Kyrnidan—even against its own people."

"Bring in the other garrisons," Alex suggested. "Lay siege to Tobias's camp."

The king's chair scratched harshly on the stone floor as he pushed himself away from the table and stood up. "I have already sent for them. My fastest rider left hours ago. However, the other garrisons will not make it here by first light." He crossed the room and looked out the window. "What is our man count here at the castle?"

"Thirty-two, including stable hands, those in the smithy, and the Calibrean guards." Michael looked to Alex for approval.

"My men are here to protect Sarah, and since this uprising directly affects her, they are at your disposal."

The king returned to his chair and pounded his fist on the table. "Still—hardly a number suitable to stand against Tobias's army—*my army*," he bellowed. He let out a low guttural moan. "I should have expected this."

"We were both blind to it, Father." Michael ran his hands through his hair as he let out a long breath. "Perhaps we would have been alerted if Tobias opposed us, but he is truly devoted to the monarchy. How were we to weed out our own supporters?"

Sarah had to bite her tongue. Tobias and his men were devoted to the *monarchy*, but they didn't support Michael or her father. Everything indicated that they were positioning themselves to seize power. Soon Michael and the king would be swept aside, and Tobias would claim the throne for himself. "What can we do to stop them?" Sarah asked.

Michael tapped a finger on the table. "Whatever we do, we must act quickly. He *will* attack at first light. He's only waiting in hope that I'll change my mind and lead the army myself. If I refuse, he'll follow through. He has already proven himself in war, and the soldiers *will* follow his orders."

"For the good of our nation, we kill our own people." The king's pain-filled words lingered in the silence that followed.

"If Tobias truly supports this monarchy," Alex said, "he *will* curb to your direct orders."

Michael shook his head. "He won't stand down. He's been placing people who share his ideals throughout the army and in our council; he's surrounded himself with those supporters. Even if we stripped him of his title and position, it would be ineffective."

Sarah silently agreed. Tobias, in his obsessive nature, would not be stopped. He wasn't going to risk Robert Moylan destroying the monarchy, and he had set up the situation so he would be in total control until that goal was accomplished.

Michael's eyes narrowed thoughtfully, and he rubbed his temples. "We must consider every available option in order to avoid disaster. I do not want the beginning of my rule to be stained by a massacre."

"Then you must consider assassination," Alex suggested in a low tone.

Sarah's stomach tightened. Assassinate Tobias? She looked at her father for a reaction, but it was Michael who spoke.

"I've already considered killing Tobias, but in order to save those at the Moylan estate, we would need to eradicate other leaders as well. Tobias carefully chose every one of the officers. Each is as ardent in their beliefs to uphold the government no matter what the cost. They will think it nothing to kill everyone at the Moylan estate in order to preserve our progress. Despite that I believe that at their core, these are good men, and to assassinate all of them in order to impose my own values—" Michael's voice faltered. "I cannot implement the very tactics that I'm trying to oppose."

The king tapped a finger on the table. "You have an idealistic heart, son, but as a ruler, you must be willing to do what is necessary. It's inevitable—some of your ideals will be sacrificed during your reign. There will be times when you will be forced to choose one of two evils. I believe this is one of those times. As much as I dislike Robert Moylan and his followers, our first obligation is to our people—including him and his followers. It is in our best interest to do whatever is necessary to protect those at the Moylan estate." The king paused then pointed at Michael.

"I know that's what you intend to do simply because it is the right thing to do. But always look deeper. Doing our duty in this may be enough to persuade influential men over to our side. If it comes down to killing Tobias and our commanders, so be it. They may support our monarchal government, but by taking this rash action, they are committing treason and, therefore, must be brought into submission."

The king paused again and looked at each of them in turn. "That said, if at all possible, I would prefer to find a peaceful way to bring this to an end without sacrificing all of my commanders. They have been wrongfully persuaded, but they are, after all, our friends and compatriots."

Michael strode over to a side table, unlocked a small box, and took out an aged scroll and several papers. "I know these battle strategies by heart." He put the papers on the table and set the crumbling scroll on top. He unrolled it and ran a finger down the yellow parchment. The king and Alex leaned forward to look at the details and diagrams. Sarah had little interest in discourses describing battle strategies, so she sat unmoving.

The men perused the writings, then Michael sat back, letting the scroll roll up on itself. "This is futile. Every approach and procedure, Tobias will also know. I could design a new plan of attack, but with thirty-two men, I see no way to subdue an army without shedding the blood of its leaders.

The king let his gaze rest on Alex. "I understand you overcame a great army by little means in your own country last year. Tell me the methods you used. Perhaps we can employ similar means to subdue Tobias."

Alex leaned back in his chair. The attack on Calibre last year had frightened the entire country, and Alex's cunning strategy had ended the war by an ingenious method, but he didn't look hopeful now. His brow creased with doubt, and his lips pulled into a frown.

"Yes. The entrapment of our enemies was a clever strategy and intricately planned. However, the method we used to subdue them was a simple siege that lasted for weeks. You don't have time for that. You must act quickly." Alex's frown deepened before he went on. "And I can see no one willing to get into a direct confrontation with the renowned army of Kyrnidan without a great deal of preparation and cunning designs. You have merely hours."

The words seemed tangible. Sarah could feel them weighing on her, suffocating and oppressing, as if they had openly declared that there was no possible solution—no hope.

The king stood again and moved toward the door. "Enough of this. We haven't time to study tactics or philosophize how thirty-two men might subdue an army. I see only two viable options. Michael, I will leave the decision to you. You may take whatever men we have left. They are too few to assault the army directly, so you may use them as bow marksmen to kill Tobias. At a safe distance, you can take him down along with every one of his commanders." He paused, his face etched with the pain of his suggestion. "Or you may go and lead the army as Tobias has requested. We will then deal with him after it's over. Either way we will cut our losses and move forward as best we can." The king's shouldered sagged. "And son, I am truly sorry our options are limited. Each path will be a painful one, but such is the affliction of one who rules. Make your choice." He walked around the table and put a hand on Michael's shoulder. "I'll leave you to think about it, but know that whatever you decide to do, I will support it."

From her satchel, Sarah pulled the little silver unicorn that Apollo had returned to her that morning. She turned it over and over in her hand, feeling its weight. When she finally looked up, her father had left the room, and Michael was slumped in his chair. She had never seen someone look so defeated in all her life.

"And I must make this choice," he muttered. "Do I kill my own uncle and my commanders?" He turned his palms up and stared at them as if they were already stained with their blood. "Martin, Aaron, Estevan . . . Samuel. They are good men. They have families." He looked up at Sarah. "Or am I to kill the Moylans? Which of my people do I kill?"

She opened her mouth intending to offer some words of comfort, but what she uttered surprised even her. "You can't rule."

"What?" Michael lifted his chin to look at her.

Sarah dropped her gaze to the unicorn and began rubbing it. Heat rushed into her cheeks as she thought of a way to explain her inept remark. "I don't think you're ready for your coronation next month. You won't be able to rule these people knowing you didn't try *every* avenue for their sakes. Surely you can't go through with either option." The words seemed to stumble over her tongue, but she rushed on. "Try to understand. We are twins, so deep inside we must be connected in some way. Do we not share the same core beliefs? Both options Father offered are wrong." She drew in a deep breath to gather her courage. "If you chose either one, I would think you undeserving of leadership. We are born into our positions, but are we not obligated to also earn them—to be worthy of them?" Her eyes briefly flickered toward Alex. "That is one reason I chose not to return to Calibre this morning. I cannot be their princess until I feel worthy of it."

The room fell silent, and from under the table, she felt Alex's hand searching for hers. She moved her arm over, allowing his fingers to wrap tightly around her own. His touch was warm and reassuring. She didn't want to look at him, but the soft squeeze of his fingers drew her gaze. He regarded her with an expression of soft understanding. It seemed as if he wanted to say something. His lips parted briefly, but Michael shifted in his seat, and Sarah looked back at her brother.

He was sitting stiffly in his chair, his arms folded, and his brow knit together in a stern manner. He offered a single nod. "All right. Perhaps we do share the same core beliefs. I do want to be worthy of my position and I'm willing to earn it, but what would you have me do? What other choice is there?"

At any other time, Sarah's heart would have leapt with joy at the realization that she and her brother were connected, that they shared the same feelings, but this admission seemed sad at the moment. She let go of Alex's hand and leaned forward, setting the little unicorn on the table in front of them. She knew what she wanted him to do; she just needed to find the courage to say it. She took a breath and pushed the words out. "There is a third option. You can revolt."

Michael moved his gaze from the unicorn up to her. "Against who? Father? Tobias? Who is it exactly I should—" Michael broke off, and a quizzical look crossed his face. "You want me to call out Tobias, don't you? You want me to fight him one on one."

"No." Sarah tightened her hands into fists. "I think you will need to fight the entire Kyrnidian army."

CHAPTER 35

MICHAEL DIDN'T LAUGH AT HER as she'd expected; instead, he held her gaze, unmoving. "You want me to fight? Head to head with Tobias and his army? In essence you want me to die a martyr. It won't make a difference."

"I don't want you to die. But fighting *will* make a difference. It will make a difference to you. You may not stop Tobias, but at least you won't have to live with killing the Moylans or your own commanders."

"Well, you are right on that account—because I won't be alive to have such thoughts."

Sarah dropped her head. She was fully aware of the risks, but it was something she herself would do—what she was actually planning to do. "Should we not do what's right despite the outcome?" She reached out and ran a finger over the unicorn. "Do you not ever feel such compulsion—that you have to do something?" She looked up at Michael and Alex. "To fight—to *really* fight?" Her brother's expression didn't change; he just stared at her. Her voice took on a harder tone. "Very well. I am going to Tobias's camp, and I will fight. I will do everything in my power to put an end to this."

Sarah was startled by the reaction she received. Both men jumped to their feet. Alex began to chide her for such an idea, but Michael paced the room, running his fingers through his hair.

"She's right." Her brother's voice boomed out, causing Alex to fall silent. He strode to the table and picked up the unicorn. "She has only voiced what I myself have felt but have not admitted."

Her heart ached for him. He had tried so hard to be what his people needed—bringing them education and sophistication—but now he was realizing that he had to be what they *wanted*—a warrior.

Michael let out a long breath. "In a way, Tobias was right too." He looked at Sarah.

"You need to prove your mettle," she said softly.

Michael nodded. "And who better to fight the Kyrnidian army than a Kyrnidian?"

Alex shook his head. "You cannot mean to take on the army yourself—"

"I'll not be taking them on by myself. I have thirty-two men who will accompany me." He pointed a finger at her. "However, *you* will not be going."

Sarah was ready to protest, but Alex broke in.

"Thirty-three men."

Sarah should have expected Alex to volunteer himself, but hearing it out loud and knowing the probable outcome was distressing. She opened her mouth, but Alex pointed a finger at her and cut her off. "*You* will *not* be going."

She folded her arms across her chest. Having never been trained in weaponry, she knew she would just be a liability, but she was willing to go and do whatever she could to help. At the very least, she would be one more body to stand between Tobias and the Moylans.

Alex put a hand on Sarah's cheek. "I am serious about this. A battlefield is no place for you. The only hope we have of surviving is if Tobias chooses to take prisoners, and I will not have you face that."

"Wait." Michael leaned over the table and picked up a charcoal pencil. He turned a paper over, and began drawing a diagram. "Being taken prisoner, I hope, is not our only option. Alex, do you remember how Tobias had thrown up spiked ramparts along this ditch?" He drew on the paper.

Sarah's stomach dropped. Tobias was more prepared than she'd imagined. He had gone to the extent of building a temporary fortification around his army. She shouldn't be surprised; after all, this was what set the Kyrnidian military apart from other nations. The army was sharpened to a knife's edge, and Tobias could expect such exertions from his men.

"I analyzed the terrain as we came and went. I believe this hill here is high enough." Michael pointed to his diagram. "Tobias's breastworks are formidable, but if we set a few archers at this vantage point—" He tapped his finger on his drawing. "They'll have an open shot into their entrenchments. As they move to defend that side, it will give us an edge long enough to cross the ditches. We'll come in here." He tapped the paper with the tip of his pencil.

Alex sat back and nodded. "It might work. But to do so you'll need to divide your men. With so few to begin with, it's unthinkable."

Sarah stood and began walking around the room. The two men watched her as she stopped and faced them. "We need more men," she said, stating the obvious. "Michael . . . when you came back from Calibre you . . ." She let her words trail off as she looked at him, still trying to gather her thoughts.

All at once, his face widened with a grin. "You're right. It just might work."

Sarah walked to the table, took his paper, and began writing on it.

"What might work?" Alex asked.

"A proclamation," Sarah said. She handed the paper to Michael to read as she explained further. "Michael sent a proclamation to the people upon his return from Calibre to quickly spread the word that I had been found. In town today you should have seen the men willing to join the fight. We may not have regular soldiers, but we have a whole country of fighting men."

"This will work," Michael said holding up the draft she had written. He grabbed the pencil. "Let's add that any volunteers should gather on the common grounds outside the village." He scribbled the note and handed the paper back to her. "Take it to the scribes and tell them to copy it as many times as they can. We will send the heralds out immediately."

* * *

Sarah adjusted the sword at her side as she watched the last of the heralds gallop out the gates toward the village. She had never worn a weapon before, and it felt heavy and awkward. She had no idea what a real battle was like, and perhaps her ignorance allowed her to think she could join in this one. But she needed to do something to aid their cause. She was confident the plan would work; however, her hopes faltered as she turned to see the men gathering in the courtyard.

Thirty-two. It seemed so few. Alex and Michael had not yet joined them, but the addition of two more wouldn't make that much of a difference. They needed every available person. She tugged at her belt, adjusting the bulky weight of the sword, then walked over and stood next to a young boy who was smacking his fist against his shield. He must have been a stable hand and looked no older than ten, yet he appeared comfortable with being allowed to join the battle.

"Where do I get one of those?" she asked pointing at his shield.

"You don't need one of those," Alex's voice growled behind her.

He walked up, wrapped his arms around her, and bent his head down, pressing a kiss to her lips. She felt his lean muscles tighten beneath the folds of his shirt, and then her breath caught as he pressed one hand against her back, while his other intertwined in her hair at the nape of her neck. After a moment, the firm urgency of his lips softened. When he pulled away, she could still feel his lingering warmth. He had never kissed her like that before. Was this his farewell kiss? Did he think they would never see each other again? She pushed the thoughts away by leaning into him and pressing her lips to his again.

When they pulled apart, Alex's lips twitched at the corners. He held the back of his hand to his mouth to hide his smile. "I should go off to battle more often if you're going to kiss me like that." Clearing his throat, he tried to look more serious. He motioned to the sword she was wearing. "It looks good on you, but you are *not* going." He pulled her close again, and she rested her head on his chest. He held her for several moments before he lowered his head and whispered, "You are worthy. Someone as loyal and devoted to their people as you are is more than worthy. Princess of Calibre and Kyrnidan."

He kissed her again. It was soft and tender this time. A moment later, they were interrupted by a gentle cough. Sarah looked at the person standing next to them. She gasped when she realized it was Michael. Gone were his puffy sleeves and feathered hat. Instead, he donned a full suit of armor. Made-to-measure, the fit was flawless, and the entire ensemble was of superior quality. Not the typical silver, Michael's suit was a distinguished black metal with a gold edging that bordered each piece and pauldron with the Kyrnidian crest emblazoned on the breastplate. He wore it well. There was a bearing about him that made one want to watch him—an ease and confidence she hadn't seen in him before.

"Sarah."

She met her brother's eyes and stubbornly folded her arms with a huff. "No."

"What?" Alex asked. "All he did was say your name."

"He wants me to take off the sword," she said.

Alex looked back and forth between them. "Have you noticed the more you two are together, the less you have to say to communicate?"

Sarah nodded. She had noticed that.

"Well?" Michael held his hand out.

She unstrapped the sword and handed it over reluctantly. "What am I to do?"

Alex slipped his fingers around hers. "We need prayers. I would like someone to keep a vigil for us in the chapel."

He looked at her in earnest. Staying behind was the last thing she wanted to do, but this was important to Alex—and it was something she *could* do. She had no talent for wielding a sword, but she could pray and ask God to protect them. "All right. I'll do it," she said.

Already silently praying, she watched Alex walk to the armory. Several minutes later, he emerged with shield and armor. He walked toward her, but Michael called for the men to mount up and take their positions. It was time to go out and meet the volunteers on the commons. Sarah's heart sank. There was no more time for farewells. She walked over to stand with her father. He had come out and given his blessing, along with some last minute advice, to Michael.

With the men in formation, Michael called the order to move out. The courtyard filled with excited cries and the clamor of hooves as the troop rode through the gates. Sarah kept her eyes on Alex. The king saluted, thumping a fist on his chest, and Sarah reached out and took his other hand. It was rough and calloused. "Do you wish to be going with them?"

He turned his head, and the afternoon sun glinted off the crown encircling his silver-copper hair. "It wouldn't be wise to send both king and future king into the same battle. Should something go wrong, the risk of leaving the country without a ruler would be too great."

Still, she saw the fire in his eyes, a hunger that couldn't hide his desire. "Unwise indeed."

He squeezed her hand. "You were right. Michael is the one who needs to fight this battle. God save him."

CHAPTER 36

SARAH LEANED ON THE ALTAR, trying to ease the pressure from her stiffening knees. She ached, but she had kept vigil through the entire night. She understood now why a squire was required to pray through the night before his knighting ceremony. Enduring the long process was empowering, yet humbling at the same time.

A soft glow filled the church as the first rays of sun caressed the horizon and slipped through the stained-glassed windows. On any other day, it would have been a beautiful sight, but today it seemed daunting as she pondered Tobias's threat. To those at the Moylan estate, the new day might mean the end of life. The sun's rays crept across the floor like an evil mist driven by the angel of death. Clutching her hands together, she continued her prayer, but now instead of asking for divine assistance for the small militia they had gathered, she turned her pleading to the protection of those on the estate. The odds certainly were not in favor of Michael's group of citizen-soldiers, and she feared what the outcome would be. Short of a miracle, those on the Moylan estate would be annihilated.

Tired and emotional, she was unable to stop the tears from falling. She begged that their plan had worked, and if not, pleaded that the Kyrnidian army had been merciful and spared Alex and Michael.

The sun had fully emerged when she heard the clopping of horse hooves on cobblestone. One lone rider had entered the courtyard. She waited, listening, hoping to hear more—prayed that more would follow.

"Please, God."

The horse stopped.

More tears. "Please, God."

Several long minutes passed before footsteps sounded behind her. The sound was ominous, and her heart fell.

"Please, God, strengthen me so that I'm able to bear this." She looked over her shoulder, bracing herself for the terrible news.

A chilling jolt ran through her. She went numb as Tobias's large frame filled the doorway. He was dressed in his usual military suit, but it was overlaid with chainmail. He was dusty and disheveled—signs that he had just come from the battlefront.

The corner of his lips twitched into a sardonic smile. "The milkmaid told me I'd find you here."

Sarah stood up. Her chest was tight, smoldering with an animosity that instantly dried her tears. For Tobias to be there signified that their plan had failed. Her hands gripped her skirts, white-knuckled, and she dared not move. Tobias walked to the front of the chapel, the sound of his heavy boots echoing against the walls. He passed by her and stood next to the table positioned beneath the window of Christ. The contrast made her want to recoil.

"I have to admit, niece, you have more influence than I originally credited possible." His words were silky and lighthearted, but she knew better than to trust his tone. His eyes met hers, and his face hardened. The next words out of his mouth wouldn't have the same innocent feel to them. "You're lucky Apollo hid you away after you were born, and you really should have stayed hidden."

The lump in Sarah's throat grew as she struggled to keep her expression passive. She needed to bury her fear. Despite the danger, she was going to hear what he had to say. She needed to know the fate of Michael, Alex, and the others.

Tobias ran a finger along the edge of the table where the candles had burned throughout her vigil. "I did try to bridge our estrangement, but you have proven difficult to work with."

"And I don't foresee it getting any easier for you," she said, glaring at him.

"Oh, it'll get easier. I will not fail where Mr. Tandy did. He didn't have the backbone to take care of you. You made him soft, and by the time he had the temerity to go through with it, you had your father's guards in your pocket. Admittedly, we hadn't expected you to be so protected in the village, but you're quite alone now, and I shall pick up where Mr. Tandy left off."

Sarah's heart raced, and her fingers tightened around the folds in her skirt as she clenched her hands into fists. "You . . . you ordered Luther to attack me?"

"Luther has been working for me since he came to Kyrnidan last year. Apparently, I pay better than the Calibrean monarchy."

The color drained from Sarah's face. Tobias was behind it after all. This is what Chad had meant when he told her that she knew who was threatening her. "It was you all along!" she yelled. "You're the leader of the Kyrnidians who want me out of the country."

"You say it like that is the purpose for our existence. It's not."

"But hasn't that been your goal? To get rid of me? You even went to the extent of meeting with Chad at the tavern and bribing him for information about me."

"That job was assigned to a colleague of mine. Not that we got anything useful. Chad was only interested in his own schemes and practically refused to help us. But that didn't matter at the time. We are a patriotic group, and we continue to look into possible threats to the monarchy."

"And I was a possible threat, so you arranged for my abduction?"

"No—that I did not do. The abduction was Luther's plan. My arrangement was to have him *kill* you, but he was too weak to do it straight out. He had *feelings* for you. He was going to try to convince you to leave with him, to never come back. When you refused his offer, he thought he could take you by force. It wasn't until you rejected him yesterday morning that he finally grew a spine and tried to follow through with my orders."

The room seemed to be spinning now. "You would kill me after all you have done to befriend me?"

Tobias looked wounded. "Don't make it sound as if I were insincere. I do love you, Sarah. After all we *are* family." A mournful look reflected deeper in his expression. "Don't think I haven't tried to find another way around this. I really have. I had high hopes that our domestic affairs would move forward uninterrupted after your arrival. I did my best to keep you out of it, but you insisted—getting involved with that council meeting. That's when you became a threat. Your death will certainly be a great hardship, but how greater the tragedy if our nation were to fall because of your actions?"

Sarah trembled. Despite their family ties, he was going to kill her for getting in his way. Every rational thought in her mind told her to turn and run, but she couldn't. Not until she knew what had happened to Michael, Alex, and those at the Moylan estate. She tightened her muscles, hoping he wouldn't see her shaking. "Do you really think I'm impeding the progression of Kyrnidan?" Her voice sounded stronger than she thought possible.

"Can you not see what is best for this country?" he retorted. "You claim to be their princess—can you not see what these people need? They need the monarchy."

"And I suppose you think they need you at the head of it."

Tobias looked baffled for a moment. "Have you lost faith in the idea of Michael ruling?"

Sarah's hand flew to her chest at the mention of her brother's name. "Is Michael alive?" she choked out.

Tobias laughed, and the sharp sound reverberated around the room. It seemed as if she was surrounded by men, all laughing at her. Her brow furrowed in confusion. Was he laughing because he thought her question absurd? Tobias had just admitted he would do whatever he thought was best for the country, even if it meant killing family. Did that include her brother? Tobias's laughter died, and he began to pinch each candlewick, snuffing out the luminaries on the table. As each one sizzled out with a hiss of smoke, she felt her hopes for Michael and Alex fade.

"I know it was you who convinced him to attack," Tobias said, turning toward her again. He traced his imposing mustache with his thumb and forefinger. "You see, one of the heralds came directly to me and told me of your proclamation. Your efforts were impressive, I have to say. Over two hundred men from the village joined your little campaign."

Sarah's heart skipped a beat. "Over two hundred?" It was more than she had imagined. That had to be the majority of the men from the village. Again, her hope found a foothold, and she walled her heart around it protectively.

"It was a doomed mission," Tobias continued. "Michael's tactics were rather good though; I didn't expect him to attack in the middle of the night. I was certain he would have waited until morning." For a moment Tobias appeared pleased.

Sarah held her breath, hoping that something had come from Michael's strike. "They had the element of surprise then? They were able to break off your assault on the Moylans—"

"Now don't be placing too much faith in that hodgepodge troop." He pointed at her. "You probably think they had a chance at succeeding with your brother's cunning strategy, but you see, I've been planning this attack on the Moylans since I learned of their rally. Of course, I intended it to go smoothly and pass with the council's approval, but when it didn't—when you put a stop to it—I still continued as planned. I had our southern garrison already on the way up here." He paused as that declaration sank in. He leaned forward, rocking on the balls of his feet, and his giant frame towered above her. "By the time Michael arrived with your pitiful two hundred—men that were too old, too young, or too inexperienced to really battle—I had two troops, more than six hundred trained and fully armed soldiers at my command."

Sarah felt tears begin to prick at the corners of her eyes. Suddenly weak, she reached out to steady herself against the altar. Tobias moved toward her. He was enjoying this—taking his time gloating. Her heart pounded in her ears and she felt sick to her stomach, but she wasn't going to let him boast any longer. Balling her hands tightly, she flung herself at him, fists flying, trying to land a blow somewhere that might cause him to feel even a fraction of the pain she felt. "Are they alive?" she screamed. "Are they? Tell me!"

Tobias caught her by the wrists and dragged her across the altar. Despite her yelp of pain, he didn't let go.

"They're dead," he said. "Once our victory was secure I left the final details of the battle in my officers' capable hands and came back here. It's perfect—Michael and his army away—leaving you alone and unprotected. What a great opportunity—and I must say, I never miss an opportunity." He paused and leveled his eyes on her. "Surprised that I would leave a battle to tend to you? Well, don't be. You keep getting in the way, and I simply need to get rid of that problem. It's best to do it before the army returns to the castle. Can't have any of your sympathizers trying to stop me."

"But you left before the battle was over, so you can't possibly know for certain. There is a possibility they still live."

"I have been in more battles than you can even fathom, and I've never failed at calculating the outcome. I'll wager that even you can predict the results of this one. Each and every one of my officers has sworn an oath to see this battle through—to let no one stand in our way until the Moylans are dead. Two hundred misfits against six hundred of the world's greatest? We both know the outcome. Every one of your volunteers is dead. Everyone at the Moylan estate is dead. However, if it makes you feel better, I did give my men implicit instructions to preserve Michael's life. They were to kill all others but not him."

Sarah looked at him in confusion. "Why save Michael when he stood in your way? Isn't that what you wanted—everyone dead that opposed you? So *you* could rule? So you could command the nation like you do the army, or your little patriotic group?"

Tobias snorted. "Are you really that dim? I have never wanted to sit on the throne. I don't want to rule. I only want what's best for Kyrnidan, and Michael is suited for that position, not me."

Tobias turned to look at the shifting light in the window. "It'll be all over by now. It would've only taken minutes to lay waste to the entire Moylan estate. Of course, they'll be cleaning up the aftermath, but I expect they'll be returning soon. The only thing left undone is my own duty—to take care of you."

A sob caught in Sarah's throat, and she sank to her knees. Tobias let go of her as she fell to the floor. She didn't want to believe Tobias, but she knew the probable outcome herself. A village militia against six hundred trained Kyrnidian soldiers who had orders to spare no one beyond Michael. They would all be dead, even Alex—her beloved Alex. It would have been a massacre, and she was to blame. She'd been the one to convince them to go. She had sent two hundred men to their deaths—including her own fiancé.

Her father had been right. They should have let it play out then cut their losses and moved on. At least there would have been fewer deaths. How could she face her father after this? How could she face the people of Kyrnidan knowing countless families would be mourning the loss of their fathers and sons—all because of her?

"Come on." Tobias grabbed her arm and pulled her to her feet. "I can't take care of this business on holy ground." He began pushing her toward the door.

Sarah stumbled as he jerked her forward. She told herself she shouldn't fight back, that she deserved this fate. With Alex gone there was nothing to live for anyway. Fighting back would be pointless. Shouldn't she just face her punishment with dignity? She looked at the doorway and something inside of her began screaming. *No! Not like this!* She struggled against him. Crying out, she twisted in his grip, trying to get away.

She screamed again, and Tobias wrapped his massive arms around her, crushing the sound. "Who is going to help you—the milkmaid? No one else is here—not a single guard."

"You can't do this!" she cried.

"For the monarchy, I will. For Michael, I will."

"And what if you're wrong? What if your men mistakenly killed Michael?"

Tobias stopped, and his face reddened. "No." He shook his head. "Michael *will* rule. This country needs the monarchy. They need him. Our people don't know what's best for them. He will rule. My men won't kill him—"

"You can't guarantee that. You know things get confusing during battle. What if someone made a mistake? Michael could be lying dead right now—a casualty of *your* battle!"

Sarah felt a shudder run though Tobias. She had pulled the right thread, and he was coming unraveled. The words were painful to speak, but she went on. "It's true; you know it. Michael can be killed just like any other man."

"No!" Tobias shook her.

She felt her bones rattle beneath his grip, but she continued on. "You can't keep people from dying." Her voice was frantic. "Even if Michael survived, what if something else took his life? What if he were to get sick again? Something deadlier than the pox? How would you keep him alive? What if there was an accident? What would you do if Michael wasn't around to lead your precious monarchy?"

"Nathaniel," Tobias choked out. "It would fall to young Nathaniel. I . . . I would just need to . . . I would just need to . . ."

"What? Change the prophecy again?"

CHAPTER 37

A COLD AWARENESS WASHED OVER Sarah as she said the words. It had only been a guess, but her uncle stiffened. Red pigment crept up his neck and into his face.

"It . . . it worked once before." He stuttered over his words.

"It was you!" Sarah gasped. "You changed it so the people would believe in a future *you* saw fit for them, one that ensured a male ruler.

Tobias shook her violently. "The prophecy referred to Michael all along. It said that *he* would unite the nation. *He* would. *The son.* I simply clarified it. *You* are the one who changed the prophecy by being born first."

"You snake!" Sarah pulled back. "You bent the will of the entire nation by misusing their belief in the high priest!"

"And I can do it again." Tobias jerked her toward the door. "But you won't be around to see it."

She struggled against his hold, but it was no use. He was too strong. A lump grew in her throat, and she tried to swallow it. She hated that she would be so easy for him to kill. At the very least, she wanted him to work for it. She gathered her strength and thrashed her arms against him, kicking out at the same time. Her foot met solidly with his shin, but he didn't even flinch.

A smile spread across his face. "I was foolish to think we could ever get along. That you could come back and we could be family."

An icy feeling settled in Sarah's chest. The remorse she had seen in his eyes before was gone. Killing her would not only be easy for him but he was now going to enjoy it.

"Tobias!"

Sarah startled at the booming voice and brought her head up. Her father stood just inside the door, his eyes ablaze, and his sword drawn. The milkmaid cowered behind him. The young woman, seeing she had done her duty, turned and ran out.

"Brother," Tobias acknowledged then gave a hearty laugh. "Don't tell me you've come to fight. At nearly ten years my senior, surely you don't think you're still my match."

Her father walked forward. "Will you have me regret giving you so much power and influence in our kingdom?"

Tobias threw Sarah to the side. She fell, jamming her wrist as she hit the floor. Despite the jarring pain, she quickly scrambled out of the way.

"You regret giving me power?" Tobias's tone was acidic. "You owe me at least that much. After all, I never tried to take the crown from you. I could have—if I wanted it. But I allowed you to keep the throne. And now you begrudge my leadership in the army? Have you forgotten who the real champion was—who really deserved and *earned* the power?"

The king's eyes flickered away. "I haven't forgotten."

Sarah couldn't take her eyes off her father. He had only muttered three simple words, *I haven't forgotten*, but they slipped from his tongue as if they were physically agonizing to speak. The bitterness between the two men was tangible, and the air seemed to pulse as the long buried rancor surfaced between them.

"You must never forget!" Tobias boomed. "After all I have sacrificed for you! It could have been me, but I held my tongue all these years—for you! For Michael!"

Sarah pressed herself against the wall and inched closer to her father. "What does he speak of?" Her father kept his eyes on Tobias, unwilling to answer. She was tired of the secrets. "What does he speak of?" she demanded louder.

"Tell your daughter," Tobias said. "Tell her that she was never supposed to be a princess—that you were never supposed to be king."

Her father flinched, but his jaw remained clamped shut.

Tobias grabbed a candelabrum from a side table and hurled it across the room. It crashed into the wall and exploded into pieces. "Tell her!"

"It was Tobias," her father said. He spoke to Sarah but kept his eyes on his brother, his expression shrouded with bitterness. "Tobias was the one who made the suggestions to improve the army. It was *his* tactics that won our battles. And I took the credit."

"You mean . . ." She stopped, unable to finish the words.

Her father flicked his eyes in her direction. "And then it was time for the council to vote in the next overlord—"

"Yes," Tobias boomed. "Only they didn't vote in another overlord, did they brother? Instead they offered you the title of king." He tightened his grip on his sword and pointed the blade. "I was young and naive and assumed your reports had given me due tribute. I had no idea what you had done until you were pronounced my king."

"I'm sorry."

"You don't mean that!" Tobias yelled.

The remorse on her father's face dissolved, any trace of regret transforming into fierce, unforgiving conviction. "You're right. I don't mean it. Although, I am sorry there was no other way. But if I had to do it over—I would do the same. I could not risk you becoming the ruler." Her father's voice escalated. "I had to do what was best for the people. I knew who you were back then and what you would have become if you had complete power. You would have ruled as a tyrant. I did it for the good of the people. They needed the better man."

Sarah nearly doubled over with the nauseous wave brought on by her father's words. How could they be so different yet have the same ideal— the same justification? Both of them—vindicating their wrongs all *for the good of the people.*

"I should never have allowed you to sit on the council or to direct the army." Her father squeezed his eyes shut for a brief moment, as if he were looking inward, then focused on Tobias again. "But all these years, I have let the guilt of my injustice toward you guide my actions. In an attempt to make up for my misdeed, I have been too lenient with you. I regret that. You haven't changed. You're still a tyrant."

"Tyrant, am I?" Tobias's voice thundered off the walls. "If I were a tyrant, I would have contested your right to the throne, but I withheld. I too want the better man to rule, and I have done everything to help Michael secure his position."

"Michael is the better of both of us," her father admitted. "But did you have to go to such extremes to ensure his position? Did you have to kill all who opposed him? Did you have to threaten my only daughter? You were the reason Apollo took her from us in the first place, God rest his soul and bless him for protecting her, but it wouldn't have been necessary if it had not been for you."

Tobias stepped forward raising his sword. "You'll allow her to ruin what we have fought so hard to achieve? You have grown weak indeed."

Sarah saw a flicker of regret in Tobias's eyes, and he lunged forward. She threw a hand over her mouth to stifle a gasp. Her father was just as quick, stepping into the attack and throwing up his sword just in time to block Tobias's powerful blow. The chapel rang with the sound of their clashing swords like discordant church bells summoning parishioners to Sunday mass.

Not daring to move, Sarah pressed her back against the wall. She now saw in her father what Apollo had seen so many years ago. He moved with an air about himself, powerful and majestic. However, age gave Tobias the advantage. He rained steady beats down upon the king until her father's strength began to ebb away with each blow.

"Stop!" she cried. Her father fell to one knee, gasping for breath. Tobias continued delivering blow after blow onto the king's sword until he was no longer able to hold it. It fell to the floor with a clang. One swift kick from Tobias sent it sliding out of his reach. Sarah took a step forward to help, but her uncle shoved her back, sending her tumbling back to the wall. She was helpless against his sheer strength. She sank to her knees with a cry. She had lost Alex, perhaps even Michael, and now her father.

"Michael is the better of all of us," Tobias growled. "He *will* rule. The monarchy will continue on through him." With a slow, deliberate movement, he raised his sword. "I will make sure of it."

CHAPTER 38

IT WAS SLIGHT AT FIRST. Sarah thought she'd imagined the faint rumble, but slowly, steadily, it increased. The low roar eventually grew loud enough to vibrate through the walls and floor of the chapel like the sound of a thousand marching men.

Tobias held his sword above his brother but hesitated as he cocked his head to the side to listen. The noise resonated with him, and his face contorted angrily. "They're back sooner than I expected." Keeping his sword at the ready, he sidestepped to the window.

Taking advantage of the opportunity, Sarah edged her way to a nearby wall niche where a metal candleholder was displayed. As soon as Tobias turned to look out the window, she grabbed the heavy sconce and hurled it at him with all her strength. Her father was already moving toward his sword. The candleholder hit Tobias's shoulder with a sickening thump, and he stumbled back with a cry of rage.

Grasping his chest and panting, the king managed to get to his sword and snatched it up. "Run!" he yelled at her.

Sarah's mind convulsed at her father's order. Fear for her own safety pulsed through her, but it was outmatched by her desire to stay and help in any way she could. Her father wouldn't back down, yet she knew he didn't stand a chance against his younger, stronger brother. Grabbing another candlestick, she threw it, but Tobias sidestepped it and replied with a swipe of his sword. Her father jumped in front of her and deflected the blow.

"Run!" he cried again.

Sarah's stomach churned. She couldn't watch him die. Her body was already moving when she made up her mind. She needed to get help. The rumbling cadence outside had drawn closer and, with it, their salvation. Someone out there would help. Tobias may be the leader of the army, but surely they wouldn't stand by as he killed their king in cold blood. With her heart pounding against her chest, she ran through the door as the sound of clashing swords filled the chapel once again.

She hit the slick cobblestones and nearly fell as she sprinted into the courtyard. Ranger barked as she ran past him. The Kyrnidian army was filling in through the gates, and she screamed for help, drawing their attention, but half of the courtyard still separated them. Her father's voice cried out in pain, making it mournfully obvious that the soldiers wouldn't get to them in time. She waved her arms, but instead of running toward the soldiers, she turned and ran toward Ranger and Tobias's horse. The tall mount was well trained; it stood, calm and steady, as she dashed up and grabbed the reins. She pulled herself into the saddle and sank her heels into the horse's ribs sending it through the chapel doors.

The pounding echo of horse hooves bounced off the walls as Sarah ran the horse across the tile floor. Her father jumped out of the way, but Tobias was too late and there was nowhere for him to go. The horse charged and hit him squarely in the chest throwing him back into the altar and sending his sword skittering across the floor.

"You!" Tobias stumbled to his feet. Sarah kept the prancing horse between them. He swiped his long, red hair away from his face and straightened up. "How dare you!"

"Of course she dares," her father called out. "She is a Delacor." He was holding a bleeding wound on his arm and leaning heavily against the wall, but he pushed himself up and tightened his grip on his blade. "You should've seen her earlier, brother—wearing a sword at her waist, ready to go to battle. The same warrior blood runs through her veins as it does ours.

Tobias's eyes twisted as he searched to see where his own weapon had gone. He balled his hands into fists and glared at Sarah. Anticipating another attack from him, she kept the horse between him and her father. Tobias tensed and lunged forward, but with a quick tug on the reins, the horse reared up. Tobias jumped away from the deadly hooves just as the sound of rattling armor and weapons burst into the room. Tobias's shoulders slumped, and he made no movement to pick up his sword. Sarah glanced back at the soldiers and nearly squealed in excitement.

Michael was at the lead. His black suit of armor was scratched and scarred from the battle, but he looked unharmed. And Alex—her heart leapt in her chest—was right behind him.

Sarah backed the horse up, letting Michael and the other soldiers in, and once Tobias was surrounded, she slid down from the saddle and into Alex's arms.

"You're all right!" She intertwined her fingers into his dark hair and pulled his face to hers, covering his mouth with kisses.

Alex pulled back and nodded toward Michael. "The credit of our survival goes to your brother."

The king walked over to Michael. He didn't bother to hold his wound, and it left a trail of dotted blood behind him. He reached out and placed a hand on his son's shoulder, nodding his approval.

Michael leveled his eyes on Tobias. "Uncle. I have always valued your advice, as you have seldom steered me wrong, but perhaps you will regret the day you advised me to prove my mettle."

"You have proven your caliber then." Tobias leaned against the altar, his expression a mixture of pride and concern. "As long as the Moylans and the other traitors are dead, I will never regret it."

"They live."

Tobias's face twisted in outrage. "No!" He pushed himself up from the altar. "It's impossible! I refuse to believe it! Every officer swore an oath— each bound their very lives to this purpose."

"And each soldier has pledged their oath to their king," Michael said.

Tobias dropped his head and shook it. "I don't believe it. The army was securely under the command of my officers when I left. They would never—"

Alex pulled away from Sarah and stepped forward. "They are trained to follow their leader with undying loyalty."

"Then they would have followed my orders!"

"They still have the ways of the warlords ingrained in them," Alex said. "They'd follow you until someone else proved their valor above yours. And that man was Prince Michael." He paused as he scrutinized Tobias. "Michael's ingenuity transformed the methods of the battle in ways that you and your barbaric officers wouldn't understand."

"I—not understand? I trained the boy myself!" Tobias roared.

"Yes. But he took your military strategies and put them to use in a revolutionary manner," Alex continued. "Your soldiers only switched their loyalty after they were surrounded. After Michael proved himself the better warrior."

The king raised a hand, and the room fell silent. "Explain what happened."

Alex gave a sharp nod. "Your son put aside the standard ideas of routine, and instead of implementing the time-consuming maneuvers, he directed us in an immediate, lively attack, which put Tobias's men on the defensive. I was completely baffled by the tactic, but it proved quite ingenious."

Sarah closed her eyes as Alex described the scene. She could picture the surprise attack in the dark of the night under the moon, stars, and torches. A group of archers positioned on a hill fired a barrage of arrows into the night sky. Not very effective against the soldiers' armor, but it distracted Tobias's men enough for the small troop to get inside the barricade.

"The least experienced in our militia were mostly young boys, and Michael compiled them into one group," Alex said. "They drew in and feigned back several times. The tactic was flawless and drew Tobias's soldiers together. Eager to do battle and with only one small group to go after, they congealed into one large mass and went after our foot soldiers. With their bulwarks scarcely guarded, we took two groups in on either side, skirting around the edges. Despite our few numbers, we were able to surround them." Tobias scoffed, but Alex continued. "Of course, they began to battle us on their edges. Numerous men were killed on both sides." He paused and looked at Sarah. He squeezed her hand, and when he continued, his voice was softer. "Luther was one of those. Once he realized I was there, fighting alongside Michael, he tried to get to me, but he met Michael's blade first." Sarah dropped her gaze and tried to wash that image from her mind. The stories of Michael excelling at fighting, being one of the best in Kyrnidan, came back to her. If he defeated Luther, then he measured up to those stories.

Alex turned back to the king, continuing his report. "Forcing the army to fight within their own barricade was another of Michael's ingenious strategies."

"Foolishness!" Tobias cut in. He looked at Michael with a hint of disapproval. "You should've drawn them out into the open. Instead you trapped yourselves inside. You were outnumbered three to one and with no escape. It was an idiotic blunder."

"It was ingenious!" Alex's breastplate rose and fell with his heavy breaths. He was losing his patience with Tobias. "Not that you would understand. You left. In reality it was *your men* who were trapped." Alex pulled his gaze away from Tobias and looked at the king. "Had they the chance to spread out, it would have been a far bloodier battle, and we would have lost. As it was, most of Tobias's army was compressed in the middle, encircled by their own men and unable to get to the edges to fight. Still, the ones within our reach battled fiercely, and many of our men fell. But at the pinnacle of the fighting, Michael stepped out and called his soldiers into formation—all of them."

The room fell silent, and the hairs on Sarah's arm stood on end as she grasped what had happened. Fighting a battle they couldn't win, Michael had stepped out. She could envision him in that crucial moment—putting himself in harm's way, pulling off his helmet so as to be heard, and calling his troops to order—not just his small militia but the entire army. He had gathered a substantial force and had bravely led them against the strongest army in the territory. This was something that resonated with the soldiers. They had seen his tactics and valued his courage, and they responded by turning to him for leadership.

Suddenly the church was filled with Tobias's booming voice. "I delight in your victory, my prince, but in such we have lost the country." He fell back against the altar as he drew his fingers down his face in despair. "Can no one see it but me? The Moylans will now have the support they need to further the descent among our people. We will never advance."

Michael stepped in front of Tobias. His wide, black armor made his presence all the more demanding. "The country would be better off with the old ways than under tyrannical rule. I will not force my ideals upon my people by eliminating those who oppose me."

A low rumble disturbed the silence that followed in the wake of Michael's comment. Steadily it grew louder.

The men in the courtyard started shouting, and Alex strode to the back of the chapel and looked out. His face pulled into a frown. "An army approaches the gates," he said.

Sarah ran to his side and looked out. The guards had just shut the gates and were barring them. The Kyrnidian army, both garrisons, stood in the courtyard, and although they must have been exhausted, they scrambled into formation, their weapons at the ready.

"The Moylans!" an officer called as he burst through the doors. "And they bring nearly three hundred armed men."

A low chuckle rose from the far side of the room. The sound chilled Sarah. She didn't need to look to know that the eerie laughter was coming from Tobias.

"Their demise is inevitable," he said. "You spared them, and now they bring the fight to you." His voice rose with fortitude, powerful and piercing. "Before the sun sets today, all who oppose us will lie in their own blood. The new monarchy will go on unimpeded."

Sarah grabbed Alex's hand. "We can't let them do this—we can't let them fight."

A darkness fell over his face. "I don't think we have a choice now."

CHAPTER 39

SARAH WALKED ALONG THE BATTLEMENTS on the outer curtain wall of the castle. She had refused to go inside as Alex and Michael had instructed her. She needed to see for herself exactly what they faced at their gates.

"No farther, Your Highness," a guard told her. Five men had been sent with her, despite her protests. She only wanted to take a look, after all.

"We have orders to not let you pass beyond this corner."

"I want to go directly above the gatehouse," she said.

"No." The guard pointed with the tip of his spear. "Beyond this point the crenels are open to arrow fire from the north side. We won't risk your safety."

Sarah's lips tightened. "Very well, but how am I to see anything from here?"

The guard motioned for her to come near. He held his shield up to protect her as she leaned out between the merlons that created the sawtooth effect along the top of the battlements. From that vantage point, she could see the company that had approached the gates. Her eyes washed over the men—all of them armored and carrying weapons. A long pole displaying a banner with the Moylan crest was raised at the front. Her eyes fell to the rider next to the flag-bearer.

"Grace." Sarah pulled back with a gasp.

Spinning on her heels, Sarah ran along the wall walk to the nearest bastion and took the stairs that led down to the courtyard where Michael was readying his men.

The two garrisons completely filled the courtyard with row after row of soldiers. They stood at attention with such precision that they resembled statues on a grid.

"The Moylans—they don't want to fight," Sarah said in gasps as she ran up to where her brother and Alex stood.

"Yes—at least that's what they claim." Michael was pushing his hand into a new gauntlet. The old one must have been damaged in the battle. At last he looked up at her. "Robert Moylan has requested a council. But remember: these are Kyrnidians. Our talks often turn into battles."

Alex regarded her with curiosity. "How did you know? You'd already gone up to the battlements when the message was brought in."

"Grace is out there with them."

"Grace? Mother's servant?" Michael asked.

"Yes, that Grace. I know our people crave combat, but women don't usually join in."

"No, they don't. Are you certain you saw her out there?"

"I know Grace when I see her."

Her father joined them. His arm was wrapped, and he now wore a chain mail hauberk under his own black suit of armor. His shoulder pauldron was missing. Sarah guessed it wouldn't fit securely over his bandage.

"Grace is with the Moylans?" he asked, confirming what he had overheard.

"Yes. It was her; I would swear it."

Her father held her gaze. "Well we won't understand any of this by standing here speculating. Open the gates," he cried.

"Maintain your position!" Michael called to the army. The order was echoed as it was passed along by the men. Sarah could sense their excitement. The air in the courtyard hummed with their urge to fight, but in their discipline, not a single spear shifted as the men awaited further orders. Their renewed respect for their prince was evident.

Sarah held her breath as Robert Moylan rode through the gates followed by his entire company. It was a brazen move—something only a Kyrnidian would do. A man from another country would have kept his men at safe distance, allowing only the leaders to come forward to talk. But this was a blatant display of Robert Moylan's convictions. He led his men in, and they crowded their way into the open space between the army and the gates, filing around the insides of the walls until they encompassed the courtyard. Sarah could feel the tension. It vibrated through the air and intensified as the two groups converged. She breathed it in, feeling her stomach tighten. If a single man on either side gave in to their cravings, there would be no holding any of them back. It was as if two fighting dogs had been brought together but held back by only their masters' hands.

Before long, every armed man was within the compound. Grace rode next to Robert Moylan on the same horse she'd procured for her and Sarah the previous day. As they stopped, she was the first one to dismount. She faced the king and curtsied deeply. "Your Majesty."

The king nodded, but his eyes were locked on Robert. Straight backed and tense, Robert exhibited a cool and unwavering expression. He made no pretense to move, and the lack of respect was obvious.

"Tobias?" he asked.

"He is . . . unavailable," the king said through tight lips.

Sarah watched Robert closely to see if he accepted the vague answer. Tobias had been locked in a holding cell for the time being, but following an investigation—which would also scrutinize every councilman and officer in the army—he would face a trial. There would be severe consequences, but what those might be, Sarah dared not guess.

Robert's eyes glinted with hatred. It was apparent he was not pleased that the man who had planned to kill his entire family and all his guests was simply *unavailable*.

Sarah discreetly reached out and touched her brother's arm. She wasn't sure if he could even feel it through his armor, but somehow he must have sensed what she wanted him to say.

"Tobias is being detained under guard," Michael explained. "He will face repercussions for his actions."

Robert's indignant expression softened, but it was still rather grim. He turned his eyes toward Sarah. His penetrating gaze bore through her, and she fought the urge to take a step back. Instead she straightened, squared her shoulders, and lifted her chin, throwing up her own mental shield against his visual blow. He examined her thoughtfully then opened a large leather pouch that hung from his saddle. He pulled out a metal plate. It was identical in shape and size to the ones hanging in the chapel.

"The lost plate," he said. He held it out for them to examine.

Michael reached out and took it. He turned the plate over in his hand, scrutinizing the details. Sarah could see the unique design—the silver pattern that resembled running water laced intermittently with golden lines. She narrowed her eyes to read the prophecy—to see how the words differed from Tobias's version. She only saw the first words: "*It shall be . . .*" Then Michael's hand covered it as he ran his fingers carefully over the engraving. "This is it. This *is* the last prophecy. Indeed, this is Cuthbert's work." Michael looked up. "Where did it come from?"

Robert cast a sideways glance toward Grace.

"I had it," she said meekly.

The king took the plate and held it close to his face as he inspected it. His eyes widened. For a brief moment, he glanced at Sarah and Michael then back to the plate. "This changes everything." His face clouded with worry, and he looked at Grace. "And how, exactly, did you come by it?"

Grace wrapped her arms around herself and lowered her head. "It's been twenty years. I was a young girl of only twelve, and my job was to wait on the councilmen in the castle. I was there that day. I had just walked out of the room when the high priest gave the prophecy. The door was not yet closed all the way, and I heard what he said. After the high priest left, I overheard Tobias arguing with Simon Cuthbert over the exact wording. It was plain enough, but Tobias insisted that the firstborn must be a son."

Sarah stepped over to her father, and he handed her the plate. The sun glinted off the metal as she held it up to read it aloud.

"It shall be the firstborn of the new monarchy who shall quiet the fears and unite the nation again."

Sarah felt a chill run through her. The prophecy was the same except it excluded the words *the son*. It did refer to her after all. Her mind swirled. She assumed that once she knew the truth, things would fall into place—that she would be able to see things clearly. But this only caused more confusion. She was the one who was supposed to unite the people. How could she do that without causing more division among her brother's supporters?

Michael took her hand and gave it a reassuring squeeze. "Grace, were these the high priest's exact words?" he asked.

The woman darted nervous glances toward him. "Yes. But Tobias insisted that the firstborn must be a boy. He said a girl couldn't understand or rule a country that had been built on wartime traditions." She wrung her hands and glanced around again. "The other councilmen agreed, but Simon Cuthbert said he would only engrave the exact words. He hurried and made the engraving, bringing it to the castle that very night. The council would not meet for another week, but he wanted it there, safe in the castle before then. He sat in the council room alone for hours. I brought him apple brandy, and he became thoroughly drunk."

Grace paused but continued wringing her hands.

"Go on, woman," Robert growled. "Tell them what happened."

"Cuthbert gave me the plate," she said. "He wanted me to take it to the house steward for safekeeping until the next council meeting." Grace's cheeks flushed red, and she looked down ashamedly. "Few of us young maids liked Grindal. He was the house steward back then." Her voice dropped quietly. "I'm sure you remember what type of man he was. I always avoided him at all cost. I hid the plate in my mattress with the intention of having Tom, the falconer, give it to him. But when Cuthbert suddenly died, I was too scared. I was certain he was killed over that plate, and I didn't want anyone to know that I had it."

"And you kept it all this time?" Sarah asked.

Grace stared at the ground. "Even after several years, I was afraid of what Tobias would do if he found out about it. By then he had widely publicized the altered version of the prophecy. When you came, I thought I could give it to you—if I trusted you. That is why I was always watching you. But at the time, you didn't want anything to do with the prophecy."

Sarah felt a pang of remorse. "I'm sorry," she said.

"I did find someone to trust though," Grace went on. "That day outside of the queen's chamber, Apollo Moylan commented that he believed it to be you who would fulfill the prophecy. I had often wondered what his personal viewpoints were, and to hear him speak to you that day convinced me that he was trustworthy. I finally decided he would be the best one to give it to—that he could do something about it. I was just gathering up my nerve, and then—" Her voice had grown husky with emotion, and she had to pause to calm herself.

"I waited too long. Apollo died before I had the chance to give it to him. I didn't know what to do, but I knew I couldn't keep the plate hidden any longer. I tried to think who would be like Apollo, and the only one I could think of was his brother." She darted a nervous glance toward Robert then ducked her head. "I knew they were estranged, but beneath all that, they were still family, and I knew at one time they were very close. I took it and went straightway to the Moylan manor, but the army had barricaded the estate. I waited, and as soon as they left this morning, I took it to Robert and told him what had happened to Apollo."

A long silence followed Grace's story; then Robert motioned toward Sarah. "My brother sacrificed everything for you—his title, his family, his reputation, and in the end, even his life." He held her gaze as he searched her face. "If you are truly the one to unite this country, then his sacrifice was not in vain, as I once believed."

Sarah's throat tightened with emotion. Robert's statement was probably the closest he would come to reconciling with his departed brother.

Michael shifted uneasily next to her. "You see her as fulfilling the prophecy then." His tone was hard and flat.

"Who can see otherwise? It's plainly stated," Robert said. "And believing in it is the only vindication I have for what my brother went through."

Once again the tension thickened. Sarah could feel it humming in the air around them.

Michael tipped his jaw up. "Are you declaring your support of her as heir to the throne?" he asked.

Robert gave him a piercing look. He slowly cocked his head to the side as if he were mulling something over in his mind before he spoke. "Look at that prophecy again, lad." He leaned forward in the saddle. "I believe in the prophecies, and that one states that the firstborn will unite the people." He paused. "However, it does not say that she will rule."

A crushing weight suddenly lifted from Sarah's shoulders, and the tension dissipated. Robert Moylan had just acknowledged that Michael, not she, would rule. She felt a wave of gratitude toward the man. He could have left it unsaid. But clarifying it would allow Michael to unite his supporters again. She could support her brother wholeheartedly and still be involved without challenging his position. She looked up at Robert, silently thanking him. He met her gaze, and she thought she saw the slightest smile pull at his lips. It was nearly imperceptible, but she could see the compassion in his eyes. He looked so much like Apollo.

Robert looked back at Michael, and his expression grew serious again. He extended a hand, and when Michael hesitantly took it, he leaned forward and said in a low voice, "This does not mean that I approve of your policies of state. But I do respect a man who defends his people."

Straightening in the saddle again, Robert gave a nod to the king and then turned his horse and rode out of the courtyard, taking his company with him. Sarah stared after him. It hadn't solved all their problems, but it was a big step in mending the country.

Her father turned to her. His eyes were bright and loving. With stiff movements, he reached up and tapped the gold band that encircled his silver-laced hair. "This crown will pass to Michael—but I believe it would fit you as well."

Sarah leaned forward to kiss him on the cheek. "We shall all be happy to see Michael wear it."

"No one more so than I," Alex said as he pulled Sarah to him and wrapped his arms tightly around her. "I think you'll be busy helping to rule another country."

"She's still the princess of Kyrnidan," Michael said. "And I have plans for her."

Sarah spun around, giving him a warning look. If he was thinking about keeping her in Kyrnidan, he had another thing coming. She pointed a sharp finger at him and opened her mouth when he cut her off.

"I'm always looking to further our foreign relationships." Michael pushed his way between her and Alex. Sarah felt angry heat rush into her cheeks. Michael might be the one who would wear the crown, but she wasn't going to let him dictate her plans.

He slipped a hand around her shoulder and grinned. "What say you, sister? Can I talk you into marrying some Calibrean prince?"

Sarah's mouth fell open. She didn't know how to respond.

Alex grabbed her hand and pulled her to him. "I think we can accommodate you." His face was only mere inches away from hers, and she could feel the entire company of people staring at them. Her pulse quickened as he tightened his grip around her waist pulling her tighter into him. "I will no longer wait for the council's approval." Alex leaned forward, holding her gaze. "I think a fall wedding will be perfect. What say you, Princess?"

"I say—" She paused. She honestly didn't care who was watching; she wanted nothing more than to spend the rest of her life in his arms. "I say yes." She reached up and pushed her fingers through his dark hair, pulled his head down, and pressed her lips to his. "Yes . . . Yes . . . Yes."

CHAPTER 40

"Mother?" Sarah paused. It was still a little strange to be calling someone other than Miranda mother. "May I ask you something?"

"Of course." Queen Natalia took a sip of her tea and then sat the cup down. "You may ask me anything."

"The first time I visited with you, in your room in Kyrnidan, you told me you harbored no ill feelings for Apollo. Can you tell me why?"

Queen Natalia looked out the window with a reflective expression. Sarah smiled encouragingly, but at the same time, she knew to be patient in waiting for an answer. She was thankful her mother had finally recovered from her illness. The queen would always be somewhat frail, but it was a blessing she was healthy enough to have made the long trip to Calibre.

"To answer that question, I think we must start with someone else," her mother said. "When I first became pregnant, Tobias was thrilled. He was certain the child would be a boy who would carry on the family line and the monarchy as a great warrior. As the time of delivery drew closer, he became positively possessed. If anyone dared to question if I carried a girl, he would rave about the prophecy and threaten that if the child were a girl, he would not allow her to live. He always favored boys. I suspect it was because of Kyrnidian beliefs and how he was raised. He assumed only a boy was capable of fulfilling the prophecy. Some thought that Tobias's threats were nothing more than passionate rants, but I couldn't feel that way. And now we come to Apollo. He shared my same thoughts, although at the time, I was unaware of it."

The queen glanced down at the cup in her hands before continuing. "Apollo was your father's closest, most loyal friend, and he had earned our trust. With Michael's birth, he saw an opportunity to save your life. He did not do so naively. He always took into consideration the consequences before he acted. And I am ever so grateful to him." She laid a hand over one of Sarah's. "As a result of his actions and his sacrifice, today I am able to sit with my beautiful daughter."

Sarah let out a deep breath, and with it went the last tiny bits of misgiving. She had grown to appreciate Apollo before he had died, but now those feelings expanded into admiration. He would forever have her gratitude. She wondered if he had known that by saving her life he was also saving his family and country. Being raised apart in Calibre had given her the means to be a mediator between the Moylans and Michael, and her negotiations had satisfied both sides of the arbitration. She supposed in that way she *had* fulfilled the prophecy. Whether or not Apollo had realized it at the time when he placed her in Miranda's arms would forever be a mystery. One thing was for certain, her mother was right: Apollo was a very wise man.

Queen Natalia patted Sarah's hand, and a moment of understanding passed between them. Then there was a knock on the door, and Margaret, who had been reading quietly on the other side of the room, moved to answer it. A moment later, Alex strode in.

"Ladies, I'm not interrupting, am I?" He leaned down and kissed Sarah on the cheek.

"Not at all."

When he straightened, he looked around the room. Sarah suspected he was looking for her baby brother. He had grown quite fond of the little toddler and doted on him whenever possible.

"Where's Nathaniel?" Alex asked, confirming Sarah's thoughts.

"Grace and Sybil took him for a walk through the flower garden." Sarah shook her head in mock disbelief. "With everything that needs to be done, I'm surprised you found time to come play with Nathaniel."

Alex took her hand. "There's nothing wrong with playing with the little tyke, especially if it allows me to see you."

"I knew it," Margaret said as she joined them. "You just wanted to get a peek at your bride before the ceremony."

"I would never do such a thing." He let his blue eyes settle on Sarah. A swirling sensation churned inside her. She liked that he still had that effect on her.

"Speaking of which—" Alex winked at her. "Shouldn't you be getting ready?"

Sarah discreetly put a hand on her stomach to settle the swirling emotions then shrugged. "I don't have a dress."

"Carlina hasn't brought it yet?"

"You know she's always been a little dramatic when it comes to presenting her very best work."

There was another knock at the door. "That must be her." Margaret moved to open the door.

The old seamstress entered, and Alex hurried over to her, offering to take the packages she carried.

"Oh no, you don't." Carlina turned away, keeping the packages out of Alex's reach. "Time for you to go. We want to keep you in anticipation until you see your lovely bride on the steps of the church."

Alex bowed to the ladies. "Very well, I have things to attend to anyway." He pulled Sarah in for a kiss. "I love you."

Sarah returned the sentiment. In just a few hours, she would finally be marrying the man she loved, and the thought elated her.

Carlina turned to her as soon as the door closed behind Alex. "Well, my dear, if you continue smiling like that, your cheeks will hurt well before you are presented as man and wife."

Sarah let out a laugh and smiled even broader. Carlina moved to a table, where she set the heavy packages, then handed a small bundle to Sarah to unwrap. Sarah pulled at the ties and wondered out loud what it could be. She laughed when she finally got the package open. In her hands lay a pair of soft, low-heeled shoes. "Finally," she said, hugging them to her chest. "A pair of sensible shoes!" She held them up, examining their simplicity and couldn't resist pressing a kiss to each shoe. "I can't thank you enough. You have no idea how thoughtful this gift is."

"Oh, that's not the best part." Carlina removed the wrapping on the large package and pulled out Sarah's wedding dress. Sarah and her mother let out a collective gasp.

"Oh, Carlina." Queen Natalia said. "I have never in all my life seen its equal."

Margaret was nodding her approval. Sarah reached out and fingered the soft, pale silk. "Carlina, it is . . ." She paused trying to find an appropriate word. "Beautiful."

"I can only take partial credit. Miranda's dress, although simple, was made from some of the finest silk I have ever worked with."

Sarah recalled the day she had been declared a princess well over a year ago. After Alex had proposed marriage to her, she had opened the dowry trunk Miranda had left her. Inside, she had found several sentimental items, a letter explaining her royal heritage, and the dress. It had been

Miranda's wedding gown. It still held its original charm, but Carlina had fashioned it into something that bespoke Sarah's royalty.

"Let's get you into this," Carlina said. "And then I have another surprise for you."

The dress fit perfectly. Sarah couldn't keep from running her hands over the fabric. It was far more than she had ever dreamed. Extra panels had been sewn into the skirt to make it fuller. The sleeves were no longer straight and plain but were embroidered with the most elegant floral pattern. More pearls had been added to the skirt and sleeves, and the entire dress was trimmed in thin, delicate lace. And as if that wasn't enough, Carlina had added a beautiful blue velvet cape that came over Sarah's shoulders, clasped at the base of her throat, and trailed several feet behind her.

"Now for the last surprise." With an air of reverence, Carlina opened a small package and pulled out a belt of pearls and blue topaz stones. She fastened it around Sarah's waist, letting part of it hang in front, where it was weighted by a silver unicorn.

Sarah blinked back tears as she reached down and tenderly wrapped her fingers around the unicorn. "Carlina, you had it repaired." It seemed a lifetime ago that she had wrenched the unicorn from the belt and given it to Apollo. Then he had returned it to her on that fateful day. "Thank you," she whispered.

Carlina put a gentle hand on Sarah's arm. "It's who you are. Now, turn around and look in the mirror."

Sarah faced the long mirror, closing her eyes briefly before looking into it. Her heart skipped a beat when she opened her eyes and met her reflection. She was beautiful—like a princess. But it wasn't just her majestic attire—she *felt* regal.

After seeing Sarah properly dressed, Carlina excused herself. Queen Natalia dabbed at her eyes with a handkerchief then left to go look in on Nathaniel before getting herself ready. Once they were gone, Sarah sat down while Margaret braided ribbons and beads into her hair.

"Thank you, Margaret," Sarah said when the finishing touches were done.

"You're so welcome, my dear. You do look divine, and the beads bring out the red in your blonde locks."

Sarah chuckled. "I wasn't thanking you for the hair, although it is perfect. I wanted to thank you for everything—for believing in me, for being my friend."

"No need to thank me. It was my pleasure."

"Won't you please reconsider and stay here in Calibre with me?"

"Oh, my dear, my family is in Kyrnidan—my parents, siblings, nephews, and nieces."

"I know. I had to try though."

Margaret patted her on the shoulder. "We'll see each other again. After all, you'll be coming to Kyrnidan on occasion, and I'll be certain to join the party when any of your family comes here to visit."

Sarah nodded, still a little sad that she and Margaret would be parting soon but grateful for the time they'd had together. She reflected on the past few years, the events that had led her to this moment, and the people who had helped her get there. Before she knew it, a tear slid down her cheek.

"Oh, dear. No crying, you'll stain the silk, and your eyes will be puffy." Margaret handed her a handkerchief. "Are you all right?"

Sarah dabbed at her eye. "I am just so thankful to have had wonderful people throughout my life. My parents, a twin brother, Miranda, Apollo . . . you." Sarah reached out for Margaret's hand. "And Alex." She gave a short laugh. "I'm getting married today!"

"Yes, you are," Margaret said with a twinkle in her eye. "Would you like a drink?" she offered the little corked bottle. "It might steady your nerves."

Sarah looked at the proffered container, and they both burst out laughing.

* * *

The air had a refreshing, crisp feel to it as Sarah walked outside. The trees wore their brightest fall colors of reds and oranges, and there were flowers everywhere. It was a beautiful day for a wedding. Sarah tingled with excitement.

The entire wedding party had gathered in the courtyard for the processional up to the chapel, where throngs of people from villages near and far had accumulated. Every member of the king's council was present to pay their respects. Each one nodded their heads toward her and bowed deeply.

Once she and Alex had returned to Calibre, Alex informed them of his indisputable wedding plans. There were some arguments, but it didn't take long for the council to give their approval. Of course, her involvement in bringing some harmony to Kyrnidan had helped in that matter. At last she had proved her mettle.

When Sarah and the following cortege reached the church, she looked around to take in the scene. Alex stood on a dais in front of the chapel doors with the priest next to him. Her parents sat on one side in beautifully carved high-back chairs while Alex's parents sat on the other side. Her stepsister, Felicia, grinned at her from her place of honor, as did Michael. Her brother now wore the simply embellished gold crown her father once had. She noted it fit him perfectly.

She walked to Alex, and his countenance brightened as he took her hand. "You're not nervous, are you?" he asked in a whisper.

"Of course not. This is easy compared to what we've already been through together." She matched his broad smile.

The ceremony was beautiful. She and Alex vowed to love and cherish each other for all the days of their lives, and then they knelt for the priest's final blessing. When they stood, they were presented as man and wife to the cheering crowd.

Alex gave her hand a squeeze, and she met his gaze. At that moment, she felt completely at ease. She had proven to others, but most importantly to herself, that she was equal to stand by his side.

Indeed, she thought, *no more opposition. At least, not today.* The crowd's cheers turned into a chant, bidding them to kiss. With that Sarah went up on her toes and pressed her lips against Alex's with all the love she possessed. She was his wife, his equal, and now his queen.

ABOUT THE AUTHORS

JENNIFER K. CLARK AND STEPHONIE K. Williams are sisters by chance but became friends by choice when a year of rooming together at college taught them how to get along. Now "play"-at-home moms, separated and living in different parts of the country, they stay in touch and support each other in their individual projects. Jennifer is busy with a monthly schedule that boggles Stephonie's mind, yet she manages to squeeze enough time out of the day to work on her passion of storytelling. Stephonie tries to maintain as quiet a life as possible with her husband, three cats, and a budding ninja. She spends her days trying to rein in an ever-growing rock collection, quilling paper jewelry, and dreaming up new stories to be written.